MW01226719

SECRETS AND MURDERS

Gale G. Pimp

Copyright © 2022 by Gale G. Pimp

All rights reserved.

No portion of this book may be reproduced in any form without written permission from the publisher or author, except as permitted by U.S. copyright law.

Contents

Three sixteen-year-old girls are found dead after being plunged off the roof of their
school. The question it poses: did they jump, or were they pushed?

While working the case, Ethan hears about an infamous serial killer that brought
havoc to Briarwood in the 1960's called the The SAD Killer. The best part? He
was never caught.

CHAPTER ONE

Three girls, splayed on the cement. Necks broken, limbs bent, dead.

The juxtaposition was uncanny. Cold weather for May, dark clouds covered the sky. Police cruisers lined the street, officers hovered around the scene. Everything played out in perfect accordance. Diverting eyes and unwanted glances, all for one reason: the bodies of three dead girls.

Detective Ethan O'Riley stared for as long as he could, then turned away. He was accustomed to seeing this sort of thing. Arriving at crime scenes and observing dead bodies was what he did for a living. Yet somehow this was different. Looking at those three girls, he felt off. As though their youth and innocence were being broadcasted on a sign above them, spinning and flashing for everyone to see. Too young. Too broken.

The perimeter had been taped off, faced with crowds of young faces trying to peek through and see what all the commotion was about. But by that point, most people already knew. Word spreads fast, after all, especially in a school with less than a thousand students.

The courtyard of St. Paul's Catholic School was crowded, kids swarming the taped-off area, trying to see for themselves what had happened. Cellphones were held above heads, shoulders nudged to get to the front. This was the most upheaval they'd ever seen.

Briarwood was a small town, population of five thousand. Nothing bad ever happened there. It was the type of town where neighbors went to each other for a cup of sugar or a borrowed egg. Where you knew every single person you passed on the street. A tight-knit community with family ties. Crime was practically unheard of. Sure, there was the odd DUI or domestic dispute from time to time – but death? Especially on those so young?

The only thing that people died from in Briarwood was old age. The way people saw it, there were only two ways out of that town: until you died of old age, or you moved far away and never looked back. The last time the town had seen an untimely death from someone under the age of eighty was a few years back, when a nineteen-year-old boy drowned in the lake. That was enough to rattle the community for quite some time. But now this had happened, and nobody knew what to think.

The three girls lying on the ground were one month shy of completing their sophomore year when their lives ended. Haddie Taylor, Anneka Wilson, and Kiera Barnes. Classmates. Best friends. Soul Sisters.

Deceased.

It was 12:05 p.m. The 911 call came through shortly after 11:00 a.m., which meant that the girls died sometime just before that. Lunch began at 11:00, so the question begged: what were the girls even doing up there in the first place? Why were they not in class?

Ethan ran his fingers through his hair, taking in another deep breath before turning around to face his superior, Major Frank Connolly. They had only arrived on scene ten minutes prior, approximately half an hour after the 911 call was dispatched. Ethan and his team were from Riverton – the closest city – approximately forty minutes out from Briarwood. Normally they wouldn't respond to a call outside their jurisdiction, but given the circumstances, and the fact that Briarwood had an almost zero percent crime rate, Riverton PD was required.

Forty minutes and the small town was already in mayhem. The school-board was doing everything in their power to prevent news from getting out. The mayor had arrived on scene and was doing her best to keep everything at bay. The last thing they needed was the local news station catching wind of things and making a dime from this devastating loss. And what would news such as this do to their small community? Surely people would be horrified to hear of something so traumatic.

Ethan focused his attention, listening to the sound of hundreds of iPhones clicking as the cameras went off. People – fellow students – taking pictures, trying to get a first look, capture that perfect, newsworthy shot.

It was a perplexing case that should have been straight-forward. From what they had gathered thus far, the girls had been plunged from the roof of the school, bodies hitting the pavement, killing them instantly. Plunged was an interesting word, because as far as anyone could tell, the cause of this plunge was still unknown.

"What do you think we're looking at here?" Frank Connolly said as he turned to Ethan. Ethan took in another breath and faced his superior. "Looks pretty cut and dry to me," he said, pushing the image of the dead girls temporarily out of his mind. "Suicide." "A triple suicide?" Ethan shrugged. "You don't think any foul play was involved?" Frank asked. "In all honestly, sir, I have no idea what to think. I'm still processing all of this." "It just seems out of sorts to me. I spoke with the principal," Frank nodded to a lanky red-headed woman, skittering around in high heels and a pencil skirt. "She says the girls were wonderful students. No sort of problems that she knows of. No bullying or signs of suicidal thoughts." "So you think someone pushed them." "Or made them jump." "But why would someone force three sixteen-year-old girls to jump off the roof of their school?" Frank shrugged. "Kids do crazy things."

CHAPTER TWO

There would be only five people working the case. From Riverton, there was Detective Ethan O'Riley, Major Frank Connolly, Officer Kennedy Cross, and Officer Jesse Tanner. From Briarwood's Police Department, there was Hal Davis. Four people was more than enough resources that could be sacrificed from Riverton PD's busy schedule.

Ethan stood on the other side of the yellow tape, observing the scene in front of him. Everything seemed to be moving quickly and efficiently. The forensics team, photographers, and medical personnel were busy at work, analyzing the scene, taking photographs, looking for anything that might arouse suspicion.

Everyone was working cautiously, eyes peeled for something that could prove useful. A weapon, gunshot residue, a suicide note, perhaps? There was nothing but the bodies, as far as anyone could tell. And the bodies stuck out like a sore thumb. Ethan had tried to drown them out, compartmentalize them in his brain so that it wouldn't be so painful to look at. Yet every single time he glanced in that general direction, the overwhelming sense of dread filled his body.

There were two forensic photographers on scene, as well as a sketch artist and an evidence recorder. The flashes went off simultaneously, capturing the images of the dead girls. Their heads, their hands, their legs, splayed out in different directions, blood seeping from underneath them, trailing down the concrete. Two of the girls were face-down, their eyes concealed from the world to see. It seemed a little less agonizing to only see the back of their heads. The third girl, however, was facing upwards; eyes closed, head crooked off to the side, allowing everyone to get a good look at the damage that had been done, the life that had been lost.

There were two officers posted on the roof of the school. The area was sealed off and a secondary scene analysis was being conducted up there. The roof was the very last location that the girls were alive, after all. They were scouting the area for anything, including the much-anticipated suicide note that everyone was certain existed, footprints, fingerprints, weapons, DNA. Anything they found was bagged and put into evidence.

Once everything was photographed and recorded, the girls were finally granted some peace by swiftly being zipped into body bags and taken to the local coroner's office for the post-mortem.

There were eight hundred students at St. Paul's Catholic School. It was up to Ethan and Kennedy to conduct the preliminary statements. Determine if the students saw anything, heard anything, noticed anything suspicious happening at the time of the incident.

Ethan and Kennedy stepped away from the crime scene and towards the crowd of teenagers that loomed nearby. The principal had organized them into small sections to allow the preliminaries to go down smoother. Ethan watched Kennedy as she walked, her dark brown hair swinging in a high ponytail behind her. She had an interesting walk, Kennedy Cross – very straight-forward and determined. She didn't like to waste time. And right now, Ethan knew that all she wanted was to solve this thing and wrap it up.

There were only two possible outcomes here. Statistically speaking, a triple suicide was extremely rare. One kid jumps, understandable. Two kids jump, okay, maybe they talked each other into it. But three? It was almost unheard of. But still, that was the conclusion that people were already coming up with. That the girls jumped. Like some sorority sister pact that they each swore on.

"I was walking through the atrium and I swore I saw something drop in front of the windows at the front," one student said. "Did you hear a scream?" Ethan asked. "A cry for help?" The student shook his head. "Nothing. I didn't even know what it was. Didn't think much of it. So I went back to class. It wasn't until after that I realized..."

"I heard someone screaming," one girl explained. "From outside. People were going to the courtyard for lunch and must have seen the bodies. Then all I heard was screaming."

"I wouldn't expect anyone to have seen anything," one of the teachers said. "They were all in class. They all should have been in class."

"Perhaps you heard a scream?" Kennedy asked. "Multiple screams? A shout for help?" The girl shook her head. "My geography class is on the first floor, not too far from the courtyard. But I didn't hear anything. None of us heard anything."

"Did the girls have any enemies?" "No."

"Do I think they jumped?" A female student echoed. "I don't know. Maybe. They were a bit fucked up." "What do you mean by fucked up?" Ethan asked. The girl shrugged. "I didn't mean them. I meant Haddie. Haddie Taylor." "You think she would have jumped?" "God only knows."

"Were you close with any of the girls?" Kennedy asked another student. "Not really. We all grew up together, so we all know each other. But I wasn't good enough for that crowd."

"Did the girls have any enemies?" "Yes."

"Were you friends with the girls?" Ethan asked. "A bit, yeah. I have biology with Kiera and Haddie. They were so... nice," the girl mumbled, dabbing her eyes with a damp tissue. "I can't believe this happened. Why would they do this?"

"Were the girls well liked?" "Oh, yes," a male student said. "Everyone knew them." "No, my question was, were they liked?"

"Did the girls have any enemies?" "I wouldn't say enemies. More like... an arch nemesis."

"Do you think the girls would have jumped? Were they depressed? Suicidal?" "Not at all," a male student said. "They were always smiling, laughing. Everyone knew those girls. Everyone loved them." "So then who would do this to them?" He only shrugged.

_____

After the preliminary statements were taken – what everyone saw and could account for – Ethan and Kennedy made their way into the school to have more in-depth discussions with some of the students. Because if anyone was to know what happened today, it was them.

Ethan and Kennedy were seated in one of the vacant classrooms, waiting. The principal – Mrs. Lang – had called in a number of students who could speak with them, hoping that something would prove beneficial.

Finally, the first student sauntered in, a petite brunette who pulled out the chair timidly and sat in front of them. "Hello," Kennedy smiled at the girl. "What's your name, love?" "Everleigh." "What a beautiful name," Kennedy said. "Thank you." "So," Ethan cut in. "How well did you know the girls?" "I knew them a bit," Everleigh said. "Well, everyone knows each other around here." "Close with any of them?" "Not really. They're group was kind of... exclusive." "How so?" "I don't mean that in a bad way," Everleigh said. "But it's not as if they were recruiting new members." "Like a club?" Ethan asked. Everleigh made a face. "No. More like an elite class. How do I put it? Popular, I guess. I hate that word." "So they were popular girls," Kennedy said. "Everyone liked them." Everleigh nodded. "What do you think happened to the girls?" Ethan asked. "Me?" "Yes." She swallowed. "I'm not sure. I'm afraid to say." "Don't be afraid," Kennedy gave her a reassuring smile. "Everyone's talking, we know. They're saying one thing or another." It was quiet for a moment. "Maybe they jumped?" Everleigh said, as though she wasn't even sure herself. "What makes you say that?" She shrugged. "Everyone else is saying it." "You don't think they could have been pushed?" She looked scared, almost. "I don't know. I mean, I guess. Anything's possible." "If you didn't know the girls exceptionally well," Ethan said. "What would make you think that they would jump off the school roof and kill themselves? They were popular, you say. Well-liked. Is there something we're missing?" She was hesitant. "Listen, I didn't know them well —" "Why would they jump?" Ethan repeated. Everleigh was quiet again. "I don't know. They could have had problems.

Things they didn't tell anybody." "Were they depressed?" Ethan asked. "I don't know." "Thank you," Kennedy interjected, shooting Ethan a look. "We'll be in touch."

They sat back and watched Everleigh exit the room. Moments later, Mrs. Lang brought in the next student.

"Hi there," Kennedy smiled at her. "What's your name?" The girl sat down at the desk. "Tessa." "Hi Tessa. I'm Officer Cross and this is Detective O'Riley. We need a bit of help from you." The girl nodded. "What can I do?" "Did you know the girls well?" "Sort of. I used to be friends with Anneka in middle school. One of my best friend's is her neighbor, so we used to hangout when we were younger." "But not Haddie or Kiera?" "No. Not really." "What can you tell me about the girls?" Ethan asked. "Um," Tessa thought. "They were nice. Polite. They were invited to all of the parties. Always had stories to tell." "Did they have many friends? Were they well-liked?" "Oh yes. Everyone liked them. But they didn't have many close friends in their little circle apart from the three of them. There were a few others that they were friends with – Gabby, Maya, Rachel, Layla. There's like, eight or nine of them that hang out and go to parties and stuff. But other than that, it's mostly just the three of them, no one else." "So they were well-liked," Ethan said.

"No enemies?" "Well," Tessa said. "I don't believe they were a fan of Beth." "Who's Beth?" "Beth Campbell. She and Haddie are kind of... how do I put it..." "Competitors?" Kennedy suggested. "Sure. Yeah, let's go with that." "Why did Beth and Haddie not get along?" "I don't know much," Tessa said. "But it's common knowledge that Beth and Haddie used to be best friends in middle school. Then something happened and all of a sudden they hate each other, and then Haddie's friends with Kiera Barnes. Then came Anneka." "How would you describe Beth Campbell?" "She's really nice," Tessa leaned back in her chair. "I had Geography with her last semester and she was super friendly. We're not close or anything, but from what I know of her, she's a nice girl." "Did anything happen between them recently?" Ethan asked. "A fight or an argument?" "Not that I know of," Tessa said. "Why, you think Beth had something to do with this?" "We're not thinking anything," Ethan said. "Just trying to get the big picture here." "You think someone pushed them?" Tessa asked, wide-eyed. Ethan and Kennedy stared at her, unsure of how to respond. Tessa spoke again. "But I thought they jumped?"

Next up was a male student: tall, lanky, shaggy brown hair. He was wearing a dark green top and beige khakis.

He walked into the classroom as though it was the most commonplace thing in the world, not walking in to talk about three dead girls with the police.

"Hi there," Kennedy began. "Your name?" "Justin." "Hi, Justin. What can you tell us about today?" He took in a slow breath. "Well, three girls ended up dead." Ethan tried to hold in his laughter. Was this guy serious? "Yes, that is why we're here," Kennedy said firmly. "Did you know them?" "Sort of. I had classes with them, but never really talked to them." "What did you think of them? Were they nice, well-liked?" "I guess. I mean, I don't think there's a single person in this school who didn't know them. Mostly Haddie, though. Everyone knew Haddie in one way or another." "What about the other two?" "They were like her followers or something." "Followers," Ethan echoed. "Interesting choice of word. What makes you say that?" He shrugged. "I don't know. Just the way it seemed to be with the three of them. It was Haddie Taylor, and the other two." "What were they like?" Kennedy asked. "How did they act at school?" He thought about this for a moment. "They were always really loud. Like, all the time. In class, in the halls, at lunch. As though they wanted everyone to know how much fun they were having." "And how would you describe their personalities?" Ethan asked. "Nice, I guess. I don't know, they were just girls. I don't know how to describe them. Everybody knew those three. I'm sure you could ask anyone else in the whole school and they'd be able to tell you more than I could."

Ethan O'Riley, Frank Connolly, Kennedy Cross, and Jesse Tanner got into Frank's car and drove to the coroner's office, which was only a short five minute drive from the high school. Everything in Briarwood was in close proximity. The school, the strip-plaza, the grocery store, the houses. Frank had warned them upon arrival: this town was small. Which could prove either beneficial or detrimental, depending on how you looked at it.

The four entered the coroner's office and were introduced to the medical examiner – Doctor Meredith Kepler. She was a gazelle of a woman; tall and slim, her hair pulled back into a tight ponytail. She was young, mid-thirties, her eyes tucked away behind her large spectacles. Today was a first for Dr. Kepler. The first time that three sixteen-year-olds showed up on her table.

Dr. Kepler had each body on an examination table. She had not yet completed the full post-mortem since that would occupy her for the next twenty-four hours. This was just a quick briefing to inform the officers of cause of death. It was presumed to be the fall that killed them, but if they were looking at homicide, the girls could have died before they even left that roof.

Ethan took a step forward and examined the girls for himself. Such small bodies, just above five feet, covered in a white sheet up to their necks. Their skin was a pale shade of blue, their eyes closed. Ethan wanted to turn away but forced himself not to. He could feel something inside him churning. The feeling to run – to get away from this place as fast as he could and never look back. He didn't want to look at their faces and see the life that was taken from them far too early.

"From what I can gather thus far," Meredith Kepler began. "The fall was approximately twenty feet onto cement. From the position that the girls landed, I'd say that two of them – Anneka Wilson and Haddie Taylor – were facing forwards when they fell, causing them to land face-down." At this point, there was nothing that Ethan knew about the victims, other than how to identify them after they landed: Anneka was the one with short, dirty blonde hair that sat just below her shoulders. Kiera had long, wavy hair that was a shade of milk-chocolate. And

Haddie had long blonde locks that seemed to fall effortlessly beside her body.Dr. Kepler motioned to Kiera
Barnes; the front of her skull concaved. "Kiera Barnes
was facing upwards when she fell," she said. "Let's begin
with Anneka Wilson. I'd say her cause of death is from
a broken neck, yet still, she has many abrasions and
lacerations to the head. All three of the girls have fractured skulls, evenly distributed between the vertex and
vertex base, as well as broken ribs," Kepler explained.
"Kiera Barnes died from a subarachnoid hemorrhage,
which happens when the blood leaks into the space
between two of the membranes that surround the brain.
Her spine is also broken, which would have paralyzed
her. Haddie Taylor died on impact, but there were a
number of things that happened here. She suffered from
extensive bilateral fractures to the ribs and cervical ver-
tebrae. The fall fractured her skull, causing extensive
damage to her brain. Her temporal bone was broken,
causing internal bleeding from the middle meningeal
artery. This subsequently led for her to die from an
extradural hemorrhage. Her neck was also broken which
would have paralyzed her breathing. But as I said, she
was dead on impact." They all stood there in silence as
they processed this information. Ethan couldn't help but

think that a fall such as this was a pretty violent way to die. At least it was quick. "Does the position in which they landed say anything about how they fell?" Ethan asked. "Not necessarily," Dr. Kepler replied. "Sometimes when a person falls from such a height, their body can turn or flip in any direction. However, given this specific height from the top of the school, I'd say that it's likely the girls did indeed fall in the positions that they landed." "Which means Kiera was the only one with her back to the edge?" "Correct." "Any sign of a struggle?" Jesse Tanner asked. "Ligature marks? Bruises? Fingerprints or hand marks on the arms, perhaps?" "No defensive wounds or skin under the fingernails," Dr. Kepler said. "No fingerprints on the skin, either, except for each other's, but that's normal. Nothing here suggests foul play. Then again," Dr. Kepler made eye contact with the officers. "Foul play can sometimes be verbal. These girls didn't have to be physically pushed to have gone over the edge." "Someone might have talked them over," Frank finished her sentiment. "Forced them to jump," added Kennedy, nodding. "But why – that's the pressing question," Ethan said. "That's what we need to figure out." "There's still the possibility that this was suicide," Jesse said. "Could be," Frank said. "But we're not calling it a suicide until all other possibilities are ruled out." "What could possibly possess three teenage girls to jump off a building?" Ethan said. "Drugs?" Kennedy suggested. "Perhaps," Frank said. "I've seen kids on some crazy things before." "Acid, speed, ecstasy," Jesse listed. "Maybe they thought they could fly." "Or they were depressed," Kennedy suggested. "Maybe they all went through a similar trauma. Maybe they all had things they were battling." "I'll need to do a tox-screen," Dr. Kepler spoke up. "That will tell us if any drugs were in their system, and will also reveal whether they were on any medications." "We're all excluding one possibility," Jesse said suddenly. They all looked at him. "What's that?" "It could have been an accident." Ethan snorted. "Three girls don't just accidently fall off the roof of their school. Come on, Tanner, I thought you were good at your job." "No, he has a point," Kennedy spoke up. "At this point, we don't know. We have to look at every single scenario. They could have went up there intentionally, just the three of them, having a little meeting or something, doing whatever girls do, you know." "No, I really don't," Ethan said. "You're the girl here. You tell us what they do." "Well," Kennedy said, thinking to herself. "My friends and I used to escape from it all. Seclude ourselves from the busyness of high school. We'd ditch the cafeteria and take our lunches to the park, or through the fields to abandoned houses." "Sounds safe," Ethan remarked. "They could have been doing God only knows up there," she ignored his comment. "They could have went up there for some privacy. To eat lunch. Paint their nails. Ditch class." "Or they could have been lured up there," Frank said. "Someone could have been blackmailing them, giving them no other option. They had to go up to that roof today. Or else they'd face some kind of consequence." Meredith Kepler remained quiet, watching the officer's converse amongst themselves. Kennedy continued with her theory that they went up there voluntarily and this was some sort of accident. "They get distracted, they're a little bit too close to the edge—" "Or," Ethan cut her off. "Someone has them cornered up there. He has a knife, forces them to keep walking until their toes are nearly off the edge..." "They're daring each other to get closer, being stupid," Kennedy continued. "Or maybe they saw something. All three of them go to the edge to see what it is," she stopped suddenly and looked up at the others. "That's what we really need to find out. What exactly was going on at the school during the exact moment those girls hit the pavement. And the why will come after." "So you really think they just accidently fell?" Ethan was getting irritated. "I don't think anything, O'Riley," Kennedy snapped. "I'm speculating, widening our horizons here. There are only three options: they jumped, they fell, they were pushed. That's it. That's all we got. And right now, we have absolutely no answers. Zero. So until we can get a better understanding of what happened here today, I'm just putting ideas out there." "It could be anything," Dr. Kepler finally spoke. "But as for cause of death, they most certainly died after leaving that roof. And their deaths were instant. They didn't suffer or feel any pain."

It was quarter past six when Ethan and the other officers headed back to Riverton for the night. They would be back tomorrow, of course. And where to begin then? Ethan knew he'd begin with the parents. Three sets, six distraught individual's whose worlds had just been turned upside-down. The idea that their child would never come home again, never wake up in their beds, never give them a kiss at the front door before leaving for school, never smile at them, never hold their hand. It was almost too much to bear.

Death was a complicated thing, you see. And not just
death, but more specifically, murder. It was horrible. It
was unlawful. It was downright immoral. And no matter what people did – law enforcement, government –
there was nothing that anyone could do to stop it. There
would always be murderers out there. Sociopaths, serial
killers, people who enjoyed the act of killing. And it
was awful. But Ethan couldn't help but think, if people
weren't being murdered, he wouldn't have a job. Murder
was necessary. It was Durkheim, after all, who said that
deviance was an integral part of a functioning society.
How would we understand the good if we didn't have
the bad? There's no justice without crime.

Ethan never pictured himself in this line of work. In
fact, he never pictured himself in any line of work really. His older sister, McKayla, was the studious one;
the offspring his parents adored more. She worked hard
in school and got a job straight out of college. It was
as though she had her entire life laid out in front of
her, and everything was as simple as a to-do list. Each
milestone she reached in her life was just a checkmark
on a metaphorical piece of paper. It all came so easy
for her. And Ethan often wondered what he lacked that
came so easily for her. They had the same parents, same

genetics. So what changed? What happened between the first child and the second child that was so drastic to create such a divergence between the two?

That kind of thinking was what made it worse for him. Overanalyzing situations, stressing about things he couldn't control. It wasn't until he, too, finished college that he realized comparing himself to his sister wasn't going to do him any good. Once he freed himself from that mindset, he was able to expand his horizons, think for himself, and decide what he wanted with his life once and for all.

It was a career that he stumbled upon. To be frank, Ethan had no idea what he was going to do with his life. His friends weren't any better. And you know what they say: who you surround yourself with determines everything. Maybe if he had better friends. Friends that were ambitious and successful. But they were just as confused and lost as he was. As though they all fed off of each other's muddled energy.

He was in a sociology class in his first year of college. The human psyche was something that interested him. The mechanics of it all, why people behaved the way they did, why people did bad things. It was the only class he took notes in and paid attention to. He grew to love it, even. And when he found himself spending his free time researching things out of pure curiosity, simply for his own personal knowledge, he knew he had stumbled upon something grand.

It was his professor who altered Ethan's life in a way that no one ever had before. He spoke to him about criminology, psychology, and the criminal mind. He told Ethan about behavioural analysts and psychologists who worked for law enforcement. From there stemmed the idea of detective work. It wasn't difficult. All he needed was to complete a degree in a specific field, whether that be criminology, psychology, or criminal justice. He chose criminology. Once that was completed, he advanced to police training at the Riverton Police Academy. He graduated at the age of twenty-five and made detective four months later. And that was what his life had consisted of for the last six years.

Ethan pulled into his driveway and unbuckled his seatbelt. He was exhausted. It had been a draining day, to say the least. And this was only the beginning. From his spot in the car, he could see the kitchen light on, illuminating the mostly-dark house. He waited, watching for any movement. Then he saw her, walking around the island in the middle of the kitchen, placing a bowl on the table. Jordan.

He got out of his car and made his way up the front steps. The door was unlocked, so he dropped his keys back inside his pocket, walked inside, and hung up his jacket. She appeared, then, like clockwork, smiling and walking towards him, her blonde hair falling over one shoulder.

"How'd it go?" she asked as she approached him, bringing her lips to his. He smelt the body lotion she always wore: vanilla, but he swore it was cotton candy. He kissed her, then pulled back and looked at her. Ocean blue eyes, always filled with curiosity and empathy. "Not the greatest." "What happened? Here, tell me in the kitchen," she took his things and ushered him into the other room, pulling out the chair for him to sit. She stood back and leaned against the island counter, holding her wine glass. Ethan grabbed the glass of water that was already waiting for him on the table and took a sip. Then he sighed. "Three dead girls. Sixteen years old." Jordan's face dropped. "Trying to determine whether it's homicide or suicide," he said. "There wasn't a note? Anything?" He shook his head. "That's the strange part. I mean, if you and your friends were going to commit suicide, wouldn't you at least leave a note? An explanation?

Tell someone what you were planning to do?" "So it's homicide, then," she said, matter-of-fact. He was quiet for a moment. "It's not that straight-forward. Everyone's saying it's suicide. That the three of them jumped together." "Why would they say that?" "Right from the get-go the mayor was saying suicide so that it didn't look bad. They don't want to scare people with the notion that there's a teenage-girl killer out there in their small town. It would frighten people, put them in a panic." "You said Briarwood, right?" "Yeah, very small town. Five thousand people." "I know it," Jordan said, taking a sip from her wine glass. "My grandmother's from there." "You don't say?" "Mhm," she nodded. "She'd always tell me stories when I was younger. Made it seem like such an enchanting place. Of course, it's been years since she's lived there. I think she left when she was young. But I'll have to tell her about this. She'll be shocked." "Yeah, from what I hear, their crime rate is practically non-existent. That's why this case is such a mess. They don't know how to react to the deaths. Murder would ruin their idyllic existence." "Yeah, and calling it a suicide is a much better approach," Jordan rolled her eyes. "In their minds, yeah. It's a coping mechanism. They don't want to face the truth. Like living in a blissful ignorance." "That's

Yet here he was, in this small town, investigating three deaths.

Ethan had seen his fair share of crime and violence in Riverton. Not that it was overly violent or had extremely high crime rates, but it wasn't perfect – far from it. There were gangs, shootings, stabbings. Downtown was the worst. Domestic disputes, theft, arson. He'd seen it all, so he was prepared for the worst. The worst was what he specialized in.

Ethan enjoyed working alone. Often times the officers and detectives were assigned partners. It made the job easier, gave you someone to lean on, always have your back. But as of late, Ethan preferred working alone. Going out into the field, conducting interviews, surveying crime scenes. He felt that having someone else there wouldn't be the most beneficial. Another body to take into account. Another human being to worry about.

Perhaps this personal preference was due to the fact that he was slightly introverted and enjoyed his solitude. Perhaps he just wasn't that fond of working with other people. Or perhaps it was due to the fact that his last partner of two and a half years died on the job and he still wasn't completely healed from it yet.

It had been three years since the incident, but Ethan was still haunted by it every single day. And since the death, Frank hadn't pushed for him to be reassigned a new partner. So for the past three years, it was just him, alone, doing what he did best.

Ethan made it to Briarwood shortly after ten a.m. He slowed down once he got off the highway and simply took in his surroundings. Green everywhere, surrounded by trees. Quaint roads, quiet streets. Elderly couples sitting on their front porch, young mother's pushing strollers, dogs chasing each other in the park. In that moment, he could understand why the mayor had been so insistent that this was a suicide. She didn't want to ruin their perfect community they had formed here. Announcing a triple-murder would be driving a steak-knife right through the center of it all. And once something like that happened, there was no coming back from it.

He glanced at the GPS and veered the car over to the next street. First up on his list: the home of Haddie Taylor. Only child to Renée and George Taylor. Mother was a defence attorney, father was a cardiac surgeon. Now, they were childless. And all the money in the world couldn't make that better.

He pulled into the long driveway of a large, Victorian house, two stories, triple garage. The entrance was huge, two white pillars extending from the ground to the second floor. The lawn was well kept and the bushes were trimmed to perfection. Ethan took in a deep breath, grabbed his notepad, and made his way to the front.

A woman answered the door, presumably Renée Taylor. She was either young or looked young for her age, he couldn't tell. She had short blonde hair that was cropped to her shoulders. Blue eyes, no makeup, dressed in all black. Her eyes were red and swollen from crying. She had a pleasant face, a face that people would enjoy looking at. He could see the resemblance from the photo of Haddie that he had in his car. Practically a spitting image of her mother. Same face, same eyes, same blonde hair.

"Mrs. Taylor?" Ethan asked as she stood there with the door open. "Yes." "I'm Detective O'Riley," he stuck out his hand. She was hesitant at first, but eventually met his grasp and gave it a light shake. "I've been expecting you," she said lightly. "Please, come in," she opened the door wider, allowing him to step inside. She closed the door behind him and he surveyed the foyer. Impeccable. "We can sit in the living room," she said to him as she turned to walk down the hallway. "Shoes on or off?" he asked. "Off," she didn't glance back. Ethan slipped off his shoes and followed her down the hallway and into the living room. She stood there for a moment, then gestured for him to take a seat on the couch. "Would you like anything to drink? Tea, coffee?" "I'm alright, thank you." She nodded then took a seat in the leather chair next to the fire place. The living room was magnificent. A glass coffee table sat in front of them, large portraits were hung on the wall, and all of the furniture looked like it cost more than his house. Ethan tried not to ruin the aura simply with his presence. "I'm so sorry for your loss," he started off. He said it with great sympathy and he meant it. He couldn't imagine the inconceivable loss of a child. Regardless of whether it was homicide or suicide – death was death. And nothing could make that better. But then he began thinking: which scenario was worse? Murder or suicide? The notion that somebody ended your daughter's life, or the realization that she chose to do so herself? Renée Taylor nodded solemnly. "Thank you. It's been –" She broke off. "I can't imagine." She closed her eyes for a moment, then opened them again. "I guess we should begin with the basics," Ethan removed his notepad from his pocket, clicked the pen. "What was Haddie like? Why don't you tell me a bit about her?" Renée sniffled, holding a tissue to her nose. He watched as she closed her eyes, smiling to herself. The memory of her daughter, still alive in her mind. "She was," Renée began. "Extraordinary." She looked at Ethan and met his eyes. "I know most parents probably say that about their children. But Haddie was different. She was so... smart. Gifted. She was incredible, intelligent, wise beyond her years. She was always so bright and optimistic – thinking about the future, her goals in life, what she wanted in this world." Ethan smiled as she spoke. He waited a moment in case she was going to continue, but she stopped there, getting lost in the memories. "And what was that, exactly? What did she want to do?" Renée focused her attention back on Ethan. "She wanted to become a lawyer, like me, but she wanted to be a prosecutor," Renée gave a slight laugh. "That was Haddie, for you. She set her goals and she worked towards them." "And your relationship with her?" Ethan asked. "Were the two of you close?" "Of course," Renée said. "We've always been close. So many mother's and daughter's fight at this stage of their lives, but not my Haddie. We were the best of friends. She told me everything. We went on holidays together, just the two of us. We had a very special relationship." "And what about your husband?" Ethan looked around the room. "He's not here, is he?" "Oh, no," Renée said. "He's out right now. It's been very... difficult for him. I'm just letting him be, giving him his space." "What was their relationship like?" "Fine. Normal. Obviously she wasn't as close with her father as she was with me. I mean, nothing compares to the relationship between a mother and daughter. But George and Haddie were close. They got along very well." She paused momentarily. "It wasn't easy for George. He always wanted a son. And after Haddie, well, we tried. I couldn't have any more children. But one was the perfect amount. That's more than I could have asked for. And George... don't get me wrong," she looked up quickly and met his eyes. "He loves her so much. More than anything in the world. But I think sometimes he envied our relationship. He wanted something like that. With a son, perhaps." Ethan nodded his head, focusing more on Renée and her voice rather than writing anything down. "What about friends? More specifically, Anneka Wilson and Kiera Barnes?" "The girls had been close for years. Growing up in Briarwood, everyone knows everyone. There are only two elementary schools, but the girls all went to St. Augustine's. They met in the sixth grade, I believe. They've been inseparable ever since." "And they all got along well?" "Yes, they were best friends." "Do you know if they ever got into arguments? Disagreed about anything?" "They're teenage girls, detective. I'm sure there was the catty drama here and there. But nothing severe. Not that I know of, at least. They did everything together. Sleepovers, birthday parties, shopping sprees, manicures, pedicures, puberty, the birds and the bees. They've been through it all, from graduating elementary school to starting high school." "So as far as you can tell, their friendship was fine?" "Yes." "Did your daughter have any enemies, Mrs. Taylor? Anyone who might hold a grudge or want to hurt her?" Renée shook her head. "No one. Everyone adored Haddie. She was always so pleasant and well-mannered," she choked. "I don't know why anyone would want to hurt her." "What about family? Do you have many here in Briarwood?" "My parents live here. George's are in England. We have some relatives out of town and such. Why?" "Does everyone get along? Or is there any bad-blood between the family?" She made a face. "No, nothing of that sorts. Everyone gets along fine. And they all love Haddie, if that's what you're wondering." "So no grudges from friends or family. Who else did Haddie interact with? Teachers, neighbors, co-workers?" "Well, yes. Practically everyone. But do

I think any one of those people killed my daughter? How am I to know?" "Did Haddie ever mention anything to you? That she was angry with someone, or perhaps scared?" Renée thought for a moment. "Not that I can think of. And I'm sure she would have told me if she was. I would have done something about it." Ethan nodded his head and glanced down at his notepad. He looked back up and met Renée's eyes. "Did Haddie ever suffer from any mental illnesses? Depression, perhaps?" "What?" Renée's face changed. "Heavens no. What are you insinuating?" "I know this is difficult, Mrs. Taylor, and please, take everything I say with discretion. But this is a –" he paused. "Investigation. Into their deaths. And I need to know... could it have been suicide?" Renée Taylor's face altered again. She was shocked. Appalled. "Of course it wasn't suicide," she said the word like it was poison in her mouth. "Haddie would never kill herself. Neither would Anneka or Kiera. This isn't some Romeo and Juliet tale. The girls didn't one day decide to kill themselves together. Somebody did this to them," she looked him in his eyes. "Someone killed my baby."

–––––

Next up were the Wilson's. The parents – Jason and Mary-Ella – divorced six years ago when Anneka was ten. Jason Wilson remarried a secretary named Pamela. Mary-Ella Wilson lived on her own, sharing joint-custody of Anneka and her two siblings, Jonah and Cloe.

Ethan sat at the kitchen table, Jason and Pamela across from him. Jason, evidently distraught, staring off in a daze. Pamela, perplexed, deeply saddened, fiddling with the tissue box between her palms. Ethan had already begun with his sympathies, which would become routine from that point on. He was waiting for Jason to respond to his question. What was Anneka like?

"She was quiet," Jason finally spoke, looking down at the table. Pamela reached forward and placed her hand on his. "Always a good girl. Respectful of others. Meek." "She didn't talk much as a kid," Pamela said. Jason nodded as if to corroborate. "She would just play peacefully with her dolls, as if the rest of the world didn't exist. The only thing that mattered was what she was doing in that present moment." "And she was so kind," Jason said, choking on his words. He had to stop to gather himself. "How did she handle the divorce?" Ethan asked. "Well, it was difficult for her," Jason said, regaining focus. "She was only ten. She was confused. Why are mommy and daddy splitting up?" "She didn't want to have to choose," Pamela said. Ethan knew by the way she spoke about

Anneka as a child that the affair between Jason and Pamela must have begun before the divorce. "We have shared custody," Jason added. "But I think she preferred being with her mother." "Well, she's a girl," Pamela gave a faint smile. "She needs her mother." "What was her relationship with you like?" Ethan said to Pamela. "Good. We got along great. I think it was hard for her at first – having a new female figure in her life. But she adjusted well. Like I said, she was very quiet, so if she did ever have a problem with me, she never voiced it." "But the two of you weren't close?" "Not entirely. We did the usual things together. But most of her time spent here was either in her room or with her friends. Or with Cloe." "How was her relationship with her siblings?" "Great. I think being the middle child was good for Anneka," Jason said. "Like she was invisible sometimes, could get away with anything. Before Anneka, we were so focused on Cloe. Don't do this, don't do that. Trying to learn how to parent and shape Cloe into someone great. And then Anneka came along and it's like we were experts, Mary-Ella and I. We had it all down pat: the diaper changing, the feedings, the storybooks and pre-school classes. She had it good," Jason paused. "And then when Jonah came along... well, Cloe was ten at that point. Anneka was six and already so independent. I think perhaps we neglected the girls around that time. All of our attention was focused on Jonah, so the girls' kind of did their own thing. We spoiled them, just in order to please them and quiet them. Anything they asked for we'd simply give them so we could focus on Jonah. And as they grew up, they all got along so well. Cloe and Anneka were close because they were together long before Jonah came along, and of course because they're girls. But despite that, they always included him in things. He was never forgotten about." Jason stopped and smiled at Ethan. "We raised them well, detective. My kids all turned out great." Then his smile dropped, and the weight of Anneka's death was back in the room, bringing with it great silence. "She seemed like a good girl," Ethan said. "But do you know if she ever fought with anyone? Had any enemies, maybe someone she was afraid of?" They both stared at him, unsure of how to respond. "You're asking us who we think did this to them," Jason said. "Essentially." Jason brought his hand to his chin, let out a deep breath. "That's the part I don't know how to answer," he said. "Because this is Briarwood, for God's sake. We're not in the ghettos of Detroit here. We live in a safe town, everyone knows each other and gets along. So who would hurt Anneka and her friends? Who would do something like this?" "So she never mentioned anything out of the ordinary? Nothing to arouse suspicion?" "Nothing at all," Jason said. "But then again, her mother would probably know more than I would. You're seeing Mary-Ella after this?" "Yes." "Good. Hopefully she can be of more assistance." Ethan nodded and formulated his next question in his mind. "Did Anneka ever suffer from any mental illnesses?" "No. No, of course not," Jason said. "It's not a bad thing, Mr. Wilson. Many teenagers suffer from ailments such as depression, anxiety, eating disorders —" "No, Anneka was fine," he interjected. "She was always happy and care-free. Quiet, but happy." "You keep saying she was quiet," Ethan said. "Did you ever think that perhaps something was causing her silence?" Jason looked at him. "No, Detective. Some kids are just like that. It's called being respectful and well-mannered." "Apologies, sir, I didn't mean to offend you." "Why are you asking if she had a mental illness?" Pamela asked. "You think she was suicidal?" "It's definitely a possibility," Ethan said. "We have to ask ourselves these questions in a time like this." "You think my daughter and her friends killed themselves?" Jason snapped. "It's still a possibility at this time —" "No," Jason said. "No, Anneka wouldn't do that. Anneka wasn't sad or depressed or suicidal, or whatever the hell you're implying. And even if she was, how do you explain the other two? Haddie and Kiera? You think they were all suicidal and just decided to off themselves at the same time? Off the school roof, for Christ sakes?" "Sir, please, if you'll let me finish –" Jason put up his hand. "I understand you're doing your job. But right now, this, this... speculation of yours. Well, it's just uncalled for. I can tell you one thing for certain, and that is my daughter would never kill herself."

_ _ _ _ _

House number three: Mary-Ella Wilson. Ethan figured that perhaps the mother could prove more useful than the father. Ethan sensed the unease and apprehension when talking about certain subject matter with Jason Wilson. For instance, the other two girls – Haddie and Kiera. Men don't pay attention to things like that, their daughter's friends, what they do for fun. No, that's a mother's job. And Ethan was hoping that Mary-Ella Wilson could provide him with more information than her ex-husband.

Mary-Ella was a mess. Her short hair was crumpled to one side, as though she'd been lying on it for hours.

Her eyes were red and glassy, evidence of the tears and dismay that had pained her for the past twenty-four hours. Cloe was at her side, aiding her mother in simple tasks, such as walking. She led her mother to the couch, one arm looped through hers. They sat together, staring at Ethan, tissues bunched into a ball, clenched between fists.

"I just came from your ex-husband's house," Ethan said once they were seated and ready to speak. "Are you up to answering some questions about Anneka?" Mary-Ella closed her eyes at the mention of her daughter's name. "Of course. Anything I can do to help you catch whoever did this." Ethan nodded and brought out his notepad. "So you believe this was intentional then? Someone did this to the girls?" Mary-Ella stared at him for what seemed like hours. "I'm not an idiot – I know what everyone is saying. That the girls killed themselves. The whole town believes it. Doesn't make it true." "What do you think happened?" "Someone did this to them. They were murdered." "Who do you think would do something like that?" Ethan asked. "I don't know, Detective. I assumed that was your job." "Did Anneka have any enemies? People she didn't get along with?" "Of course not. She stuck to her close group of friends. Haddie Taylor and Kiera

Barnes – those two were her best friends. She had a few others as well. Rachel Dunn, Gabriella Pratt, Maya Bowman. But no enemies. Anneka was a sweet girl. Got along with everyone," her voice faltered and Cloe leaned in closer to her mother. "Do you know if she was ever bullied at all?" "Not that I'm aware of. I'm the first to admit that parents are not perfect. Especially parents of teenagers. There are probably lots of things that we miss. And it's our jobs not to miss it. But bullying? I sure hope I didn't miss that." "So Anneka never mentioned anything to you? No visible signs of depression or self-harm?" Mary-Ella shook her head. "Not at all." "Cloe," Ethan said. "Did you notice anything? Or did your sister ever mention anything to you?" "No, nothing. We were close. Anneka always came to me for advice or just to talk. I swear, she told me everything. And if there were any problems, I'd know. But there was nothing. No boy problems. No girl drama. No bullying." Ethan jotted this down. "It's just odd," Cloe spoke again. "All three of them. Together. Have you ever seen anything like that before?" "No. I haven't," Ethan said. "And you're right, it is odd. That's why this case is so peculiar. Two people, it could be a possibility, especially in this fashion, the location, etcetera. But it was three of them.

Three is very rare for suicide, statistically. And there was no note. No indication that the three of them did this themselves." Mary-Ella began to cry again. Cloe rubbed her mother's arm and handed her more tissues. "If someone did this to them," Ethan began. "They did it for a reason. I'll need to find out everything I can about the girls' lives. Who they communicated with the most, if they had gotten themselves into some sort of trouble," "Isn't that victim blaming?" Mary-Ella asked. "Why is this their fault?" "I didn't mean—" "People kill for all sorts of reasons," Mary-Ella said. "Clearly someone had it out for those girls. And the reason for that is not on them." "Yes, I understand that," Ethan said. "But the entire situation is very perplexing. It happened at school, during school hours. If someone wanted to harm those girls, they could have planned it differently. On a weekend, in the evening. But they chose to do it in broad daylight where everyone would see." At those words, Mary-Ella broke down again. What Ethan didn't say aloud was that the whole scenario was very odd for a murder. Perhaps they really did jump. Ethan watched her for a moment, then cleared his throat. "I'll leave you for now," he said as he stood. "But I'll most likely be back very soon. When I return, I'd like to have a look around Anneka's room, if you don't mind. See if there are any clues or indication as to why the events of yesterday happened. Do you know if she kept a journal or a diary?" Mary-Ella wiped her eyes and looked up. "I'm not sure. We'll have to look around." "If you do, try not to move anything. Leave all her belongings as they are. I'll be back possibly later today or tomorrow. Until then," Ethan paused. "Well, again, my condolences. And just try to stay strong. It's a terrible time. If you remember anything else, or think of anything that you believe might be useful, please don't hesitate to call me," Ethan handed Mary-Ella his card.

House four: the Barnes. Just down the road from the Taylor's, the Barnes lived on a four acre property with a large pond and a horse stable. Patrick and Vivian Barnes came from old money and didn't bother trying to hide the fact. Locals said they flaunted their possessions, ensuring that everyone was aware that they were The Barnes. Kiera was their eldest, followed by her younger sister, Kelsey. Chocolate brown hair and striking blue eyes ran in the family; a chocolate lab to go along with their aesthetic.

But as far as Ethan could tell, today they were just a regular family, grieving the loss of their daughter. Patrick and Kelsey sat on the couch of their elegant living room. Vivian entered moments later, carrying a tray with mugs of tea. She handed one to Ethan, who had insisted that she not bother getting drinks for everyone, but eventually obliged once he realized she wasn't going to give up. He went with earl grey.

Vivian sat down on the couch next to her husband. None of them touched their teas. Ethan took a small sip, then placed it on the glass table that sat in the center of them, assuming his would go untouched from that point on as well. Tea, like most things in the Barnes home, was just a formality.

"Why don't you tell me what your daughter was like," Ethan said, fiddling with his pen between his fingers. It was just after two-thirty. At least this was the last time he'd have to do this dance today. "Kiera was brilliant," Vivian said, then stopped as the tears came. "I'm sorry," she held a tissue to her eyes. "I just... I still can't believe she's gone," her voice broke and she began sobbing. Patrick placed his hand on her thigh, a look of sorrow engulfing his face. Kelsey sniffled, trying to hold back her own tears as she watched her mother. "I'm sorry,"

Vivian said once she collected herself. "Don't apologize," Ethan told her. It was quiet for a moment. "What was the question again?" Vivian asked. "Just tell me about Kiera. Your relationship with her, her friends, what she was like." "Kiera. Yes. Well," Vivian began again. "Kiera was always so full of life. If you asked anyone who she was, they'd be able to tell you. Full of life and ambition. Always smiling and laughing. She truly was remarkable." "She always had this big smile on her face," Patrick said. "When she was in the eighth grade she had to get braces. And she swore that she would never smile with her mouth open again. But that didn't last long. Not even the braces could contain her smile. She let it shine for the world to see." "And she was funny," Kelsey added. She was two years younger than Kiera – only fourteen. "She always knew how to cheer me up and make me laugh." "The two of you were close?" Ethan asked the sister. She looked exactly like her. Kelsey nodded. "Two peas in a pod," Patrick said. "We were so glad the girls were close," Vivian explained. "You never know with girls. One day they're princesses, the next, they're pulling each other's hair out," she smiled slightly. "But not Kiera and Kelsey. They got along so well, even when they were babies." "What about her friends? Did Kiera get into any disagreements or arguments? Ever have any enemies?" "No, not at all. The girls," Vivian said. "You know, Haddie and Anneka, they were her best friends. The three of them spent all of their time together. And they never fought. They were all such polite, respect-ful girls." "And a part from that friend group, did she have many other friends?" It was quiet for a moment as the three Barnes thought about this. "You know, I can't really think of anyone else right now," Patrick said. Vivian agreed. "Come to think of it, she didn't have many other friends. Just Anneka and Haddie." She paused. "But when you have a friendship like that, how many others do you really need?" "What about boyfriends?" Silence again. It was Vivian who spoke first. "Boyfriend? No. Kiera was focused on her schoolwork. She wanted to go to Yale." Ethan looked at Kelsey, hoping perhaps she'd speak up, in case she knew something her parents didn't. But she only glanced at him, not saying a word. "Did any of the girls have boyfriends?" Ethan asked. "Haddie," Vivian said. "She was dating Oliver Harris." "Everyone thought they were going to get married," Kelsey added. Ethan internally scolded himself for not finding this out sooner. Why didn't the Taylor's mention a boyfriend? Perhaps it was because Ethan never asked. Why was he just thinking of boyfriends now? This was crucial information. He jotted down the name, Oliver Harris, and made a mental note to pay him a visit. "So if the girls didn't have any enemies," Ethan said. "Who do you think would do something like this? Who would want to hurt them?" It was quiet again. "Honestly, Detective," Patrick said. "I don't know. I don't know who could have done such a thing. I don't know who killed my daughter –" he closed his eyes and brought a hand up to shield his face. "Kelsey," Ethan said, looking at her. "Did Kiera ever mention anything to you? Anyone she was angry with? Scared of?" Kelsey shook her head. Ethan looked back at the parents. "Did Kiera ever experience any mental illnesses? Depression, anxiety, eating disorder...?" "No," Vivian said quickly. "No, Kiera was perfect. Nothing of that sort." Again, Ethan looked to Kelsey hoping she'd interrupt with some more information. But she remained silent. Perhaps he'd have to speak with her later. Separately. "Well," Ethan said as he stood. "I'll leave you for now, obviously give your family some time to mourn and be together in this time of tragedy. But I will most likely be back either later today or tomorrow, if that's alright with you." "Of course," Vivian said, standing as well. "Anything we can do to help you find the monster that did this." "I'll need to look through Kiera's room, see if there's anything that can indicate what exactly happened yesterday. So please, if you are able, leave everything as it is." "Of course." Ethan nodded his head and Vivian led him to the door to see him out. Once he was outside, he glanced back and met her eyes. She was staring at him so desperately, pleading with him, silently, to find her daughter's killer. The only problem was, Ethan still wasn't sure if that was another person, or if it was Kiera herself.

CHAPTER FOUR

It was just after three o'clock. Ethan was having mixed feelings about each of the families he had spoken with so far. Of course all parents speak highly of their children. Of course all parents of a deceased child speak highly of them. But with these families, everything seemed too perfect. No enemies. No arguments. No boyfriends – with the exception of Haddie Taylor – and no known mental illnesses. In fact, every time Ethan mentioned mental illness or suicide to the parents, they got defensive. As though he were a terrible person for even suggesting such a thing. Was this simply a coping mechanism to deal with their daughters' deaths, or were there things they were keeping from him?

Ethan didn't know what to think. When he first arrived on scene the day before, he knew that something was off. The dispatch call had detailed that three girls were plunged off the roof of their school. His initial assumption was that they'd been pushed. But then getting to the school, hearing what everyone was saying – they were all convinced it was suicide. And that began to muddle his perception of the case.

With the absence of a suicide note and no plausible cause for suicide, all fingers were pointing at this being a murder. But even then, it was a rare and unusual homicide. Broad daylight, roof of the school. It wasn't pre-mediated. If the killer had planned this out, they could have done a much better job. This implied that the killing was a last-minute decision, perhaps even accidental. Something happened on that roof yesterday morning. Someone got those girls up there and either pushed them or had them jump. But who would do that? To all three of them? And more importantly: why?

Perhaps it was a teacher, someone who worked at the school. A key role-model in the girls' lives. That might make sense, given the circumstances. A teacher or someone who worked at the school would have had access. It could have even been another student. Or multiple students. They would have seen the girls every single day, observed them, knew their habits and patterns. It would be convenient if the killer was someone in the school. Easy to narrow down. But that still left motive. Why would someone do that? What did those girls do to deserve what happened to them?

The next step in this investigation was social media. It was the twenty-first century, after all. Millennials were practically glued to their phones and laptops. The internet was almost as good of a tool in solving a crime as DNA evidence. Teenagers put everything on the internet – their relationship status, who they are and aren't friends with, what books they're reading, the thoughts in their heads. If Ethan wanted a closer look into those girl's lives, social media was the key.

First he began with Kiera Barnes. Her Facebook name was listed as Kiera Mae Barnes. Profile picture was a self-portrait (a selfie), and she was smiling, bright-eyed, brown hair flowing over her shoulders.

She had 348 friends. Lives in: Briarwood. Studies at: St. Paul's Catholic School. He scrolled down her timeline. Posts from friends, videos she shared, mobile uploads. She had made a status three days ago about how much she loved Leonardo DiCaprio. More posts revealed that she was in support of the Cancer Society, was participating in a Relay for Life event in two weeks, and loved Oreos.

A girl named Sierra Green posted on her wall an inspirational quote, most likely found somewhere on the internet. "Optimism is the faith that leads to achievement. Nothing can be done without hope and confidence."

There weren't many personal posts, mostly just shared links from friends. There were check-in points from when she went somewhere, and mobile uploads of Kiera and the girls. Ethan clicked the photos and scrolled through. All three of them in a forest. The photo was taken from behind, the three of them walking through the trees. Another shot – a selfie – of Kiera and Haddie, sticking their tongues out. Photos of them at a party, holding up red solo cups, wide smiles.

He exited out of the album and found her Instagram. Mostly selfies. Selfies with the other girls. A picture of a coffee mug and her feet in fuzzy socks. A shot of her finger nails, freshly painted. A clear Starbucks cup, filled with red liquid. A bathtub, filled to the rim with bubbles. Quirky little captions.

Ethan clicked out of Instagram and went back to Facebook to find Haddie. Her name was simply Haddie Taylor. 657 friends. That was nearly the population of their school. Her profile picture looked professionally taken; a shot of her posing on a beach. White sand, turquoise water. Must have been somewhere tropical.

Her cover photo was a pink sunset over a lake. As he scrolled down her timeline, he saw another link to the Relay for Life page, probably a mutual thing between the girls. A photograph taken at the school, presumably, of Haddie kissing a giant poster that read: Kiss Away Cancer. A tagged post from Gabriella Pratt thanking her for the birthday wishes. Then photos of Gabriella and Haddie at a party together, pink ribbons and balloons surrounding the room.

Another post from a friend – Layla Bowen – a photo of the two of them standing at the beach, posing for the camera. Haddie had shared a post the week prior titled: 10 Reasons why I Love my Mother.

Ethan scrolled down further and found photos of Haddie and Oliver, holding hands, him kissing her on the cheek. There were photos of Haddie and her parents, Haddie in a field beside a horse, Haddie doing a handstand in a grassy field. Not many status posts at all.

Her Instagram page consisted of selfies, artsy shots of sunsets and scenery, and photos with the girls. He clicked one of the photos; it was of Haddie, Kiera and Anneka, all smiling into the camera. Ethan felt strange looking at it, as though the three of them were staring directly at him. So happy, so alive. Their eyes were silently willing him to bring them justice. To find out what happened to them.

Lastly he found Anneka Wilson's Facebook page. Her profile picture was a selfie: a closed-mouth smile, her short blonde hair over one shoulder as she turned sideways for the camera. Her cover photo was a black and white photograph of New York City.

The first few posts on her timeline were photos. It was an album titled Photography. In it she had posted all of the photos she had taken. They were good, Ethan noticed. Really good. There were landscapes, portraits, shots of her dog. Photographs bursting with colour – red sunsets, green forests. And then there were black and whites. Abandoned houses, furniture, trees, silhouettes. The photos were stunning.

As he scrolled down her timeline, Ethan noticed that there were no status updates, only photos she had taken, along with posts from friends. There was a photo she added of her and her father captioned love you dad.

Then, going back farther, more photographs from the previous summer. Vacation, the beach, seashells, Haddie and Kiera. And that was it. There wasn't much else to see.

He looked up her Instagram, which proved to be exactly what he assumed: Purely photography. Mostly the same photos he had seen on her Facebook with a few newer ones, the last one posted four days ago.

Most teenagers posted everything about their lives online. But other than photography, Anneka hadn't posted a single thing. Was that strange? Possibly. But perhaps she just preferred to keep her life private. That wasn't a crime. There was nothing wrong with that. In fact, Ethan appreciated people who didn't post their entire lives on Facebook. He found it quite bothersome when Jordan's friends would post essays on their statuses, going off and ranting about things that no one else cared about.

Ethan closed the internet tabs and sat back, taking a sip from his coffee cup. As far as he could tell, all three of the girls lived happy, normal lives. But then again, social media wasn't the best representation of one's mental health. People post when they're happy – they don't post when they're sad. It also didn't tell him who hated them and wanted them dead. Ethan would return to the subject of social media later. He would also need to get their phone records and see who they were in contact with the most. That would prove useful. If there was anything they were hiding – or anyone – Ethan would find out.

–––––

The next stop on Ethan's list was the boyfriend's place, Oliver Harris. It was 4:15p.m. He only had so much time of investigating left for the day before he had to meet with Kennedy and Jesse to discuss their findings then head back to Riverton. He had already begun mapping out tomorrow's agenda: Return to the victim's homes, search the girls' rooms, talk to the teachers, neighbors, and anyone else close to them. But right now, it was the boyfriend.

Oliver Harris was a good looking kid. Ethan could see why Haddie Taylor – who was your picture-perfect ideal of the high school cheerleader – was dating the guy. Everyone thought they were going to get married, Ethan remembered Kelsey saying.

"I'm very sorry for your loss," Ethan said to Oliver, who sat on the couch in his living room. Oliver's mother had answered the door, looking just as distraught as the other mothers of the day. She excused herself and gave them privacy as she busied herself in the kitchen. "Thanks," Oliver said. The kid looked numb. Like he'd been crying all day, but didn't want this detective to sense any sign of weakness. "How long had you and Haddie been dating?" Ethan asked, tapping his pen against his notepad. "Um," Oliver took in a breath. "About two years, maybe?" "How did the two of you meet?" "That's a dumb question." "What do you mean?" "Everyone knows each other here. The question isn't how. It's when. When you meet someone." "Okay. When did you and Haddie meet?" "Well, we kind of grew up together, living in the same neighborhood and all. We were never close friends or anything. But then I guess, when high school started, I began to notice her... in a different way. You know?" "And she noticed you too." "Yeah." "So you started dating." He nodded. "What did her parents think of that?" Ethan inquired. "Her parents love me. And my parents adored Haddie. The daughter they always wanted. I have three brothers, so." "What was she like, Haddie?" Oliver took a moment to answer this. "She was fun. Loud. Charismatic. Everyone noticed her. Everyone loved her." "And you," Ethan said. "You loved her?" "Of course I loved her." "Did the two of you ever fight?" "Obviously. Doesn't everyone? I'm not saying we were perfect. There were things she did that I didn't agree with. And of course the same goes for me. We bickered and disagreed. But at the end of the day, I loved her more than anything." "You two were close. You would know if she had any enemies, anyone who might want to hurt her." Oliver was quiet for a moment. "Yeah, I suppose I would. But I don't. I don't know a God damn thing." "She never said anything to you? Never mentioned anything unusual?" Oliver shrugged. Ethan stared at him. "Oliver, what do you think happened to Haddie?" "Call me Ollie. I hate Oliver. Sounds so conservative." "Ollie," Ethan said. "What do you think happened?" Oliver was quiet for a moment as he gathered his thoughts. "Someone pushed them?" "You say that like it's a question." "It is a question. How the hell am I supposed to know?" "You were her boyfriend," Ethan said. "Did she jump? Did Haddie kill herself?" He was quiet again. "No." "Are you sure?" "Why would she jump?" "You tell me." "Haddie wasn't crazy, okay? She wouldn't jump off a building to prove a point." "Prove a point? What are you talking about?" Oliver was quiet again. "Ollie," Ethan said. "What are you not telling me?" "Nothing." "Oliver." He looked at Ethan, flattened his mouth into a line, thought about it. "She was just... I don't know. She could be a bit dramatic sometimes." "How so?" "Like, if something happened to her, it was the end of the world. And she thought everyone believed it too. Like she was Miss Center of the Universe." "Were things not good between the two of you recently?" "Not at all, things were great. Haddie's always been that way. If you know her, you know what I mean." "Drama queen?" "Yeah. And very attention-seeking. All eyes on Haddie. But I just... I don't know. I don't think she jumped. My point was, if you think she did jump... she wouldn't have." "To prove a point?" "Yeah." Nothing he was saying was making sense. "What kind of point would Haddie be trying to prove?" Ethan asked. Oliver shrugged. "I don't know. She's a girl. She wanted people to notice her. Girls are always trying to prove something. That they're better and smarter. That they mean something to the world. That they matter." "Do you think Haddie mattered, Ollie?" "Of course she mattered. She mattered to me. I didn't care if the whole world loved her or not. I loved her. I cared." He was quiet again. "But that wasn't enough for her." "She wanted more." Oliver nodded. "She wanted fame, fortune, celebrity status. Briarwood wasn't good enough for her. She wanted to go to Hollywood, make it big as a singer or an actress." "Big dreams, little town." "Yeah, exactly. She hated it here. Briarwood did nothing for that girl. It didn't deserve her. She could have done anything. Been anyone. Been with anyone. Yet she chose me. She loved me." He was quiet again. "So she didn't jump." Ethan said. "She didn't jump."

Ethan left Oliver's house and headed for his car. Talking with Oliver proved more beneficial than he initially suspected. Oliver opened up new possibilities about Haddie Taylor. Things family members would never say. Not because they were untrue, but because parents don't think of their children in a negative light. Not that what Oliver said about Haddie was negative – it was realistic. Ethan could understand more about her now, get a better understanding of the type of person she was, get inside of her head. Dramatic. Attention-seeking. What did Oliver mean when he said to prove a point? Would she have done something like that for attention? Pushed herself to the edge of suicide to make somebody notice?

Why did you jump, Haddie? Ethan thought to himself. Or... what did you do to make somebody push you?

It was just after five when Ethan arrived at the local diner to meet with Kennedy and Jesse. They were having an end-of-day meeting to go over the information that each of them had gathered thus far – evidence, interviews, plausible explanations. Ethan felt that Cross and Tanner had it easy. They were officers, after all, and he was the detective. While they obtained preliminary information and gathered things like evidence and witness testimony's, Ethan had to talk to everyone, go through the case step-by-step, rack his brain for hours on end about culprits and suspects and logic. Who did it and why. That was the tough part – analyzing it all and trying to put a finger on the right thing with one hundred percent certainty.

The diner was one of the only ones in town. It was a quaint place, only two waitresses working. The place wasn't busy. Ethan found them at a booth near the back and slid in across from them. Kennedy and Jesse already had food and drinks in front of them. A coffee sat there waiting for Ethan.

They made brief small talk then got right down to business. Each of them went over everything they had gathered. Ethan filled them in on each of the families, the boyfriend, the Facebook pages. He listened intently as Kennedy spoke, then Jesse. Once they had all finished speaking, it was quiet, a gap in the conversation.

"So, your final thoughts of today are...?" Ethan said to both officers. Kennedy sipped her coffee, eyeing Ethan through slit lids. "Right now, I'm going with suicide." "Even after everything I just told you?" Ethan was taken back. She nodded. "This town is too small to have a murderer lurking around." Tanner snorted. "That's ignorant of you," he said. "As a cop, I mean. No town is too small to have murderers." "Now you're just starting to sound like the rest of the town," Ethan said. "You're giving up that easily, eh?" "I'm not giving up," Kennedy said, placing her coffee cup on the table. "I'm thinking logically. And what makes logical sense is that those three girls had some crazed suicide pact and killed themselves together." Ethan rolled his eyes. "There's no such thing as murder here," Kennedy said. "Everyone I talked to is lovely and decent and had only nice things to say about the girls. Everyone is like family here. I can't imagine anyone who would want to hurt them." "Then clearly you haven't heard about The Sad Killer," Tanner remarked. Both Ethan and Kennedy looked at him. "The what?" "The Sad Killer," he repeated, taking a bite from his sandwich then licking his fingers, which were doused in mustard. He reached for his water and took a gulp. They waited patiently. "Don't worry," Tanner said. "Before today, I hadn't heard of him either." "What the hell is a Sad Killer?" Kennedy asked, reaching for a fry off of Ethan's plate. Tanner cleared his throat then wiped his mouth with a napkin. "I was talking to some locals today. One of them was saying how they hadn't seen this many deaths since The Sad Summer. I said, what's The Sad Summer? Well, turns out, during the summer of '65, there was a serial killer here. Seven men murdered between April to August." "Here? In Briarwood?" Ethan asked, even though, yes, Tanner had clearly just said that. But he needed clarification. Tanner nodded. "So what ever happened to him?" Kennedy asked. "The killer, I mean." "That's the good part," Tanner smiled as he leaned forward. "They never found him." "Get out," Kennedy pushed back into her seat and laughed. "That's unnerving!" "Gotta love a good serial killer story," Tanner said. "Especially when they go unsolved. Like the Zodiac. Man, those cases just get to me." "So this guy,"

Ethan said. "Kills seven people in 1965. And gets away with it. Scot free. No one knows who he is?" "Or was," Tanner said. "Probably dead by now. It was a long time ago." "Fifty-one years isn't that long ago," Kennedy said. "He could still be alive." "Depends how old he was during the murders," Tanner said. "Why do they call him the Sad Killer?" Ethan asked. "Oh, right," Tanner leaned in again. "So get this. At each of the murders, the guy writes sad. Just like that. S. A. D. Sad." "What, you mean like written in blood or something?" "No, in marker. On the ground. Or the wall. I don't know. I only just heard about it." "So they called him the Sad Killer. Because he was sad?" Ethan asked. "Yeah. Listen, I don't know, O'Riley. I'm no expert on this shit. Go ask the Briarwood Lieutenant or something." "Maybe I will," Ethan said. "Sounds interesting." "Oh, here we go," Kennedy rolled her eyes. "O'Riley's going to go digging up old case files, trying to hunt down the Sad Killer." Ethan shook his head and laughed. "I'm just curious, that's all." "Why do you have a thing for serial killers, anyway?" Kennedy asked him. "They intrigue me." "Should we be concerned?" Tanner joked. "Yeah, of course. Next thing you know, I'll become a serial killer. As long as I get the notoriety, of course." Ethan joked back. "That's the thing I don't get," Tanner said. "What?" "The serial killers who don't get caught. I mean, most serial killers are psychopaths, right?" "Yeah," Kennedy said. "And one of the main characteristics of psychopathy disorder is narcissism," Tanner explained. "So most serial killers either end up outing themselves, or agreeing to turn themselves in simply for the notoriety of it all. It's like they can't help it. They want to be caught, because they want to be known. It's all a part of their illness. So the serial killers who are never caught, like Zodiac, for example... How do they live with themselves? Knowing that no one will ever truly know who they are. That they will never get the full recognition that they deserve." "Very true," Kennedy said. "It must drive them insane. Well, lucky for us, O'Riley is the opposite of a narcissist, aren't ya, Ev?" she punched his shoulder. "We won't ever have to worry about you becoming a serial killer."

They finished up at the restaurant, paid their bill, said their good-byes, and headed to their cars. They'd be back again the next day, repeating the same routine. Ethan checked his watch; it was almost six-thirty.

His mind was still swirling from the conversations. He was appalled at how quick Kennedy had been to dismiss the homicide option, so easily persuaded into believing whatever the town said. She was a good police officer, but he couldn't quite figure out why she was giving up and rolling over so easily.

The three of them had been working for Riverton PD together for the last few years. It had been Jesse Tanner who had joined the taskforce first, two years before Ethan. Then it was only a year after Ethan joined that Kennedy came along. They worked the odd case together here and there, but generally, he didn't see them too often. Ethan had developed quite the rapport with Kennedy Cross – KC, as he called her – going over cases together, getting her opinion on things. She was smart and diligent, and Ethan respected that. Tanner was good in his own ways. He had a knack for finding out truths that no one else could. And he never left a task unfinished. Together, Ethan was sure that they could solve this thing – although, most of that weight laid heavily on Ethan's shoulders, not theirs.

Just as he got in the car and started the engine, his cellphone rang. He dug into his pocket and put it to his ear. "O'Riley," he said. "Detective," said a familiar female voice. "It's Doctor Meredith Kepler. The medical examiner." "Oh, hi. How are you?" "I'm fine, thanks. Do you think you'd be able to come down to the coroner's office?" "Right now?" "Yes." "I was about to head back to Riverton. Is it urgent?" "Yes." Ethan paused. "Alright. I'll be there in five."

He was there in six minutes. The parking lot to the small building was empty except for the sole Mazda parked at the back. Ethan entered the building and headed down the stairs towards the morgue. Meredith Kepler stood in her white lab coat, facing him as he walked in. Ethan could see one body lying on the table, the white sheet covering everything but the face. It didn't take him long to determine which girl it was – the bashed-in skull gave it away.

"What's wrong?" he asked once he got close. Meredith unhooked her hands, which she held in front of her. She walked closer to the examining table as she spoke. "I was doing the autopsy on all three of the girls this afternoon when I noticed something quite alarming. I thought you should be the first one I notify, given the circumstances." "What is it?" Ethan asked, his heart-rate accelerating with anticipation. "It's Haddie Taylor," Meredith said, peeling her eyes away from the body on the table and

meeting Ethan's gaze. She pursed her lips together, unsure of how to proceed. "She was four weeks pregnant
when she died."

Chapter Five

CHAPTER FIVE

Haddie was pregnant. Four weeks pregnant. That was barely pregnant at all. But still pregnant, nonetheless.

On average, women don't discover that they're pregnant until at least six weeks. If only Haddie Taylor had lived for two weeks longer. Would she have found out then? Or... Did she already know?

Did Oliver Harris know?

All of these questions swarmed Ethan's head. He drove back to Riverton in silence, trying to process it all; Meredith Kepler as she spoke the word pregnant. Ethan's eyes widening, then diverting to the body lying on the table. Haddie Taylor. Her beautiful head smashed in. Her tiny stomach, flat and without flaw.

There was a fetus in there. A little baby, yet to be a baby, never would become a baby. It would simply be a fetus indefinitely, never having the chance to grow and have a life.

Did Haddie know?

That was the biggest question of all. Because if she didn't know, what would she have done with it? Kept it? Put it up for adoption? Aborted it?

And if she did know... well, that brought forth even more daunting questions. Most specifically: Is that why she jumped?

But then why did Kiera Barnes and Anneka Wilson jump as well? Unless they really were pushed. Or coerced. Forced off the edge of St. Paul's.

Did Oliver know? Perhaps not. But if he did, would he have mentioned it today? Told Ethan what was going on? Would he have pushed her? Then pushed the other two to get rid of witnesses?

This baby changed everything.

Ethan would have to go back tomorrow and talk to him. But wouldn't that break some sort of confidentiality? She was dead, after all. But still.

Would it matter if he was the father? Would he have a right to know?

Ethan arrived home in a similar fashion as the night prior. Jordan had made roast chicken and a ceaser salad and was busily rushing around the kitchen, whistling to herself as she set the table. She didn't need to do all of the things that she did. But she did them regardless. And with joy.

Sometimes Ethan felt bad. Guilty, almost. Jordan was by no means stay-at-home-wife material. She was pro-feminist and anti-patriarchy. She believed that women should be in the work-force just as much as men. But still, that didn't stop her from cooking and cleaning, and doing whatever other duties she desired. Ethan pointed this out to her once. She got mad at him, claiming that it was only going against feminism if the woman didn't want to do it. If she could work and cook, then why wouldn't she? She also pointed out that Ethan could cook, too, if he wanted to. He didn't, but she never complained.

"Long day?" she asked when she noticed how quiet he was. "Hmm?" he looked up at her from across the table. "Yeah, just tired, that's all." "How's the case going?" "It's complicated." "I can follow." "No, I don't mean that," he said, putting down his beer. "The people are complicated. The whole scenario is complicated." "What do you mean?" "I'm getting certain things from the parents, different things from the boyfriend. Then the medical examiner tells me she was pregnant." "Who was pregnant?" "Haddie Taylor." Ethan wasn't sure how much of his cases he could legally discuss with Jordan. But he always told her anyways. "That's one of the girls from the roof?" she asked. "Yes. Haddie, Anneka and Kiera." "How old were they?" "Sixteen." "And one of them was pregnant?" "Looks to be that way." Jordan made a face somewhere between astonishment and sorrow. "It's so sad. Tragic, really." "It is. And I still have no idea if they jumped, or..." "Or if they were murdered," she finished for him. He nodded. "Is that all that's on your mind?" Jordan asked. "You're awfully quiet." He met her gaze and forced a small smile. "I'm fine. Really. It's all just getting to my head." She returned the smile, then grabbed his plate to begin clearing the table.

Ethan helped her tidy up, then grabbed his beer and headed into the living room to turn on the television. Anything to get his mind off this case and give him a bit of reprieve. That was probably the most difficult part about being a detective. You never truly left the office. It followed you home, followed you everywhere. Never giving you rest, never giving you peace of mind. Every waking second is spent thinking about victims or cases, solved and unsolved. They stay with you, haunt you, taunt you. It's miserable, but that's how it goes.

He needed to get away from it all because he knew it was bothering Jordan. When Ethan was upset, Jordan was upset. Like he said, they were in sync. So even if he tried to fake it and be happy, his misery would spread on to her, wallowing in between them like a disease. Sadness. Dismay. Death.

He needed to stop thinking about it because Jordan was catching on that something else was amiss. And although she already knew about his own personal tragedy, he didn't want her to have to bring it up again. To attempt to console him about something that one can never truly heal from.

Ethan barely thought about it himself. It was too difficult. So he did his best to push it away, suppress it to the deepest parts of his mind. But then there were times like this when a situation so tragic arises, and the similarities were uncanny.

It was his old partner – the one who died three years ago. The one whose death still haunted him and affected him each and every day. The reason he still hadn't moved on and got reassigned a new partner. The reason he preferred to work solo.

Detective Olivia Mackery. Died March 22, 2013. On duty. She was shot, twice. Two bullets to the chest. She wasn't wearing a vest. Didn't think she had to. It was a house call, to check in on a witness. Nothing serious. Nothing life threatening. Nothing to wear a vest for.

The damage was done. Punctured lung, internal bleeding. Nothing the doctors could do. She died within six hours of being shot. She, along with the baby she was carrying. Their baby.

She was five months pregnant at that time. She shouldn't have even been on duty. She should have taken work off, went on maternity leave. But Olivia was dedicated to her job. She loved what she did, took pride in her work. And it was just a simple house call. Nobody could have saw it coming. Especially not Ethan, who was with her the entire time. From the moment the bullet left the gun, to the moment in the hospital room, when he held her hand, cried on her chest as he held her belly, whispering to his child who would never be born.

Olivia Mackery. O-Mac, everyone called her. They met at the academy. She was fresh out of college for criminology. Her hair was a light shade of blonde – like vanilla pudding. Her eyes were emerald green, and they seemed to get brighter every time he looked at them. Or perhaps it was her personality that made her eyes shine so bright. She was always smiling. Always so happy and optimistic. It's a wonder how they became friends, really. Ethan was dull. Pessimistic. Didn't see the good things in life. Not until Olivia, that is.

When they met, it was as though his world had opened up. The air was fresher, the sun was brighter. Everything seemed to matter more when she was around. She made everything seem so good. So golden. She made everything matter.

It was forbidden for partners to date – for anyone at the precinct to date, really. Conflict of interest, distraction, etcetera. But that didn't stop them. They simply kept their love affair a secret. Nobody knew. Nobody had to know. It was just the two of them. O'Riley and O-Mac against the world. Ethan and Olivia. O'Riley and Mackery. Olivia O'Riley. That's what her name would have been if they married. O.O.

But of course, they never married. They never even had the chance to start their life together. Because she got pregnant. And nobody knew it was Ethan's. Nobody knew that they were even together. Not until she died. Then everyone knew. And everyone knew about the baby. The baby he would never have. Never get the chance to have. Because that opportunity had been ripped away from him without a choice. Olivia never had that choice. Because Miles Brady took that choice away from her when he fired his gun.

It was a boy – that much they knew. They were going to call him Luka. Five months along and that baby already had more love than some children have their whole lives. But Luka never got a chance. Olivia never got a chance.

And now, that was all that Ethan could think about since he saw Haddie Taylor on that table, Meredith Kepler saying the words pregnant. Did Haddie know?

Ethan hoped not. Because if she did... if that girl knew that she was pregnant and willingly took her own life anyway... He couldn't even think about what he'd do.

He was on the road again, back to Briarwood: day three. First, he would go back to the school. Talk with teachers, students, friends of the girls. Then he'd return to the homes of the girls, look around, keep an eye out for anything useful. Maybe talk to the neighbors, see if they had anything to say.

Ethan was trying to think critically. There were only two possible scenarios. If the girls killed themselves and this was a group suicide, there had to have been a reason. Depression, drugs, peer pressure. What makes three perfectly healthy teenage girls suddenly kill themselves? Was there a much larger picture that he wasn't seeing? Did something traumatic happen to the three of them? Something they could no longer cope with?

Then there was scenario B: they were pushed or talked off the edge. And in that case, there was the even more pressing question: who wanted them dead?

Ethan arrived at the Briarwood station to meet with the team and go over formalities. Frank and Jesse Tanner were seated at the table already. Ethan entered the room and pulled out a chair. Kennedy walked in after him, opening up her briefcase and tossing a scatter of paperwork on the table before anyone could say a word. They all looked at her.

"We got some news from the medical examiner," Kennedy said. "Go on, then," Frank nodded towards the paperwork. Kennedy waited a moment before she spoke. Dramatic pause. But Ethan already knew what was coming. "Haddie Taylor was pregnant," Kennedy said. "Get out," Jesse said, leaning forward and grabbing the sheets of paper. Frank leaned over to examine the documents as well. Ethan remained silent. "You want to look, O'Riley?" Kennedy asked him. He didn't make a move. Then her face changed. "You already knew." He nodded. "Kepler told me yesterday," Frank and Jesse turned to him. "And you didn't think to mention this?" "I had a lot on my plate," Ethan said. "Meaning?" Kennedy asked. "Cross," Frank snapped. Frank knew. He had worked with Olivia for years. Been there when she died. He knew why this would be bothering Ethan. "Well, have you looked into it?" Kennedy asked. "Who was the father?" "I'm assuming it's the boyfriend, Oliver Harris," Ethan said. "Get on it, then, alright?" Frank said to him. Ethan nodded. "Will do." "What else do we have on the agenda today?" Frank asked. Kennedy went on about what she and forensics were looking into. Jesse confirmed that he would be out with Hal Davis for the day. Finally Ethan spoke. "I'll be talking to people at the school. Friends, teachers. Then I'm going to look at the girls' rooms. See if there's anything that stands out." "Like a suicide note?" Kennedy scoffed. Ethan didn't answer her. "We'll meet back here at end of day," Frank said. "Best of luck out there."

Ethan waited in the office of the principal, Mrs. Rebecca Lang. She was a tall, lanky woman with dark red hair. She wore small, burgundy rimmed spectacles, kept on a chain around her neck. She entered the room moments later in a flurry, closing the door behind her and walking over to her desk to take a seat across from Ethan.

"How is the investigation going, Detective..." she paused. "I'm sorry, I've forgotten your name." "O'Riley. Detective O'Riley," he said. "Still in the early stages, unfortunately. I just wanted to go around the school, perhaps talk with some teachers and students. Is this okay to do now? Or would the lunch hour be a better time?" "No no, now is fine. Do you need my assistance with anything?" "I should be fine, thanks," Ethan smiled and stood. "Actually, just the names of the girls' teachers would be a great start."

Rebecca Lang got the information for Ethan, then printed it on a sheet of paper for him. He grabbed the sheet and headed down the hallways of St. Paul's.

His first stop was with the girl's homeroom teacher, Mrs. Hawthorn. Fortunately they were all in the same class. Hawthorn was in the empty classroom alone, grading papers.

"You must be here about the girls," she said once Ethan entered the room. "I am. Detective Ethan O'Riley," he stuck out his hand. She stood from her desk and shook his hand. "Mrs. Hawthorne. But please, call me Miranda." "Miranda," Ethan said, leaning against one of the desks. "What can you tell me about Haddie, Anneka, and Kiera?" She took in a breath as she sat back down and adjusted in her chair. "Well, they were good girls. Didn't get into trouble. You know, some of the kids around here often resort to drugs and alcohol when they can't find anything better to do. It's a small town, so they get bored very easily. The girls never succumbed to such stupidity. I can always tell which of my students are the bright ones." "And the three girls – they were bright ones?" "Well, yes. All three maintained good grades. Always had their homework and assignments completed on time. As far as I can tell, there was nothing astray in their lives. Good home and family life. Good school life." "How did they interact with each other in class? And with other students?" Miranda thought about this for a moment. "Usually the students work independently for most things. But whenever there was group work, it was always the three of them together. They'd arrive to class at the same time and they'd leave together. They associated with the other students at times, but as far as I can tell, the three of them just kept to themselves." "So you never noticed any problems in the classroom with other students?" She shook her head. "No, everyone got along great." "What about boys? Did any of them talk with boys in the class?" "I know Haddie had a boyfriend. Oliver Harris. Other than that, I think they might have had a few male friends, but nothing that's out of the ordinary." "What about other teachers?" Ethan asked. "Did the girls ever have problems with teachers or staff? Get in trouble? Detentions? Talk back in class?" "Not that I'm aware of. You'd have to ask the others to get a better idea, I presume. But as far as I can tell, the girls lived seamless lives." "I'm sure they must have had some problems," Ethan said. "They were teenage girls, after all." "If they did, I wasn't aware of it. Either that, or they did a pretty damn good job at hiding it."

─────

By the time Ethan finished speaking with the teachers, it was already lunch hour. He couldn't say that he was too pleased with the results. Every one of them had said the same things: The girls were good, studious kids who worked hard and didn't cause any trouble. He wished that there was a better way to get an understanding of what those three were like.

Ethan wandered through the courtyard, which just twenty-four hours prior, was taped off and scattered with police officers. He made his way down the hallway and into the cafeteria. It felt strange to him, being back in high school. The atmosphere, the busyness of it all. The tables, the cliques. He headed to one of the tables near the front of the room where a number of girls were seated, eating their lunches.

"Hi there," Ethan said as he loomed over them. "Anyone here that was friends with Haddie Taylor?" They all stared at him, momentarily silenced by his visible level of authority. Finally, a girl a few seats down spoke up.

"You're looking for them," she extended her arm and pointed across the cafeteria. He followed her gaze and locked eyes on what he assumed was the table she was referring to. "Those girls there?" Ethan asked to confirm. The girl nodded her head. "Thanks." He walked over and repeated the motions. There were four girls, two on each side of the table. "Yes?" said one of the girls. "I'm Detective O'Riley. You were friends with Haddie, Anneka, and Kiera?" They all nodded. "If it's alright with you, I'd like to talk to you about the girls," Ethan looked around the room, crowded with people and food trays. "Would you mind coming outside, to the courtyard, perhaps?"

The four looked at each other, then shrugged, simultaneously gathering up their purses and leading the way, Ethan following behind.

They got outside and made their way over to one of the picnic tables. The sun was shining and the weather was warm. One of the girls hopped up on the table, crossing her long legs that flowed from beneath her short, striped Catholic uniform skirt, and lit a cigarette.

"Can I get your names?" Ethan asked, holding his notepad in front of him. "Gabby," said the brunette with green eyes. "Full names would be great," Ethan said. She rolled her eyes. "Gabriella Grace Pratt." The girl next to her giggled. Golden brown skin, dark curly hair. She looked at Ethan. "Maya Bowman." The one sitting on the picnic table smoking the cigarette spoke next. "Sadie West." The last girl, tall, tanned, red hair cut shoulder length, "Rachel Dunn." Ethan took their names down, then faced them once again. "No offence," he started. "But giggling and sarcasm aren't usually indicators that one is mourning the loss of their friends." That hit a nerve. Altogether, their smiles dropped. Gabriella dropped her gaze. Sadie put her cigarette out on the table. It was silent for a moment before Gabriella spoke up. "Everyone deals with grief differently." "How so?" Ethan asked. "Obviously we're sad," she said. "We're fucking devastated. Haddie, Kiera, and Anneka were our friends. Just because we had a little giggle just now doesn't mean we're not broken up about it. We're eating lunch for Christ sake. We're allowed to smile and talk normally again." "Gabs is right," Maya said. "You can't tell us that we're not sad. Because we are. You just caught us at an off time. Things were getting back to normal today. People returned to school, the crying seized." "Okay, my apologizes," Ethan said. Not even five minutes with these girls and he was already succumbing. "So what did you want to ask us?" Sadie said, tilting her head sideways, examining him. "Why don't you tell me what your friendship was like," Ethan said. "With the girls?" "Yes." Rachel cleared her throat. "That's a weird question." "How so?" Ethan asked. "How does someone explain what their friendship with someone is like? Uh, we were friends. What more can I say?" "How close were you with them?" Ethan asked. "Not as close as the three of them," Sadie spoke again. "So I've heard," Ethan said. "Why were they so exclusive?" "Beats me," Sadie replied. "It was always the three of them, since middle school. There was always something about them, something that no one else could compete with. Sure, we were all friends with them, but our friendship couldn't compare with what they had." "Did you all get along?" "Yeah," the four girls said simultaneously. "No fights or arguments?" It was quiet for a moment. "Everyone fights sometimes," Rachel said. "And we're girls. We're always bickering about something. But for the most part, everyone got along fine. Nothing too detrimental." "Do you know if the girls had any enemies? Anyone who might want to hurt them?" They all shook their heads. "So as far as you can tell, the girls got along with everyone? They had no one on their bad side?" "Not really," Maya said. "No one who would want to kill them." "But possibly someone who wasn't in their good books?" Ethan asked. Again, more silence and blank stares. "What can you tell me about Beth Campbell?" Ethan said. Rachel made a face. "Beth? Why do you want to know about her?" "I hear she and Haddie didn't get on so well." "Obviously," Gabriella said. "Everyone knows that." "Yes, can you tell me why that is?" The girls shrugged. Sadie exhaled a breath of smoke from the second cigarette she had lit. "Beth is a bitch," she said simply. "She hangs out with those other two. Audrey and Megan." "Haddie and Beth were best friends once upon a time," Maya explained. "But Beth is psychotic. She told her parents all these lies about Haddie. The school had to get involved. It was a mess." "And when was this?" Ethan asked. "Seventh grade." "And they still hold onto this grudge from all those years ago?" "It's not a grudge," Gabriella said. "Like Sadie said, Beth's a bitch. Why would Haddie want to be friends with someone like that?" Ethan nodded, trying to understand the logic of teenage girls. "Did anything happen between the two of them recently?" Sadie laughed audibly. "If you're thinking that Beth Campbell pushed them off the roof, then you really should take up a different profession." Ethan stared at her. "Alright, so other than Beth, no enemies you've failed to mention?" They all shook their heads. "What about teachers? Or faculty? Were the girls involved with anyone?" "Like, dating a teacher?" Maya asked. "Sure," Ethan said. "No, I don't think so," Rachel said. "Any teachers they hated or had a vendetta against?" "Just Mr. Jackson," Sadie said. "But everyone hates him." Ethan glanced back down at his notepad, thought for a moment. "What did your time spent with them usually consist of?" Ethan asked, hoping to prompt more discussion. "Whatever we felt like," Gabriella replied. "Go out, party, drink..." Ethan suggested. They all looked at each other. Sadie said, "We just did whatever. Okay?" "Sometimes we went out," Maya said. The others looked at her. "We'd go to the mall. Go for long drives together. Anneka was really into photography, so we'd like, go out places and take photos. You ever hear of urban exploring?" "I'm familiar with it." "Yeah, we did that kind of stuff," she said. "Get into any trouble?" Ethan asked. "No," Gabriella replied. "What kind of girls do we think we are, Detective?" "That's what I'm here to find out." "Haddie was like, queen of everything," Rachel said suddenly. The others looked at her. "What do you mean?" Ethan asked. "You know, like, the queen. The ruler. If anyone was going to win Prom King and Queen, it was Haddie and Ollie." "So they were the it-couple, then." "Yeah, exactly," Rachel said. "Everyone wanted to be Haddie. Or be friends with her. Be known by her." "But we loved her," Gabriella said, shooting a look at Rachel. "It was just difficult sometimes, being friends with Haddie Taylor," Rachel said, and Ethan finally felt like he was getting somewhere. "Don't listen to her," Sadie said, rolling her eyes. "Difficult for Rache, maybe. Haddie wasn't like that with us. She was our equal. We were all friends here." "Yeah, but those three were... different," Rachel said. "Define different," Ethan said. "Like, closer, I mean," Rachel replied. "A bond that none of us could compete with. They grew up together, knew each other like the back of their hand. We all met when we started high school," Rachel motioned to their group of four. "We all hung out and got along well, but those three were always... well, best friends." "Why would the girls have been up on the roof that day?" Ethan asked. "Was that out of the ordinary?" "No," Gabriella said. "The three of them went up there to hangout sometimes. Talk, eat lunch." "None of you ever went up there?" "No," Gabriella said. "It was their spot." Ethan took in this information. If the girls were pushed, somebody must have known that they'd be up there. And if they weren't pushed, then that just meant that the girls chose one of their favourite hangout spots to kill themselves. "What do you think happened to them?" Ethan asked, and for the first time, the girls were actually perplexed on how to respond. "I don't know," Rachel said. "I honestly don't." "Do you think they jumped?" Ethan asked. "Did they ever say anything that would make you think something was amiss? You girls were their closest friends. Did you notice any signs? Suicidal thoughts? Depression? Rebellion?" "No," Gabriella shook her head. "They wouldn't have jumped." "What makes you so sure?" Ethan asked. "Because," she said matter-of-fact. "When you live the kind of life that they did, you don't just end it by jumping off a roof."

The bell for third period sounded and the students packed up their things to head back to class. The general consensus thus far: the girls lived happy, normal lives. They were not depressed or suicidal, and they wouldn't have jumped. Yet at the same time, no one could tell him if they had any enemies or whether someone would want to hurt them. Either Ethan was missing something, or these girls were keeping a lot of secrets.

The cafeteria was now empty with the exception of three girls: Beth, Audrey, and Megan. They waited in the hallway while Ethan took turns speaking with them individually.

First up was Audrey Mitchell. She sat across from Ethan at one of the empty cafeteria tables, fiddling with her fingernails. The janitor was hovering in the background, sweeping beneath the tables.

"Did you know the girls?" Ethan started, observing the girl in front of him. Petite. Circular face dusted with freckles. Light brown hair. Hazel eyes. "Of course I knew them," Audrey said. "Everyone knew them." Her face was composed, solemn. "Tell me what they were like." Audrey took in a breath as she thought about this. "They were unique, I'll put it that way." "Can you elaborate?" "Sure. Haddie was everything. There was something about that girl that everyone just seemed to love and envy. I'm not sure why," she said, picking off a chip of her nail. "I mean, yeah, she was beautiful, but her personality wasn't all that great." "Why do you say that?" Audrey shrugged. "She just wasn't the nicest person. I mean, I didn't know her that well. I didn't particularly want to. But my best friend used to be close with her. And, well, she's told me stories." "I'm assuming you mean Beth

Campbell." Audrey nodded. "What happened between those two?" "Oh, it was years ago," Audrey said. "But it was all Haddie Taylor. She was a very manipulative girl. Even when they were little. And she was known for being a compulsive liar. I mean, if you're always telling lies, how can anyone believe anything you say?" "Can you give me specifics?" "I'm not the person to ask," Audrey said. "You'd have to talk to Beth."

Next up was Megan Phillips. She sat there in front of him, light brown hair streaked with highlights, eyes framed with mahogany glasses. They suited her, brought out the intensity of her hazel eyes.

"Megan," Ethan said. "Are you alright?" She sniffled and nodded her head. The girl was on the verge of tears. "I'm just..." she paused. "Still shaken up from this whole thing. I mean, three girls just died." Ethan gave her a moment to collect herself. "Were you close with any of them?" Megan sniffled again and met his eyes. "No, not really. But I mean, I didn't have to be close with them to feel bad? They jumped off the roof!" she began to cry again. "What makes you so sure that they jumped?" She stopped for a moment, perplexed by the question. "What do you mean? That's what everyone's saying happened." "But that's not necessarily the truth.

Hence why my team is here investigating." "Oh," Megan seemed utterly surprised to hear this news. "You're saying that it wasn't suicide?" "We don't know. That's why I'm here talking with you." "What else could have happened to them?" Megan asked. "Perhaps there was foul play involved." "Like, somebody pushed them?" "Could be. Do you know anyone who would want to harm the girls?" "No! Not at all. This is a high school. I don't know about you, but I don't know any murderous teenagers in Briarwood." "Okay, well," Ethan took in a breath. "What can you tell me about the girls?" Megan thought for a moment. "Anneka was very pleasant," she said. "I've had a few classes with her. She was quiet, but a nice girl. Kiera? I didn't know her too well. She was very loud. And Haddie? Well, everyone knows Haddie. She was nice, but a little bit snooty if you ask me. Like she was somehow better than the rest of us. She looked down on everyone with her nose up," Megan looked at Ethan. "Oh god, I feel so horrible for saying that. I mean, those girls are dead, and here I am saying negative things about them!" "Don't worry about that," Ethan said. "Any details are great. People tend to idolize the dead and only say nice things, when in all honesty, no one is perfect. There's always more than what meets the eye. So it's more than acceptable to hear both positive and negative things about the girls, especially when this a potential murder investigation. I need as much information as I can gather to get the bigger picture and see who might have a possible motive." "Oh my god," Megan said. "So this really is, like, a murder?" "Like I said, it is undetermined at this time." Megan nodded. "Is there anything else you can think of?" Ethan asked. "Anything at all?" Megan took her time thinking. "Hmmm, well I guess there's one thing worth mentioning. It happened last month, at Wren Kreigler's party. There was sort of a blow up between some of the girls. Beth and Haddie, in particular." "What happened?" "Beth thought that Haddie was flirting with her boyfriend, which was totally not the case. Beth was drunk and overreacting. And then words were exchanged, everyone was yelling. Audrey and I had to take Beth upstairs to calm her down. Next thing I know, Haddie is leaving and getting in the car with Corey Gibbons. That's Beth's boyfriend. And he was drinking. Not only drinking, but he was drunk. And she was getting in the car with him! I looked at her and thought to myself, does that girl have a death wish? I mean, who does that? Gets in the car with someone who is drunk?" "But is that suicidal, or just reckless?" Megan thought about it for a moment. "Probably both."

Finally, the one he had been waiting for. Beth Campbell sat in front of Ethan, her white blonde hair pulled back into a pony tail. Her eyes were bright and glassy, as though she had been crying.

"Are you alright?" Ethan asked her. She nodded her head. "Yes. I'm fine. Just trying to process this still, that's all." Ethan stared at her, studying her reaction. "I understand you didn't get along with the girls. Haddie Taylor in particular." Beth made a noise and rolled her eyes slightly. "I'm not surprised to hear. Of course everyone's already blabbering about that. Petty drama, really. Haddie is dead and all people can talk about is our past." "Which is quite rocky if I'm correct?" She stared at him. "I guess you could say that." "Why don't you tell me your side of the story, Beth. Since everyone else has gotten to speak before you." She nodded and cleared her throat. "Haddie and I used to be best friends. Like, inseparable. We were younger, though. And things just didn't work out between us. She became very catty. And dramatic. I simply couldn't handle being friends with her anymore.

So we ended our friendship. It was all very amicable," Beth explained. "It was for the best. We went our separate ways. But what I can tell you about Haddie Taylor is that the girl was very controlling. Always demanding things and expecting people to do whatever she wanted. And she was very particular. Like, everything had to be her way or no way. If I'd suggest something or make plans for us, she would freak. As though she had to approve everything we did to align with how she wanted it." "And you were how old? Eleven?" "Twelve, actually." "Alright," Ethan said. "What else?" "Well," Beth said. "As you probably already know by now, everyone loved Haddie. And Haddie loved the attention. She lived for it. But she was also very competitive. When we were friends, it was like we were compcting. Always. Even if we were just getting ready to go out to the mall or something, she always had to look better than me, be dressed better than me, be better than me." "So you two stopped talking. And you never reconciled in high school?" Beth shook her head. "No. Like I said, it was best that we each went our separate ways." "What can you tell me about the others? Anneka and Kiera?" "I didn't know them well. But Kiera," Beth paused. "I think she just wanted desperately to fit in. More than anything. She was always trying so hard to keep up with the latest trends, be in everyone's good books. I think she was a bit self-conscious, to be honest. Even though she had no reason to be. Kiera was beautiful. But she was very self-conscious. And I think that really affected her. Especially being best friends with Haddie. I mean, do you know what that does to a person?" "Being best friends with Haddie Taylor?" "Yeah." Ethan didn't respond. "What about Anneka?" "Anneka, well, I don't really know much about her. She was very quiet and introverted. It's a wonder how she kept up with Kiera and Haddie. I didn't know her well so I can't tell you much. But she seemed pleasant. Like a sweet girl. Never did anything wrong to me, so there was no reason for me not to like her." "What do you think happened to the girls, Beth?" She stared at him for a moment, considering her answer. "Everyone keeps saying they jumped." "Why would they jump? Were they unhappy? Suicidal?" "I don't know," Beth said. "Everyone has their secrets, things they don't share with the rest of the world. I can't tell you why they would jump. But I can't tell you why anyone would push them, either, so, there's that."

He was in her bedroom – Haddie Taylor's. It was everything you'd imagine a sixteen-year-old girl's room to

look like. Mature, elegant, tidy. The walls were painted a light shade of beige. Her theme was pink. Pink
everything. Pink comforter, pink cushions, pink lamp,
pink fuzzy carpet, pink garbage can. And everything
that wasn't pink was dark brown. Brown pillows, brown
carpet, brown nightstand.

George and Renée Taylor stood in the doorway, watching Ethan walk around their daughter's bedroom slowly,
hands clasped behind his back. He was an observer. An
outsider, intruding on the last little piece they had left of
their daughter. An invader.

"What are you looking for, exactly?" Renée said. Ethan
turned to face her. "Nothing in particular. I just want to
get a sense of what your daughter was like. What she did
in her spare time. Who she kept closest to her."

The image of Olivia flashed through his mind. Her pregnant belly. Ethan shuttered and turned away from the
parent's, wondering, did they know?

He walked over to her desk and opened the drawer. It
was quite mundane: pencils, pens, sharpeners, rulers.
He was hoping to see a journal or a diary. Perhaps something to give him a better understanding of it all.

"Did your daughter keep a diary or anything?" he said to them. "I'm not sure," Renée said. "If she did, she probably wouldn't have told us," she forced a small smile. "You know how teenagers can be."

He took a step back and observed the walls. There were hearts everywhere, as though it went along with her pink theme. Hearts on the wall, hearts on her desk, a heart shaped pillow in the center of the bed. He leaned over her desk and picked up her school book, which had her name written multiple times over the front, surrounded by more hearts.

He held up the book. "She loved love or something?" he asked. "Pardon?" Renée took a step forward, hesitantly, as if entering her daughter's room was like passing through some sort of force field. George remained at the door. Ethan held up the book for her to see, then motioned around the room. "She had a thing for hearts?" "Oh," Renée seemed to laugh with relief once she realized what he was referring to. "That," she took the book from Ethan's hands. "Her initials are HART, so she puts it everywhere, metaphorically. As though she is the heart. HART. Haddie Anne Renée Taylor." Ethan nodded his head. "I see," She handed him the book and he placed it back on her desk.

Ethan continued going around the room, lifting up pillows, peeking inside the closet. He had to admit, it was uncomfortable searching the room with Haddie's parents standing there, watching him. What did they expect him to do, make a mess and destroy everything? He just needed to do his job.

Kiera's room was next. At least Patrick and Vivian Barnes gave him some space while he searched. There, he was actually able to maneuver a bit better, sleuth with more emphasis.

Ethan repeated the same routine he had executed in Haddie's room. He went through Kiera's drawers, searched the bottom of her closet, checked behind the books on her bookshelf. And when he felt something thin and rectangular hidden behind the books, his heart leapt in his chest.

He grasped it with his fingers and pulled, revealing a little pink diary. Of course, it had a lock on it. Ethan quickly scrambled around the room, looking for a tiny key to fit the tiny lock.

When he came up empty handed, he poked his head outside the door, ensuring the Barnes weren't hovering, then smashed the tiny lock as hard as he could with the stapler that sat at her desk. It opened wilfully. She won't be around to wonder what happened to it, he reasoned with himself.

Part of him felt guilty for invading a teenage girls' diary. As though he were entering her private space — the deepest, most intimate parts of her mind. This is where she spilled all of her secrets. The things she loved, the things she hated, boys she crushed on, teachers she despised, plans for the future. It made Ethan wonder if he would ever be doing this again someday, perhaps to his own daughter. Did Jordan want kids? They'd talked about it briefly once or twice. Jordan knew not to bring up the topic of children, especially after Luka and Olivia.

But he needed to move on. It had been three years. He had been with Jordan nearly two. He was thirty-one years old. She was twenty-eight. They'd have to think about children soon if that was in their foreseeable future. He would need to move on with his life, get married, and start a family once and for all. And if he was blessed with a daughter, then maybe this really would be him in the next fifteen years, snooping through her room, reading her diary.

He stopped flipping through the pages when he saw a name that he recognized. At first he thought it might have been out of context. Perhaps Kiera was referring to Haddie and her life at some point. But Haddie's name was nowhere on the page. He flipped forwards, backwards, trying to gain a sense of navigation through this crazy, vast diary. Perhaps he had been mistaken.

But he was not mistaken. From that page on, nearly every single entry was about the same person. That same name, reappearing over and over again.

Oliver Harris.

Chapter Six

CHAPTER SIX

Ethan sat in front of him, watching as he fumbled with the water bottle he held between his palms. His dark brown hair was shagged over to one side, his eyes facing downwards. When he finally looked up and made eye contact, Ethan wondered just how many other secrets this kid was hiding.

"Anything you'd like to tell me?" Ethan said. "What do you mean?" Oliver placed the water bottle back on the table. Ethan stared at him defiantly. "Regarding this case. Haddie, Anneka, and Kiera. Apparently people around here are quite good at keeping secrets." Oliver furrowed his eyebrows. "Look, I don't know what you want me to say –" "How about the truth?" Ethan said. There were so many things he needed to know, about the baby, about Haddie, and now, apparently Kiera. "The truth?" Oliver said, then sat back in his chair. He picked up the bottle again, looking down at his hands that rested on the table. "Isn't that a loaded question." "I don't believe so." "Isn't the truth just our perception of what we believe?" Ethan thought about this. "The truth isn't an experience, altered from person to person. It's a fact, Oliver. Why don't we start there – with the facts?" Oliver looked up at him. "Did you know?" Ethan asked. "Did I know what?" "About the baby?" "What baby?" It was quiet again, a shift in the atmosphere. Perhaps it was just Ethan who felt the shift. He had just inadvertently revealed personal information about the deceased, Haddie Taylor. Haddie Anne Renée Taylor. Who covered her room in hearts. Who would have been prom queen. Who was adored by practically everyone. Who was four weeks pregnant when she died. "What are you talking about?" Oliver sat up straighter, giving Ethan a look of utter confusion. Ethan cleared his throat. "Tell me about Kiera Barnes." "What baby!?" Oliver said again.Fuck. "She was pregnant, Oliver. Haddie was pregnant." He watched as Oliver's eyes widened, his mouth falling open slightly. He leaned back in his chair, slowly bringing his hand to his forehead. Ethan allowed him a few moments of silence. He allowed this boy – this sixteen-year old boy whose girlfriend had just died, whose life had just been changed forever – to process this information. Then Ethan spoke. "So, I'm assuming you didn't know." Oliver's eyes snapped forward, landing on Ethan's. "Of course I didn't know. How do you know?" "The coroner." "Holy fuck," Oliver muttered to himself. "She was only four weeks. She may not have even known herself yet." Oliver was quiet again. "Oliver?" Ethan said. No response. "Ollie?" "Yeah?" he said, looking up. "What are you thinking?" Oliver was quiet for a moment before he spoke. "This is bad. So bad." "I know –" "No," Oliver interjected. He looked at Ethan, holding his gaze. "That baby wasn't mine."

Ethan stood outside of Anneka Wilson's house. He needed to go inside, tell Jason and Pamela that he needed to have a look around her bedroom. He had already searched through both Haddie and Kiera's, now all that left was Anneka. But unlike the other two, Anneka had two bedrooms he would need to search.

Ethan paced the sidewalk, his conversation with Oliver playing on a loop through his head.

"What do you mean the baby wasn't yours?" Ethan had asked, perplexed. "How would you know that?" "Because," Oliver said. "I just... do." Ethan nodded his head in silence. "Because you and Haddie... you weren't –" "Not anymore. Not really." "Things weren't good between the two of you?" "It's complicated." "I'm a detective. I do complicated for a living." Oliver sighed, leaning forwards and placing his hands on the table in front of him. "I suspected that Haddie was cheating on me, back in February. We'd been together for a year and a half then, and things were starting to change. Not drastically or anything, not enough for anyone to really pick up on, but I could tell. She was growing distant, acting weird." "How so?" He shrugged. "It's hard to explain. She just wasn't the same Haddie. And so I thought that there must be someone else." "Did you ever see her with anyone else?" "No." "Then why would you think that?" "Just the way she was acting with me. Like she didn't care anymore. As though her time was being occupied elsewhere. With someone more important than me." "And she never said anything? Anything that would indicate she was cheating on you?" "She didn't have to say anything. I've known that girl my whole life. I just knew." Ethan stared at him for a moment. "When did you start seeing Kiera Barnes?" "What?" "Don't try to lie your way out of this one. I want the truth, that's all." Oliver was quiet. "I guess it must have been March. Mid-March, maybe?" "So almost three months ago." "Yeah. I don't know. We just kind of... you know." "I get it. Your girlfriend's gone AWOL. You think she's cheating on you. So you start seeing her best friend," "No, it wasn't like that," Oliver insisted. "God, that makes me sound like a horrible person. I didn't just choose Kiera on purpose. We were always together, you know? With Haddie and Anneka, and sometimes the others. We'd all hangout. Kiera and I got close. Especially when Haddie started going off, doing her own thing." "And so you just assumed she was cheating on you although you had no confirmation of this." "I do now." "Because of the pregnancy," Oliver nodded. "I'm sorry," Ethan said. "This must be tough for you." "It is. I loved her. I really did. Despite everything. She was my first love. Nothing can ever compare to that."

Now Ethan was filled with more questions. Was Haddie aware that her boyfriend and best friend were having a secret love-affair? Did Haddie know about the baby? Who was Haddie cheating on Oliver with? And lastly: was that enough motive for Oliver to kill Haddie?

Ethan was distracted from his thoughts when an elderly man materialized on the sidewalk in front of him, waving a hand in front of Ethan's face as if to wake him from his evident daydream. The man looked to be about sixty, early seventies. He was wearing a plaid shirt and a fedora.

"Good afternoon," the man said once Ethan's attention was on him. Ethan was momentarily stunned. "Hi." "Walter Fitz," the man stuck out his hand. "Detective O'Riley," Ethan said, meeting his grasp. "Can I help you with something, Mr. Fitz?" "I couldn't help notice you just standin' out here. What in God's name are you doing, son?" Ethan wondered how long he had been standing out there. And how that might look to other people. "I'm investigating the murder's at St. Paul's," Ethan said. "Murder now, is it?" Walter said. "I didn't know if it was suicide or homicide or whatever the hell else ends in cide." Ethan hadn't meant to say murder – the conclusion was still undetermined. "Apologizes, it's still unclear as to what happened." "You a detective, eh?" Ethan nodded. "From Riverton." "Riverton!" Walter said enthusiastically, but slow, annunciating each syllable. "What's Riverton doin' sending their detectives down here to Briarwood?" "The case," Ethan said. "Not many deaths happen around here. Well, undetermined deaths, that is." "That's for sure," Walter said. "We aint seen no murders like that since the Sad Killer." Ethan's attention was grabbed. "So I've heard. What can you tell me about that?" Walter seemed pleased to have the invitation to speak more. "Oh, boy, The Sad Summer. What a summer that was." "One of the officer's working the case mentioned it yesterday. Said the guy killed seven people that year? Was never caught?" Walter nodded his head. "Sure bet. The summer of '65. I'll never forget that year. I was nineteen. Got my first car that spring. Was dating this beautiful girl. Wendy, her name was. Yeah, then the first murder happened. Musta been April, I believe. Or May. Anyway, it was a hot one, that summer. Everyone calls it The Sad Summer. Because of The Sad Killer. That's what we called him. Because he wrote that at each of the crime scenes. Sad, aint it?" Ethan nodded. "But kind of unsettling," Walter continued. "Why write sad? Did it make him sad?" "He knew the investigators would see it," Ethan explained. "So he most likely left it on purpose. A signature of sorts." "Makes sense," Walter said, thinking this through. "The last body was found in July or August. It must have been a seasonal thing – the murders, that is. Because once fall rolled around, the body count ceased. Everyone was waitin', frightened for their lives that they would be next. But nobody else died. The Sad Killer had ended his reign. And no one has heard from him since." "That's interesting," Ethan said, watching Walter intently, curiosity getting the best of him. "Did you ever have any suspicions of who it might have been? Anyone you knew, maybe? Briarwood is a small town, after all." "Oh, hell, course I did! Everyone had their theories. Nobody ever done proved it though." "The population must have been, what, two thousand back then?" Ethan asked. "Something like that." "So not a lot of people to choose from," Ethan thought to himself. "One killer, seven bodies. And no one ever found out who he was." Walter laughed. "That bothers you, dunn't, son?" Ethan smiled involuntarily. "Just slightly. It bothers me when crimes don't get solved. It's a pet peeve of mine. So now this will bug me." Walter laughed again. "Hey, maybe while you're in Briarwood, you'll crack the case once and for all." Don't give me any ideas, Ethan thought to himself.

Anneka's rooms – both of them – came up clean. Nothing suspicious or out of the ordinary. Well, as far as Ethan could tell, at least. He wasn't a teenage girl. How was he supposed to determine what was normal and what wasn't?

By the looks of things, the room at her mother's house was her safe-haven, the place she favoured most. It was more personal, more inhabited somehow. Her bedroom at her father's place was crisp and clean. The bed made neatly, nothing lying around out of place. Too clean, almost.

Some of Anneka's school books sat on her desk beside her laptop. A notebook was opened to a page on math equations. Her phone charger extended from the socket on the wall to behind her pillow. Shopping bags were piled in the corner.

It was eerie, looking at the bedrooms of the dead girls. Everything seemed so normal. All of their belongings left untouched and unfinished, as though at any moment, they could walk back in and resume their lives like nothing had changed.

As far as Ethan could tell, Anneka's room was average. Nothing here suggested that she was depressed or suicidal. Especially given the fact that Ethan had searched all three – four – rooms with that specific notion in mind and came up empty handed. But were suicidal thoughts really all that tangible?

If they did jump, why not leave a note? Why not leave one last bit of communication with your family and loved ones? It was true that not everyone left suicide notes, but still, for three young girls to kill themselves and not even leave an explanation behind... It just seemed odd.

Ethan was conflicted. More and more things were pointing him in one direction: that the girls were pushed. So why was he having such a difficult time separating himself from the suicide theory?

They reconvened at six-thirty, Ethan, Frank, Kennedy, and Jesse. They met at the diner, yet again, to go over the day's findings and leave room for discussion regarding the case. Ethan liked the diner. It was quaint and reminded him of something that he couldn't quite put his finger on. He felt nostalgic for a town in which he never lived.

The four of them ordered their meals and dropped their menus in unison, handing them to the waitress.

"So, tell me what we got so far," Frank said, lifting his beer to take a sip. "Forensics doesn't have anything new," Kennedy began. "There's tons of DNA on that rooftop. I guess people went up there for all sorts of reasons. But near the edge is where we found stuff from the girls. A hair, shoe prints, saliva." "Saliva?" Jesse said. Kennedy shrugged. "Girls spit too?" "What about anything else up there?" Ethan asked, remembering Sadie West and her tobacco addiction. "Cigarette butts, maybe?" "Alcohol bottles," Jesse added. "Or drugs." Kennedy shook her head. "No drugs. No alcohol. I think there were a few cig butts up there, but there were lots of things on that roof. I could ask them to run tests on the stubs, see if we get a match to one of the girls. But what does that prove – that they smoked? So what?" "Okay," Frank said. "O'Riley, what do you got?" "I've spoken with the families, friends, teachers, neighbors. They all said sim-ilar things. The girls were great. Nice, studious, friend-ly. Although," Ethan paused again. "Perhaps everything wasn't as simple as people are making it out to be." "How so?" "I'm getting mixed signals from the friends and the boyfriend of Haddie Taylor. The parents and teachers have only positive things to say about her and the girls. And then there's this other group of girls who say Haddie was pretentious and controlling. They seem to think that Haddie was this superior being to them all. Even the boyfriend said that she could be a bit dramatic and attention seeking at times. Oh, and I just discovered that he was cheating on her with the best friend, Kiera Barnes." "Oh my God," said Kennedy. "Because he suspected that Haddie had been cheating on him," Ethan finished. "What is with kids these days?" Kennedy laughed. "It's a complicated mess," Ethan said. "Not much I could gather about Anneka or Kiera. People had lots to say about Haddie." "But do you have anything solid, O'Riley?" Frank asked. "Any evidence to suggest suicide or foul play? We're really stuck in the middle right now." "I don't think it was suicide, no," Ethan said. "And why is that?" "They lived good lives. They had friends, boyfriends, family who loved them. They had money. They were popular. And there was no suicide note. That's the biggest thing, really. Most teens who commit suicide leave a note. An explanation, an apology – something. These girls didn't leave anything. In fact, all of their bedrooms suggest that they were planning on returning home that day," "So you think we're dealing with homicide, then?" Frank asked. "Yes. I do." "May I butt in?" Jesse asked, looking from Frank to Ethan. Just then, the waitress appeared, carrying four plates. She unloaded them from her arm, placing the meals in front of them. Kennedy dug into her burger immediately.

Ethan and Frank smiled at the waitress as she left, then waited for Jesse to continue. "Hal Davis and I have been talking to locals, looking through Briarwood's history. We're thinking that this could possibly be the result of an initiation gone wrong. More specifically, a cult of sorts." "Please tell me you're kidding," Ethan said as he reached for his drink. "Why?" Jesse said. "In all honesty, it's a probability." "Please," Frank said. "Elaborate." "Well, these girls, they could have been into satanic rituals, devil worship, human sacrifice —" "There is no indication of that whatsoever," Ethan interjected. "Just because they didn't have it written all over their walls, doesn't mean they didn't do it," Jesse said. "Kids hide many things from their parents." "They weren't like that," Ethan said. "You didn't even know them," Jesse said. "Quit acting like you know everything just because you're the only detective here." "You're right," Ethan said. "I am the detective. And while you guys look at evidence and logistics, I talk to the people. I immerse myself into their lives and find out everything I can. In all likelihood — and no offence, Tanner — I think I would know if these girls were into devil worship." Jesse stared at him. "I'm just giving you an update on what Hal and I believe." "Great, you do that —" "Thank you, Tanner," Frank silenced them both, then picked up his burger. "Hey," Kennedy said in between mouthfuls. "You guys ever see that movie where everyone gets some disease that makes them kill themselves?" "What?" "Yeah," she swallowed her food. "With uh, what's her name... Zooey Deschanel. And Mark Wahlberg." The three men stared at her, not a clue as to what she was talking about. "There's this virus or something," Kennedy continued. "That made everyone commit suicide. Terrible movie," she laughed. "But, imagine." "Imagine what?" Ethan asked. "A virus like that," she said. "That makes people kill themselves." "No," Ethan said. "I can't imagine. Because it doesn't exist."

Going from Briarwood to Riverton made it easier to divide work from home. During those forty-five minutes Ethan spent driving home each night, he had time to think and recollect himself. He allowed himself those forty-five minutes to think about the case, slowly unwind, and eventually, stop thinking about it completely. But who was he fooling if he said he didn't still think about the case at home? It was all he could think about. He needed to know what happened to those girls. And it was even more pressing now that the possibility of homicide was growing.

Not only was the current case on his mind, but Ethan couldn't help but let his thoughts wander to The Sad Killer. After he finished eating dinner with Jordan that night, he opened up his laptop and began Googling.

He read the basics – what the local had already told him. During the summer of 1965, seven young to middle-aged men were found murdered in their homes. Cause of death ranged from stabbing to strangulation to suffocation. This unsub clearly didn't have a method of preference, which was unusual since serial killers normally tend to stick to just one.

There was no correlation between the men, other than the fact that they all lived in Briarwood, a small town just off the grid from modern society. It was rare beyond belief. Briarwood didn't have murders. The crime rate was so low that they barely had a police department. They had a few deaths per year from people falling through the frozen lake in the winter time. But Briarwood didn't see murders, let alone serial murders.

The strangest part was that after August 1965, the murders ceased completely. No more men were found dead. No more sad's anywhere to be seen. It was as though the killer simply packed up and vanished. Or perhaps something else happened to him...

Regardless of why he stopped killing, Ethan became invested in this case from the moment Jesse Tanner first mentioned it to him. It suddenly became apparent to him that it would become his responsibility to solve those murders from fifty years ago and put a name to The Sad Killer once and for all.

Chapter Seven

CHAPTER SEVEN

Day four. Already his initial sense of being in Briarwood was disintegrating and a new one was being formed. In fact, Ethan O'Riley quite enjoyed it. The quietness of it all, the remoteness. It was a nice break being away from Riverton. Perhaps he could convince Jordan to move out here. Okay, perhaps not Briarwood. But another small town would do.

Ethan quickly erased that thought from his mind. Jordan was all for the big city. She'd had her eyes set on New York for as long as he'd known her. It was her childhood dream to move to the city and make it big as a writer. Together, they'd find a quaint apartment in Manhattan, get a cat or a small dog. She, a NYT best-seller; he, a NYPD detective, best in the business.

Ethan had a list of things that he needed to do today. He was meeting with Tanner and Davis regarding their cult theory. Ethan was opposed to it, but Frank was forcing him to hear what they had to say, get another opinion. It was ridiculous and Ethan knew it. The entire town was already convinced that the girls had killed themselves, and now here was Tanner bringing yet another suicide-related theory forward; that the girls were involved in some sort of cult and their deaths were a sacrifice – martyrs, of sorts. But that's not the kind of girls they were, and Ethan was sure of this. It wasn't an initiation and it wasn't a human sacrifice.

He needed to dig more, find out everything he could about those three girls, as well as everyone else in this small town. If the girls were pushed, then it was most likely someone at that school. Students, staff, teachers. At least that limited his range slightly. He had already spoken to the teachers. What more could they say? As of now, there was only one potential suspect with a motive, and that was Oliver Harris. What Ethan also needed to find out was who Haddie was having this secret love-affair with. This mystery-man was the father of her unborn child, and that in itself would be another possible motive – if he even knew about the pregnancy, that is.

Ethan would need to go back to the four friends –
Gabriella, Rachel, Maya and Sadie. There would be
more information to gain from them. Did they have
anything to do with the girls' deaths? He'd need to speak
with them one-on-one to get a better sense, see if they
left anything out.

Ethan arrived at the Briarwood police station. It was
cute, really, how quaint it was, the minimal staff they
required. He walked down the hall and found Frank
speaking with Briarwood's Chief Superintendent, Jason
Gregory.

"Morning, gentlemen," Ethan said as he stood at the door
frame. "O'Riley," Frank motioned him inside. "Come, sit."
Ethan walked forward and took a seat at the desk across
from Jason Gregory. He was older – sixty, maybe? Dark
hair that was on the fringes of grey. "How's it going?"
Jason said to Ethan. "Not bad. I'll need to speak with
more people today, determine more about the girls and
their personal lives." "Just tell me straight, son," Jason
said. "Murder or suicide?" "I can't say for certain as of
this moment." "But what do you think?" Ethan took in
a breath. "I don't think it was suicide, no." Jason closed
his eyes and pinched the bridge of his nose, clearly
unpleased with Ethan's response. "You're hoping for

suicide," Ethan stated, not a question. Jason looked at him. "Do you understand how bad this will look when people start thinking there's a murderer in Briarwood?" "Jason —" Frank interjected. "Sir," Ethan said at the same time. "I understand that. And I am doing everything in my power to figure out what really happened up on that rooftop. But in all likelihood — and we have to be realistic here — I don't think that those girls killed themselves." Jason stared at Ethan, studying his face, thinking of what to say next. "Alright," he finally said. "You do what you need to do. You need more resources, you come to me. I'll do whatever is needed to get this case solved and under wraps already. Four days is long enough to be undetermined whether this was a suicide or not." "And in the case of a murder," Frank said. "Well, we'll need to crack down on this. Fast." "Will do, sir," Ethan nodded, then stood. "Oh," he turned to Jason once again. "I just had one question." "What is it?" "You familiar with The Sad Killer?" "Course I am," Jason said. "The only serial murderer Briarwood's ever seen." "And never caught," Ethan said. "You ever had any suspects?" "A few," Jason said. "Why the sudden interest?" "A local mentioned it to me yesterday. It's intriguing, that's for sure." "I'm not sure if I'd call seven dead men intriguing —" "Sorry," Ethan said. "Lack of a better word." "What are you thinking, O'Riley?" Frank asked, raising an eyebrow at him. "Perhaps we could talk more about this later," Ethan said to Jason. "Go over some of the files?" "Why? You trying to solve this thing or something?" "Like I said, I'm just interested." Jason and Frank stared at him. "Sure. Come see me before end of day. You'll need to give me an update anyway. Alright?" "Sounds good. Thank you, sir," Ethan said, and then he left.

Ethan met Jesse and Hal at the coffee shop down the street. Spread out on the table in front of them were images of what Ethan could only assume to be the devil, as well as photographs of symbols; a star surrounded by a circle, more symbols and crosses.

"Why are you so convinced this is ritualistic?" Ethan asked Hal. Briarwood was his town, after all. He would know more about the town's history than Ethan and Jesse. "The deaths are strange, you see," Hal said. "Three deaths at the same time. Of teenage girls? That just doesn't happen around here. Only one logical explanation," he nodded to the photographs. "Well I'm sure there's more than one —" Ethan started, then stopped when he saw Hal's face. "Listen, Detective," Hal said. "You're not from here. You're from Riverton. I'm sure you're used to seeing death all the time up there. But here, this is a big deal for us. Especially since it was young girls. They all jumped off that roof. They did it to sacrifice themselves to Satan." "I really don't think so," Ethan said, fiddling with one of the photographs. "I looked around their rooms, talked to their parents and friends. None of them mentioned anything of the sorts. And there's no hard evidence that points to it, I'm afraid. No photographs, symbols, or anything like this," Ethan gestured to the photographs. "Around their personal belongings." He paused to gather his thoughts. "And even if they did participate in some devil worship, wouldn't they have left something at the scene? Something on that roof?" It was quiet. Hal stared at Ethan, clearly enraged by Ethan's disregard of his well thought out idea. "How about this?" Hal leaned forward, resting his arms on the table. "You keep doing your thing, we'll keep doing ours." "Perfect," Ethan said as he stood. "All I hope is that we find out what truly happened to those girls."

Ethan was making his way back to the high school. He was planning on speaking with the four girls again, hoping they could provide him with more information. Perhaps one of them knew about Haddie's secret relationship.

He was about to turn onto the street of the school when his cellphone rang. He didn't recognize the number, put answered regardless.

"Detective O'Riley," he said into the phone. "Hi," said a female voice. "This is Cloe Wilson. Anneka's sister." "Cloe, hi. Is everything alright?" "Yes. I just," she paused. "You said to call you if I wanted to talk about my sister. I think I'm ready."

He was at the Wilson's house within ten minutes. Cloe answered the door, dressed in jean shorts and a white t-shirt. Ethan surveyed the place to see if Pamela or Jason were around. Jonah, he presumed, would be in school.

"Your dad or Pam home?" Ethan asked. "They're out. Busy running around, confirming funeral arrangements ." "Right. The funeral was tomorrow. "What can I do for you, Cloe?" "Can we sit and talk?" she motioned to the kitchen. Ethan nodded and followed her there. She must have been at least twenty or twenty-one, he presumed. Five years older than Anneka. Cloe sat at the table, biting her lip and fiddling with her thumbs. Whatever she wanted to say, she didn't know how to start. "Is everything okay?" Ethan asked. She looked up at him then, her eyes looking almost glassy. "Yeah," she forced a small smile. "It's all just so much for me. Having Anneka gone." "I can't imagine." "She was my best friend. We did everything together, since we were little. And now it's like a part of me is gone too." Ethan remained quiet. What words could possibly relay his sympathy? Cloe sniffled. "I wanted to talk with you," she said. "Because I think you need to be aware of something." "What is it?" "Anneka. She had been acting strange these last few months. Not her usual self." "Did something happen?" "I'm not sure. My sister had always been quiet. But it's like something changed in her. It wasn't just that she was quiet. She was distant. Comatose. Like she lacked her passion for life." "Do you think she was depressed?" Cloe shrugged. "I don't know. But... I think she started hanging around with a new crowd of people." "What makes you say that?" "Well, it was just..." Cloe paused. "This one time, she told me that she was out with Haddie and Kiera. But then later that day I ran into the two of them at the mall, and they said they hadn't seen Anneka all day. So I started watching her, taking notice of things.

She'd leave the house at random times, miss dinners with the family, show up at mom's house when she was supposed to be at dad's on certain nights. All of that on top of her strange behaviour – I was concerned." "Did you tell anyone? Your parents?" She shook her head. "No. They're so busy and I didn't want to worry them. And besides, I didn't think that there was anything to worry about. Not until Tuesday..." "When you first heard the news... you thought she jumped?" "I didn't know what to think. My sister and her two friends found dead outside of the school? Fell off the roof of the building? Everyone was saying they jumped. It wasn't even a question of murder or not. How can people just conclude a situation without even knowing the full story?" "The people here aren't used to death," Ethan said. "They feel more comfortable with the idea of suicide. It's less scary." Cloe nodded her head. "It just doesn't make sense. If Anneka was depressed or suicidal, why wouldn't she tell me? And why would Haddie and Kiera jump as well? There must have been something going on. Something only the three of them knew." Ethan thought back to his conversation with Oliver Harris. He too said he noticed a behaviour change in Haddie, back in February. Then he started seeing Kiera Barnes the following month. Could something have happened back then? Something drastic and monumental that altered all of the girls in one way or another? "What did Anneka want to do when she finished high school?" Ethan asked suddenly. Cloe was caught off guard by the question. "Um," she adjusted in her chair, sitting up straighter. "She wanted to be a photographer. Or a journalist. She loved that kind of stuff. She was always so artsy and unique. I never understood why she hung out with those girls." "Haddie and Kiera?" "Yeah. Don't get me wrong, I grew to love those girls like sisters. But the three of them were so different. First you have Haddie, who is this majestic butterfly of a human being. She's extroverted, popular, beautiful. So full of confidence and life. Then there's Kiera, who's sort of like Haddie, but not. She's like Haddie's shadow, almost. But Kiera had her own traits too. She was daring and brave. Bold and quirky. She always spoke so fast and was full of energy. Everyone had trouble keeping up with that girl. And then you had my sister. Quiet, peaceful little Anneka. She was an introvert, loved her alone time. But she also loved spending time with those two. They did everything together. She spent more time with them than she did with me. And I always felt like Anneka was sort of like an outcast who accidently got pulled into their loop. Like their friendship happened serendipitously. They met when they were young, so they grew up together. But who they became – who they were when they were on that rooftop on Tuesday – I don't know how the three of them maintained it." "Maintained what?" Ethan asked. "Their friendship."

Cloe led Ethan down to the basement. It was finished, with drywall and carpeted floors. She opened the door to a room and walked inside. Ethan followed.

It looked to be a spare room of sorts. Or a lounge room. There was a bed made up against the far wall, bean bag chairs on the floor, stacks of paper, paintbrushes, and art materials. A pink mirror propped against the wall.

"This was Anneka's creative space," Cloe explained. "Before my parents divorced, it was a spare room. But once all of my mom's things were cleared from the house, this room kind of became Anneka's. She would come down here to get away. To just be alone and let her creative juices flow." They both looked around the room. "Why are you showing me this?" Ethan asked. "Because," Cloe said, walking towards the far wall where the bed was. "I was down here a few weeks ago, trying to tidy up the place," Cloe knelt down to the floor and reached underneath the bed. She pulled out a cardboard box. "When I found this," she lifted off the lid and pulled out a small, zip-lock baggy. Ethan took a step closer to get a better look, but he didn't need to. The bag's contents were obvious. It was marijuana. "You're saying that belonged to Anneka?" he asked. Cloe nodded. "I told you, I suspected she was hanging around with a new group of people. Maybe they were druggies." Ethan reached forward and Cloe handed him the bag. "Marijuana is hardly anything to be worried over," he said. "But I'm going to have to take this." She nodded. "I know. I just thought I'd show you. So now you know." Ethan examined the zip-lock bag, then surveyed the room once again. Anneka's space. The place Anneka came to be Anneka. "Now I know," he said.

So Haddie was pregnant, Kiera was seeing Haddie's boyfriend, and Anneka was smoking weed. Guess it's true when they say there's more than meets the eye.

Ethan waited in the school office while Mrs. Lang paged the four girls down to her office. Ethan would need to speak with them again, one-on-one this time. People act differently in group settings. He hoped that speaking with them individually would perhaps prove more use-ful.

The first to enter the office was Maya Bowman. Her thick, dark hair was pulled back into a tight ponytail. She hardly wore make-up, but she didn't need it.

"You have more questions," she said once she was seated. "Yes. I'm hoping you can help me." "I'll do my best," she crossed one leg over of the other. "Who were you closest with in your little circle?" "Gabby." "Not Haddie, Kiera, or Anneka?" "No. Like I said, the three of them were kind of exclusive. Everyone was friends with one another, but we each had one or two people we were, or are, closer with. Gabby and I are that." "And who was closest with Haddie?" Maya thought about this for a moment. "Other than Anneka and Kiera? Probably Rachel." "And what about Anneka?" "Like I said, she was closest to Haddie and Kiera," "So the two of you weren't particularly close?" "Not compared to the others." Ethan nodded. "Did you notice a change of behaviour in any of the girls recently? Say, in the last few months? January or February, perhaps?" "Not really," Maya fiddled with her fingers. "Beginning of the year is new semester, so of course there's always that. I know Haddie hated one of her classes – English, I think it was. Anneka and Kiera were happy to have Geography together." "But nothing out of the ordinary happened that you can recall? No breakups, fights, accidents?" "What do you mean, accidents?" "I don't know," Ethan said. "I'm just throwing ideas out there." "No," Maya said. "Nothing happened. Everything was fine."Fine for who? Ethan thought.

Next up was Rachel. Ethan had a feeling that she would prove more useful than the others, simply based on the conversation they had had previously. Gabriella was sarcastic. Sadie was rebellious. Maya was willing but still held back. But Rachel was honest. She wanted to help with the investigation and she had simply spoken the truth – or what she believed to be the truth, at least.

"Hello Rachel," Ethan said once she took a seat. "How are you?" "I'm alright," she forced a small smile. "The funeral is tomorrow." "I heard. Are you going with your parents?" Rachel nodded. "I'll meet the girls there." It was quiet for a moment. "I just wanted to talk to you again," Ethan said. "You seemed eager to help out yesterday and I just thought I could ask you some more questions." "Of course," Rachel said. "Anything I can do to help." Ethan placed the pen to his notepad, hesitated, then said, "Did anything happen to the girls earlier this year? In January or February, perhaps? Or even sometime before then?"

"What do you mean?" "Any fights, breakups, drama, a mid-life crisis?" "Not that I can think of. Why?" "People have mentioned that the girls began acting strange a few months ago," Ethan said. "Oh." "Were you close with Anneka?" "Somewhat, yes. We all hung out together once in a while. Anneka and I had two classes together last semester." "She was a quiet girl, wasn't she?" Ethan asked. "Not with us." "Really?" Rachel nodded. "Anneka was tamer than most, I will say that. But everyone thinks she's this quiet, meek girl who doesn't have a say in anything. That's not true at all. Anneka had a voice. She just chose when to use it and when to remain silent." "Did she ever get into fights or arguments with the others?" "No. Anneka got along with everyone. If there was ever drama with the girls, Anneka was never involved. It was usually Haddie or Gabby or Kiera. Or Sadie." "They butt heads often?" "They all have clashing personalities," Rachel said. "Dominant. Aggressive. In charge. You can only have so much of one person before it becomes too much." Ethan nodded his head. "Did Anneka seem distant to you these past few months? Secluded, maybe?" Rachel thought again for a moment. "I really don't know." "Did she ever mention anything to you that would make you think that she was depressed?" Rachel was hesitant.

"No." "What about drugs?" Rachel's face altered. "No." "You flinched when I said drugs," Ethan said. "What do you know?" "Nothing." "Rachel." She was quiet. "Please, I'm just trying to do my job. You won't get in trouble for saying anything." She was quiet again and Ethan could tell that she was thinking this through. Finally, she spoke. "I don't know anything about drugs, per se," Rachel said. "But I'm pretty sure Anneka was smoking weed." "Weed is a drug." "No it's not. It's a herb." "Alright." "And it's medicinal." "She was taking it medicinally?" Rachel shrugged. "I don't know. I'm just saying. Marijuana has been proven to help people." "So you confirm that Anneka was in fact smoking pot?" She didn't respond. "Rachel." "Yes. Okay. But she made me promise not to tell anyone. She didn't even tell me, actually. I caught her smoking behind the school one afternoon. She said that she was really stressed and it helped calm her nerves." "And she didn't elaborate?" Rachel shook her head. "I just let it be. Whatever helps, you know?" "Why would she be stressed?" "I don't know – school? Family life?" "And other than that, you never noticed anything suspicious or strange about Anneka?" "Maybe she was a bit quieter than usual," Rachel said, thinking. "I guess she had her own problems that she was dealing with." "And weed helped her with that?" "Apparently."

What would the motive have been? Ethan was racking his brain, thinking of reasons why someone would want those three girls dead. If Ollie or the mystery man wanted Haddie dead, that's one thing – but why kill all three? Were they all just there at a bad time? Collateral damage? Did they seem something they shouldn't have?

Widening the horizons, who else would want to harm the girls? Was it a personal vendetta? Did the girls do something to someone? Get themselves into some sort of trouble? Or were they simply just innocent victims in all of this?

He needed to take what information he knew so far to think strategically. Haddie was pregnant, this was a fact. Oliver claimed to have not known and said the baby wasn't his. Could he have been lying?

This was all assuming that Haddie herself knew about the baby. There was still a good possibility that she didn't have a clue and this pregnancy had zero correlation to her death.

And there was still Anneka and Kiera. Someone wanted all three of them dead. Why would someone want one girl – or three girls – dead?

They must have known something they shouldn't have. Or perhaps something did happen all those months ago. They saw something. There was a fight. They owed someone money. They did something bad to the wrong person and that someone came back for revenge.

This was all speculation. That was the worst part about being a detective – the not knowing. The speculating and not having certainties. Because when you're work-ing a case that involves the mysterious deaths of three sixteen-year-old girls, there are no straight answers.

Ethan knew what his next step was. He needed to figure out who this mystery man in Haddie Taylor's life was. Then he needed to uncover what really happened all those months ago that no one was willing to talk about.

CHAPTER EIGHT

It was almost five when Ethan returned to the Briarwood station, knocking twice on the Chief's door. Jason Gregory opened it and welcomed him inside.

Jason walked around to the other side of the desk and took a seat, motioning for Ethan to sit across from him. "How'd it go today, O'Riley?" "Getting bits and pieces, here and there." "What are your thoughts on the cult angle, devil worship?" "With all due respect, sir," Ethan said. "I think it's a load of crap." Jason smiled at this. "Why's that?" "Well, as I explained to officer's Davis and Tanner, there are no signs of this in the girls' lives whatsoever. They may have gotten into their own sorts of trouble, but devil worship was definitely not one of them." "What sorts of trouble?" Jason asked. "That's what I'm still trying to determine. Teenage drama, girl stuff. Everyone has their secrets." "Indeed," Jason said. "And it's your job to figure them out. Can you do that?" "I'm doing my best. These things take time, especially when I can't seem to get a straight answer out of anyone." Jason nodded. "Your partners – Cross and Tanner – left a little while ago, headed back to Riverton. They'll be back for the funeral tomorrow. I'm assuming you'll be there as well." Ethan nodded. "I will." "Good." It was quiet for a moment before Ethan spoke up again. "You said I could talk to you about The Sad Killer?" "Tell me – why are you interested in this?" Jason asked. "It was fifty years ago." "I guess something about it is just drawing me in. It bothers me that the person responsible was never caught." "I'll tell you now, just about every cop in this town and his brother tried to solve that case, put a name to the killer. No one ever could. What makes you think you're going to be any different?" "I never said I wanted to solve it," Ethan lied. "I just want to see for myself what all the hype is about." Jason smirked, then pushed his chair back and stood. "Come with me then. We're going to need to go way back."

They left Jason's office and headed to the evidence room at the back of the building. Jason headed directly for Cold Cases.

He scanned the shelves, looking through the chronologi-
cally ordered boxes for 1965. When he found the box, he
grabbed it and brought it back to his office. He unloaded
each file from the box onto his desk, spreading them out
for Ethan to see.

"We don't get many murders here," Jason said. "Let alone
serial murders. So this one stands out. Everyone knows
about The Sad Summer." "Did you work the case?" "How
old do you think I am, son?" Jason laughed. "I was sixteen
at the time of the murders. Fortunately for you, my dad
was a cop. He worked the case and told me everything
he knew." "So what can you tell me?" Ethan asked. "I've
heard the basics. I want the technical. The details. The
evidence." Jason was sorting through the files still. Then
he grabbed one and slapped it down in front of Ethan.
"Start reading."

Ethan picked up the file. Inside were black and white
photographs of a crime scene. A dead body, blood everywhere. He scanned the page and found the victim's
name: Mark Irving, thirty-two-years old. Seven stab
wounds to the chest and stomach. Died from severe
blood loss.

"That was the first," Jason nodded towards the file. "April 23, 1965." "Did he have a family? Kids?" Jason shook his head. "He had a girlfriend at the time, but nothing serious. His parents died when he was young. No one left to mourn him once he was gone." "Tragic."

Ethan continued to skim through the file. He came across another photograph. On the ceramic floor beside the body, one word: sad, scribbled in black marker, all lowercase. This must have been the signature that was the catalyst for the infamous name: The Sad Killer.

"Why do you think he wrote the word sad?" Ethan asked, looking up from the file. Jason gave a slight shrug. "Remorse? Sadness?" "He didn't want to kill those men, but he felt obligated to?" Ethan suggested. "Like it was his duty." "Something like that." Ethan looked down and continued reading the file. "And the killer used a knife," Ethan noted. "That's quite personal, for a kill." "Indeed." "You think the killer knew the victim?" "We didn't think so. And there was no correlation between any of the victims. Of course a couple of them went to school together. But this is Briarwood. Everyone went to school together." Ethan nodded, thinking it through. "Seven stab wounds, seven victims. Do you think the number seven has any symbolism?" "Doubt it. Probably just a coincidence. There was no other record of the number seven anywhere other than those two things. But good eye." "It looks a bit sloppy," Ethan noted, observing the crime scene photos. "Whoever did this must have been an amateur." "We figured it was the unsub's first kill. Not just during The Sad Summer, but their first kill in general. You're right – the stab wounds are messy. Hesitant, almost. The first one," Jason leaned forward and pointed to the photo. "Was in the center of his sternum. Then it got messy from there. His abdomen, his heart, his lung. The first incision was the deepest. You can tell the killer went slow and steady as the knife penetrated the skin and entered his chest. Then the following stabs were overkill. Anger. Aggression. Stab, stab, stab." Jason handed Ethan the next file. "Victim number two: Mike Darbyshire. Age twenty-seven." Ethan opened the file and scanned through the photos. No blood this time. Cause of death? Asphyxiation. "He changed his M.O," Ethan noted. "Probably still getting into the swing of things. Testing the waters, experimenting, trying to find the mode of killing he preferred," Jason said. "Irving was the first. Stabbing. It's quick, aggressive, and unplanned. The second kill, Darbyshire," Jason nodded to the photographs. "This one the unsub took his time on. Planned

it out, chose a victim, executed his plan thoroughly."
"That's unusual," Ethan said. "Most serial killers stick to
one method. If it weren't for the word sad at the crime
scene, do you think these two cases would have even
been connected?" "Maybe not," Jason said. "But two men,
five years apart in age, turn up dead within a month
of each other? I'm sure police would have linked the
murders eventually. But it doesn't matter whether we
would have linked them or not. He killed again only
two weeks after Darbyshire." Jason handed Ethan the
third file. "Patrick Brooks, age forty-two. Husband and
father of two." "That's quite the age jump," Ethan said.
"Ten years on the first victim," Jason said. "But still a
pattern. All the men who were killed were between the
ages of twenty-seven and fifty-four. This unsub had a
type." "Men," Ethan said. "Is that unusual?" "Not particularly. Most victims of serial killers are women. Usually
young. But there have been quite a few serial killers
who target men." "He could have been gay? Had some
kind of hatreds towards men – maybe a misandrist?"
Ethan suggested. "Given the age groups, I'd say the unsub
was somewhere between thirty and fifty. Am I correct?"
"You are indeed. Back then it was predicted that the guy
was anywhere between thirty and fifty, white, middle

class, male. As I've already told you, they believed this was his first time killing. He was getting the hang of it, trying new things, graduating from amateur status to professional hitman by his last kill." "The age group is odd to me," Ethan said. "The majority of serial killers who do kill men usually target youths and teens. Take Jeffrey Dahmer for example. Killed 17 young men. Jason Wayne Gacy killed 33 teenage boys. Gacy sexually assaulted his victims, and it was believed that Dahmer was gay." "You're right, sexuality definitely could have been a factor. Perhaps the unsub was homosexual and was taking out his rage and aggression on these men. Maybe he was rejected. Perhaps he had daddy issues. He just wanted control of a situation. And yes, the age factor is a bit strange. Dahmer and Gacy both targeted teens, along with The Freeway Killer, Patrick Kearney. Killed 43 young men and teenagers in the 70's. Raped them before killing them. I'm guessing our unsub either wasn't interested in youths, or was older himself. There was no indication of sexual misconduct on any of the men," Jason leaned forward to grab more files. "But age could be irrelEthant. There have been other serial killers who have targeted middle-aged men. Mexican serial killer Juan Corona. Or Dennis Nilsen, who was a necrophiliac, and killed 15 men between 1978 and 1983," Jason continued. "Adolfo Constanzo, human sacrifice." It was quiet for a moment. "There are some fucked up people in this world," Ethan finally said. Jason let out a small laugh. "You can say that again. Here," he handed Ethan four more files. "Victims four to seven. Robert Baldwin, age forty-three. Jason Morgan, age fifty. David Hill, age thirty-eight. And finally, Paul Monoghan, age fifty-four."

Ethan opened up the files, skimming over the photographs and evidence logs. Stabbed. Stabbed. Strangled. Shot. The killer's grand finale was a single bullet to the head.

Then nothing else after August of 1965. As if the killer just dropped off the face of the earth, disappeared forever, and was never heard from again.

It was Friday night, so they decided to go out for dinner. Jordan's favourite restaurant was a place called Belle Notte, meaning beautiful night in Italian.

"I like Rosie. And Bella is very cute and dainty," Jordan said. They had somehow landed on the discussion of baby names. Jordan's friend was pregnant and wanted name suggestions. Jordan happened to be an expert. "What about Katie?" Ethan suggested. Jordan made a face and shook her head. "Way too mainstream. Come on, Ev, this generation already has enough Katie's and Jessica's and Sarah's." "What's wrong with mainstream?" Jordan gave him another look. "We need unique names. Different names. Like Apple." "Apple?" "You know, Apple Martin? Gwyneth Paltrow and Chris Martin's daughter?" "Never heard that one before." Jordan laughed. "Okay, Apple is a bit of a stretch. But Kaia is nice. Or Reign. Summer, Autumn –" "Winter, Fall." Jordan laughed. She twirled her fork around her pasta and lifted some into her mouth. Ethan watched her. "What were you like as a teenager?" he asked suddenly. She finished chewing then took a sip of wine, eyeing him. "What do you mean?" "I'm just curious to know what teenage girls are like." "Is this about the case?" "No," Ethan paused, Jordan's eyes on him. "Okay, yes." "Ev, we agreed no work talk at dinner." "It's not work talk! Just tell me what you were like." Jordan rolled her eyes. "I don't know, I was just an average girl. I had friends, boyfriends. We had fun, skipped school, did the usual stuff." "What's the usual stuff? Did you drink? Do drugs?" "We drank, yeah. But I never did drugs. Maybe pot a few times." "Keep any big secrets?" "Where are you going with this?" Ethan sighed, moved the food on his plate around. "I'm just trying to get into their heads. These girls," he paused. "They had a lot of secrets. And I'm trying to figure out how and why they died." "I thought you were certain it wasn't suicide." "I was. I mean, I am," he took in another breath. "I'm still not sure. There are so many factors. So many things to take into account." "Like what?" He gave her a look. "You know I can't tell you details." She nodded her head and took another bite of pasta. "Anyways," Ethan said. "I'll find out more tomorrow." "Why tomorrow? It's Saturday." "The funeral." "You're going?" "Yes. We all are. I'm hoping I can talk to more people there." "Ev," she said. "That's a bit insensitive. At least wait until the service is over. These girls just died and you want to be interrogating everyone?" "No, not interrogating. Talking." She nodded but remained silent. "Have you ever heard of The Sad Killer?" he asked suddenly, putting down his knife and fork. "Is that a movie?" "No. It's a serial killer –" "Oh, come on Ethan. One night. That's all I ask." "He killed seven men in the summer of 1965," Ethan continued, relaying the facts. "Was never caught." "Okay? Why is this relEthant?" "It happened in Briarwood." "The murders?" "Yes. That's why I asked if you'd heard of him." "I didn't

know Briarwood had murders." "Exactly. It's practically unheard of, which makes it all the more unsettling.
Especially since no one ever solved the case." "So what,
that's your job now?" He laughed. "I was reviewing the
case with the Chief tonight. It's all very interesting." "Oh,
yeah, murder is so interesting." "You know what I mean."
"I do," she took another sip of her wine. "My boyfriend
is a nutcase who loves murderers." "Not true," he said. "I
love you and you're not a murderer." "That you know of,"
she winked. "It's fascinating though. I think I'm going to
talk with one of the old reporters on the case, see if I
can get more information." "Seriously?" she was clearly
not impressed. "Yeah. It was fifty-one years ago, but most
of the people from that summer are still in Briarwood.
No one ever leaves that place." "My grandmother did."
"Right, your gran lived there," Ethan remembered. "Why
did she leave?" Jordan shrugged. "I don't know. She was
born there. It was a small town. She left, got married, had
my dad." "I guess Briarwood isn't for everyone." "Guess
not," she said. "Okay, let's change the subject." "Let's."
"You're still able to get off work early on Tuesday, right?"
she asked. "What's Tuesday?" Her face altered and Ethan
knew that look. He had forgotten something. And now
he was screwed. "Your birthday!" he quickly remem-

bered. How could he forget his own girlfriend's birthday? "Of course. Sorry. Just a bit distracted, that's all. Yes, of course I'll be there. Dinner at your parents place. Yes yes." "Good." "Hey," Ethan said, conjuring a new thought. "Your grandmother will be there, right?" "Yes." "Maybe I can talk with her, see if she remembers anything from that summer." "You're seriously going to harass my grandmother about your serial killer fetish?" "She lived there! Maybe she can give me insights." "She's never mentioned it before." "Well, I'm assuming grandmothers don't usually tell their grandkids bedtime stories about murder." "You could give it a shot, I guess," Jordan said. "She loves talking with anyone. Give her your ear and she'll talk it off." Ethan laughed. "Perfect. I look forward to it."

Chapter Nine

CHAPTER NINE

It's a given that nobody likes funerals. They're dark and depressing and serve as one reminder: life is too short. It can be taken away from anyone – anytime, anywhere.

Nobody wants to attend the funeral of a sixteen-year-old girl, let alone three of them. Ethan could feel the calamity in the air. Rows of people dressed in black. Sobs and whimpers, sniffled noses and tissues. Today was everyone's time to say goodbye.

It was a sunny day – beautiful weather for mid-May. George and Renée Taylor stood near the front of the church, greeting each person who came over to give them their condolences.

A few feet away from the Taylor's were the Barnes. Vivian and Patrick were standing in front of a large mosaic photo collage that some of the girls' classmates had made up. They were marveling at it, taking in each and every photograph of their daughter and her friends. Kelsey was nowhere to be seen.

Near the back of the room were the Wilson's. Pamela stood off to the side slightly as Jason and Mary-Ella Wilson spoke to people, Jonah and Cloe beside them, red eyes, damp cheeks.

Ethan spotted Oliver Harris speaking with a few other students from St. Paul's. He debated making his way over, but remembered Jordan's words and decided to wait until the service was finished. The funeral would be over, but this investigation was far from it.

Everybody took their seats and the priest made his way to the podium at the front of the church. He turned on the microphone and cleared his throat. All eyes were on him.

"We are gathered here to say farewell to three daughters of God," he began. "Anneka Elizabeth Wilson, Haddie Anne Renée Taylor, and Kiera Mae Barnes. In the Name of the Father, and of the Son, and of the Holy Spirit, we ask to bring peace and faith to the families who are suffering an immense loss. Our Father in heaven, we thank you that, through Jesus Christ, you have given us the gift of eternal life. Keep us firm in the faith, that nothing can separate us from your love. When we lose someone who is dear to us, help us to receive your comfort and to share it with one another. We thank you for what you have given us through Anneka, Haddie and Kiera. We now entrust ourselves to you, just as we are, with our sense of loss and of guilt. When the time has come, let us depart in peace, and see you face to face, for you are the God of our salvation. Amen."

Once the service was over, everyone headed outside to watch the caskets be placed in the ground. Usually in a murder investigation, the time it takes to examine and release the body to the families can vary. However, Meredith Kepler finished examining the bodies to the fullest extent and released them yesterday. That way, the girls could have a proper burial and finally rest in peace.

Friends and family walked forwards to place a flower on the coffin, sprinkle some dirt on top. Everyone's hearts nearly broke when young Jonah Wilson walked forward to say his final goodbye to his sister.

The reception afterwards was held at the Barnes' home. Large enough to hold everyone with enough property to go along with it, everyone made their way across town to gather once again.

The aura had shifted slightly. Most of the tears had ceased and people were trying to remain optimistic. Rather than crying and sequestering themselves, people were congregating to discuss the girls. Reminiscing on the happy moments, the memories.

Mary-Ella was talking to a few of the mother's from the school about Anneka and the girls when they were in elementary school. The phases of hair styles they went through, their gradation trip that went horribly wrong. There was laughter and smiles, which made Ethan feel reassured knowing he was about to begin the questioning, yet again.

Ethan spotted the girls he spoke with the day prior and made his way over. Gabriella, Rachel, Maya, and Sadie were standing near the staircase talking with a few other girls he didn't recognize.

"Ladies," Ethan said as he approached them. "My condolences." They nodded their heads solemnly, muttering "thank you." "This is the detective working the case," Rachel explained to the other girls. "Detective O'Riley," he said. "Brittany," said one girl. Followed by, "Layla."

And, "Gemma." "How are you all holding up?" Ethan asked. "Alright," Maya forced a small smile. "It was tough," Gabriella said. She was hardly wearing any makeup and looked substantially different, a look of exhaustion in her eyes. "Any news on the investigation?" Rachel asked. "Making progress," Ethan said. "I wanted to ask you some more questions. Perhaps you three may be able to help as well," he said to the others. Brittany. Layla. Gemma. He recognized one of the names from the Facebook page. "Anything we can do to help," Layla said. "We've already gone over a lot," Ethan said. "I'm just trying to trace this all back to something. A problem or incident that might have occurred in the past that altered the girls in some way. Some people have noted that the girls were acting differently these last few months. Did any of you notice anything within the days leading up to Tuesday? Even the night before, or the morning of?" It was silent for a moment as the girls all thought collectively. Gabriella spoke first. "Now that I think of it," she said. "Haddie seemed a bit bitchy on Monday. We were supposed to go out for lunch, but she cancelled on me. Said she had other things to deal with." "Why didn't you mention this before?" Ethan asked. "I completely forgot. It wasn't until you mentioned weird behaviour just now." "Alright," Ethan said. "What about Anneka or Kiera?" The girls remained quiet. "I don't know if this has any relEthance or not," the girl, Gemma, said. "I have biology with Kiera and Haddie in first period. They're usually lab partners. But on Tuesday morning, Haddie asked the teacher if she could switch." Everyone turned to Gemma. "What?" Rachel asked, notably taken back by this comment. "What the fuck?" Gabriella echoed her astonishment. "This was Tuesday morning?" Ethan asked. "You're sure?" Gemma nodded her head. "Are you close with the girls?" Ethan asked her. "Not particularly. I mean, we're friendly. I see them around the regular crowd at school, at parties and stuff. But we don't hang out much." "So you all agree that this is odd?" Ethan said. "Haddie wanting to switch lab partners?" "Um, duh," Gabriella said. "Haddie and Kiera are always lab partners." "Something must have happened," Rachel looked concerned.

Ethan didn't need to be a teenage girl to figure out what had happened. He already knew. Haddie must have found out about Kiera and Oliver. It was the only plausible explanation.

Or so he thought.

He had just left the group of girls and was about to move on elsewhere when he heard voices being raised. He recognized the male voice as George Taylor. Ethan followed the voices, heading towards the commotion until he was standing directly in front of them. George and Renée Taylor, talking – or rather, yelling – at Oliver Harris.

"What's going on?" Ethan said as he approached them. George noticed Ethan, then shook his head and walked away. Oliver looked stunned. He took this opportunity to escape, leaving Renée as the only person remaining to speak with Ethan. "What's going on?" he said to her. She shook her head, tears forming in her eyes. "It's nothing." "Mrs. Taylor," he said. "Did something happen? Can we go somewhere to speak?" he noted how busy the main floor of the Barnes' home was. She looked up at him, hesitated, then said, "Come with me." She led him down the hallway to the office on the main floor. Renée walked inside and closed the door behind them. Ethan watched as she walked towards the desk, paced around, then turned to face him. "What is it?" he asked. "Did you know?" she said to him. "Know what?" She hesitated again. "About Haddie. About..." she broke off, began crying again. The baby. Ethan approached her.

"The M.E told me the other day. What do you know?" She wiped her eyes and looked at him again. "That she was four weeks along." Ethan nodded. "That's why you were speaking with Oliver." "He says the baby wasn't his." "I know. He told me that too." "You talked to him?" "I did." She was quiet for a moment. "I don't believe him. He says Haddie was cheating on him. That isn't true and he knows it." "I'm not so sure," Ethan said, then bit his tongue. He needed to speak with caution. This was Haddie's mother he was speaking with. She was on the defence regardless of what he said. "How would you know?" she snapped. "Apologies, ma'am," he said. "Listen, I'm trying to figure out what happened to your daughter, and that involves talking to a lot of people. I don't believe that this was a suicide. I am looking into anyone who might have had a problem with Haddie and may have wanted to hurt her," Ethan paused. "You said she didn't have any enemies, correct?" Renée shook her head. "Everyone loved Haddie." "This is very crucial, Mrs. Taylor," he said. "Did anything happen within these past few months? Something monumental and trauma-tizing that would have affected the girls negatively?" "I don't know," she said. "They were good girls, Detective. They didn't get into trouble. They didn't have any problems or issues with people. I don't know what sort of thing you believe might have happened." Ethan took in another breath. He already knew that speaking with Renée Taylor would prove useless. She was holding onto this perfect image of her daughter, the idea that Haddie could do no wrong. Haddie would never cheat on Ollie. Haddie would never cause trouble or get into fights. "I'll let you be, for now," Ethan said. "But please, if you think of anything else – anything at all – that may prove useful, don't hesitate to call me. I need to know everything if I'm going to find out what happened to your daughter."

_ _ _ _ _

Ethan was roaming around the main floor of the house, maneuvering between the crowds of people. He was looking for Oliver Harris. The house, as he noted before, was spectacular. It was so busy, crowds of people congregated in almost every square inch of the house. Where could Oliver have disappeared to so quickly?

Just then, he felt someone tug on his arm. He turned around to see Kelsey Barnes standing behind him. She was wearing a long sleeve black dress that sat just below her knees. Her dark hair was pulled back in a headband

and her crystal blue eyes were glossy with tears. She was a spitting image of Kiera.

"Detective O'Riley?" she said faintly. "Kelsey," he said, turning to face her. "What's the matter?" "I heard you talking to Mrs. Taylor in the office," she hesitated. "You want to know about Haddie and Ollie?" Ethan stared at her. "Can we go somewhere to talk?"

Kelsey led him upstairs to Kiera's bedroom. She closed the door, instantly blocking out the sounds that echoed from the rest of the house, and sat on her sister's bed. Ethan stood there, uncomfortable at the fact that he was alone in a dead girl's bedroom with her four-teen-year-old sister.

"What do you know, Kelsey?" She looked at him and hesitated. "I knew about my sister and Ollie," she said, which surprised Ethan. "Kiera tried to hide it at first, but I knew something was up. She was so happy and giddy all of the time. She told me she was talking to a guy, but wouldn't tell me who. Eventually I figured it out." "How?" "I made her tell me." Ethan nodded. "You said you two were close." "Best friends. So I was hurt that she didn't trust me enough to tell me sooner," Kelsey was quiet for a moment. "She made me swear not to tell anyone. Said Haddie would kill her if she found out," she quickly stopped, wide-eyed at the realization of what she'd just said. "Anyway, I told her that it was wrong. She was seeing her best friend's boyfriend! And that's when she told me that Haddie was doing it too." "Doing what?" "Seeing someone else." "Kiera knew who Haddie was seeing?" Ethan asked. "No, she didn't know. Ollie didn't even know. It was just a suspicion he had. But he was so certain, Kiera told me. Otherwise he would never have started things with my sister. If Haddie had just stayed faithful to him..." "But you know something," Ethan said. "That's why you wanted to talk to me." Kelsey looked up and met his eyes again. She nodded. "What do you know?" he asked. Kelsey sighed. "I don't know anything for certain," she said. "But if you want more information about Haddie Taylor, then you should probably talk to Bentley Carter."

CHAPTER TEN

Bentley Carter – what a name. The guy was two years older than Haddie, in his final year at St. Paul's. Once the reception was finished, Ethan made his way over to the Carter residence. A woman, presumably the mother, answered the door.

"Can I help you?" she asked, shielding herself behind the door. "Mrs. Carter?" "Yes?" "I'm Detective O'Riley with the Riverton PD. Is your son, Bentley, home?" The woman stared at him a moment. "What is this regarding?" "The deaths of the three St. Paul's girls." "Why would you need to talk to Bentley about that?" "Mom, it's alright," A boy, who Ethan presumed could only be Bentley, emerged from behind his mother. "Stay inside, it's fine," Bentley said to her. His mother was hesitant. Mother-bear mode, once again, Ethan thought. Finally, she left her post at the door and disappeared down the hallway. Bentley came onto the front porch, closing the door behind him. "Detective O'Riley," Ethan said, sticking out his hand. "Bentley," the boy met his grasp and gave him a firm shake. He was a good looking kid. Tall, muscular build, light brown hair, dark eyes. Ethan studied him, noting that this was the mystery-man he'd been searching for. If what Kelsey Barnes told him was true, Bentley Carter had been secretly seeing Haddie. And that meant this was most likely the father of her baby. "It's been brought to my attention that you were acquainted with one of the girls – Haddie Taylor." Bentley didn't respond right away. "Alright." "What can you tell me about your relationship with her?" "We went to the same school. I saw her around a few times, but I didn't know her too well." Ethan eyed him. "You don't need to lie, Mr. Carter. I'm aware of your secret relationship." Bentley tried to hide his unease, but Ethan could see it. "Let's just make things easier for the both of us," Ethan continued. "What can you tell me about Haddie?" Bentley debated answering, then finally gave in. "It wasn't anything serious. We kind of started seeing each other occasionally." "You knew about Haddie and Oliver Harris?" "Didn't everyone?" "Why were you interested in a girl like Haddie?" Bentley shrugged. "She's interesting.

Gorgeous. We had fun together. She said she was getting tired of being with Ollie. Said she wanted something new. Something exhilarating, were the exact words she used." "When did your relationship begin?" He thought about this for a moment. "It must have been at the end of December. Around New Year's." "And you were still seeing each other up until Tuesday?" "When she died? No, she broke things off with me a couple weeks ago." "Did she?" Ethan said. "Any particular reason?" Bentley shook his head. "Didn't say. She ended things just as quickly as they started," he paused for a moment. "To be honest, I thought I would be the one to end things between us when it came time. I didn't think I'd actually fall for her. And then she just goes and dumps me." "To be with Oliver?" "Who knows." "Do you know if she was seeing anyone else?" He looked appalled. "You mean other than me and Oliver? Yeah, no." "During the last few months, does anything in particular stand out that would cause a drastic change in Haddie's life? Anything that might have happened that affected her negatively? Was she sad? Depressed?" "You're asking if I think she killed herself?" "Do you?" He shook his head again. "I don't know what to tell you. I show up in the cafeteria on Tuesday only to find out that Haddie and her two friends are dead. Everyone was saying they jumped. I don't know why they would do that. Especially Haddie. She wasn't like that at all. She was happy. Genuinely happy. Maybe confused sometimes, but she would never kill herself." "So what do you think happened?" "How would I know?" he paused for a moment. "Did someone do this? Did somebody kill them?" Ethan thought about how to answer this question. "It's a possibility. But if they were pushed or talked off the edge – threatened in some way – I need to know everything about them to understand the full story. Who they interacted with, any issues that they had. Was someone after them? Were they in trouble? Did they know something they shouldn't have?" "Haddie never mentioned anything. She was always up to something. But nothing too serious. Or dangerous." "What do you mean, up to something?""You know, just being Haddie. She was always pushing people's buttons, testing them. I don't know if she fucked with the wrong people, or got herself into something deep." "She never mentioned anyone who was out to get her? Anyone who could have held a grudge against her or the girls?" He shook his head again. "Have you talked to her friends? Gabby and them?" "A bit, yeah. No luck there. No one can tell me anything useful. And if they do know something, they're not telling me." Bentley nodded. "Try talking to Oliver. He probably knows more than I do." "I've spoken to him. He said Haddie was distant the last few months. He suspected something was off." Bentley took in another breath. "I don't know what to tell you. Haddie was everything. And now she's nothing. I'm still trying to grasp that concept, understand how that can be." "Call me if you think of anything," Ethan handed Bentley his card. Bentley took it and nodded. "Will do."

Ethan drove back to the Briarwood station and headed directly for Jason Gregory's office. Jason wasn't in. Right – it was Saturday. People would be at home, tying to rest or take a break from this case.

He asked the secretary if he could have access to the evidence room. She happily obliged and let him in.

Ethan found the 1965 box and took it to the spare office near the front of the station. He began unloading the files, skimming through the paperwork that he and Jason had reviewed the night before. It was Saturday, he reasoned with himself. The funeral had just finished. He was just taking a little break, that's all. He would return to the investigation and interviews tomorrow. After all, he felt as though he was at a stand-still, going in circles. Nobody could tell him anything useful, and when they did have something new, or a name, like Bentley Carter, it didn't prove useful anyways.

What were those girls hiding? What were they doing on the roof that day? He would need to reconvene tomorrow. Right now he had other things on his mind. And that was The Sad Killer.

Ethan knew he shouldn't be looking into this. He was called to Briarwood to solve the triple deaths, not a case from fifty years ago. But there was something so alluring about it. Something that was tempting him to peek into those files and learn more. If he was going to find out who The Sad Killer was, he would need to immerse himself into that time period, know the victims, think like the unsub. And in order to do that, he needed to do exactly what he was doing now with the triple deaths at St. Paul's. He would need to speak with any surviving friends and family members of the victims. Reporters, investigators, locals – anyone he could find, he would speak with. After all, this was Briarwood. Most people who lived here in 1965 were still here, settled down for retirement and taking it easy.

Ethan found multiple newspaper clippings from the summer of 1965, new information surfacing each time a body was found. The writer was the same person for each story: Martin Gallagher.

With a quick Google search, Ethan found an M. and L. Gallagher at 26 Dystel Street. They were still here in Briarwood. He placed the files back into the box, stuck it in evidence, and headed out.

It was almost four o'clock when he reached the Gallagher's home. It was a small, cottage looking house. Green grass, white picket fence out front. The garden was beginning to bloom for spring, dozens of Daisies and Marigold's sprouting out from the ground. Ethan walked up the narrow pathway and knocked twice on the door.

Moments later the door opened to reveal a petite elderly woman, white hair and glasses. "Mrs. Gallagher?" Ethan asked. "Yes?" "I'm Detective Ethan O'Riley from Riverton PD. Is there any chance that your husband, Martin, is home?" "What is this regarding?" "Just an old case that I believe your husband could be of some assistance with." She nodded her head and turned around. "Martin!" she called. "You have a visitor," she turned back to Ethan and smiled. "Would you like to come inside?" "Sure," he stepped into their home. "I'm Linda." "Pleasure to meet you." Just then, an elderly man came tottering down the hallway with a cane. "Well this is a surprise," he said once he laid eyes on Ethan. "What can I do for you, son?" "He's from Riverton," Linda said to her husband. "He's a detective." "A detective," Martin repeated. "What's a detective from Riverton doing at our doorstep?" Ethan smiled. "I was actually hoping to speak with you about The Sad Killer. I know you were a reporter at the time." Martin's face changed, a spark of recognition. "What do you want to know about that? Musta been, what? Fifty years, now?" "Fifty one." Martin laughed. "Please, come in." Ethan followed them into the living room, settling down on the sofa. He looked around the room, observing his surroundings. Fireplace to the left, coffee table to the right, dozens of picture frames everywhere. "Would you like anything to drink?" Linda asked. "Coffee, tea?" "Coffee would be great," Ethan said. "Two cream, one sugar." Linda nodded and headed off into the kitchen. "So," Martin said, settling into his chair. "What would you like to know?" "Well," Ethan said. "I'm intrigued. This guy killed seven men in the summer of 1965, then completely dropped off the grid and was never heard from again. Never caught. What do you think happened to him? You worked closely on the case as a reporter. Surely you must have some theories." "Oh, I did," Martin grinned proudly. "It was one of the first stories I ever worked. Well, big stories, anyway. Nothing ever happened here in Briarwood. I'd report on the usual stuff: events, politics, the women's march. But when the murders happened – well, that gave us all something to do." Linda returned to the living room holding two mugs. She placed them on the table that sat between Martin and Ethan. "We had never seen anything quite like it before," Martin continued. "I mean, sure, you hear the stories, watch the news. You see crime happening elsewhere. You hear about murderers. But to have one in your own town? Especially a small place like Briarwood? It was unheard of." "That's particularly why I'm interested," Ethan said. "With such a small population, I'm sure there were suspects. Why was no one ever charged?" "Nothing solid. I'm sure you've heard by now that there were a few arrests. They thought they had the guy at one point, but didn't have enough sufficient evidence to charge him." "Did you ever have any suspects in mind?" Martin laughed again. "I was sure it was Phoenix Arnold. He was one of the first ones arrested on suspicion. I think he was dating the ex-wife of one of the victims. They thought the wife hired Phoenix to kill them, or something along those lines. The guy seemed guilty. I always suspected it might have been him." "But why kill the other six? If it was truly the wife and him? Doesn't make sense." "I know," Martin said. "I also know that most serial murders are committed by strangers. The police shouldn't have been looking at anyone close to the victims. It must have been arbitrary." "Can you tell me anything about the victims? You were there at the time; what were they like, the men?" "I didn't know any of them personally," Martin said. "Of course I'd heard of them all, seen them around a few times. Briarwood is small, remember, so everyone knows everyone somehow. Anyway, the first victim, Mark Irving... I remember him clearly. He was a few years older than I was – a real Casanova. Young, charming, Briarwood's bachelor. Ask Linda, all the women adored him." Linda nodded in agreement. "He was a ladies man. Good guy, nice looking. We were all so shocked when he turned up dead. Murdered." "And you must remember," Martin said. "We'd never really seen a murder in Briarwood before. So when Mark turned up dead, the town turned to pandemonium. The police believed it was a robbery gone wrong. But the murder... it was overkill if you ask me." "Seven stab wounds to the chest," Ethan relayed.

"Exactly. A burglary? No, they would have just shot him or stabbed him once, taken his things and left. So anyhow, the police believed it to be an isolated incident. Until three weeks or so later, the next body turns up." "Mike Darbyshire." "Yes, him." "What did you know about Mike?" Martin took in a deep breath. "Well, not much. He was closer to my age, I believe. I was twenty-eight at the time. He was a good guy, born and bred in Briarwood. I think he may have had a girlfriend or fiancé at the time. Again, nice fella. No one could figure out what was happening to these men." "It was peculiar," Linda said. "As though all of these men were being targeted for some reason." "Did any of the victims know each other?" Ethan asked. "Perhaps they all attended the same clubs or went to the same bar to hangout?" "There was no correlation," Martin said. "That was the strangest bit. Arbitrary and individualistic." "Perhaps they were into drugs," Ethan suggested. "Or gambling, even. Got into some trouble, owed someone money. And when they couldn't pay their debts, someone came after them?" "Maybe. But if that was the case, nothing else ever came from it." "Do you know anyone else who was involved in the investigation that I should talk with?" Ethan asked. "Hmm, only other person I would suggest is Constable

Fraser. He was in charge of the investigation back then. But he must be in his late eighties by now. I haven't heard from him in years." "How can I find him?" "You could always ask the men down at the station. Jason Gregory will help you with that," Martin said. "He's a good man, Jason." "Yes, I've had the pleasure of working with him these past few days." "You're here for those girls, aren't you?" Linda asked. Ethan nodded. "Everyone's saying it was suicide." Linda added. "See, that's called misinformation," Ethan said. "Whenever there's a death, it's crucial that no conclusions are drawn from lack of evidence. Everyone in this town has been saying its suicide. That is undetermined." "Right," said Martin, looking Ethan over. "We could have another murderer on our hands."

It was Saturday night. Ethan should have been on his way home to Jordan by now, but he couldn't seem to pull himself away from Briarwood.

He had spoken to the Chief and was able to track down Gus Fraser, the constable in charge of The Sad Killer investigation back in 1965. If anyone was going to be able to help Ethan solve this, it was Fraser.

Ethan found his house and knocked on the front door, hoping that a) it wasn't too late, and b) he was home. Gus Fraser was thirty-four when the murders happened, making him eighty-five today. Ethan could only hope that he remembered enough from back then and was willing to speak about it.

A young woman answered the door. A granddaughter, perhaps. "Hi," Ethan said. "Would this be the residence of Gus Fraser?" "This is," the woman smiled. "How can I help you?" "I'm Detective O'Riley. I was looking at an old case and was wondering if I could go over some things with Gus, since he used to be the constable." "I can certainly go ask him. Gus is always up for visitors. I'm Sarah, his PSW." "Sure, that would be great." Ethan stepped inside and closed the door. Sarah disappeared down the hall. He looked around the foyer, surveying the house. Picture frames lined the walls, cabinets with antiques. There was a faint smell of cinnamon in the air. Sarah reappeared a moment later. "He said he'd love to talk with you. Come this way," she motioned for him to follow her. They reached the living room and Ethan could finally lay his eyes on Gus Fraser. He was older, that was for sure. White hair, brown eyes behind a pair of glasses. He still managed to look good for his age. Sarah disappeared into the kitchen and let them be. Ethan took a seat on the couch, keeping his eyes on Gus. "What did you say your name was?" Gus asked. "Ethan. Ethan O'Riley. I'm from Riverton, here investigating a triple death." "Those girls over at the school," Gus said slowly, methodically. "Tragic, really." Ethan nodded. "The reason I'm here —" "The Sad Killer," Gus finished for him. "Yes. I was hoping you could be of some assistance." "I was the constable in charge of the case," Gus said. "But I'm sure you already know that," he gave a wink. "What is it you want to know?" "I guess just the preliminary information. What can you tell me?" Gus took in a breath, scanning his memory. "It was a long time ago." "You remember much?" Gus stared at him. "Of course I do. That case was one for the history books." Ethan nodded and waited for Gus to continue. "Well, as you probably know by now," Gus started. "The killer had a particular taste. Men between the ages of thirty to fifty. The method of killing ranged from asphyxiation by pre-venting the victim from breathing, to strangulation with ligature. Two were stabbed to death." "Tell me about the first victim," Ethan said. "How he died." "Let me think," Gus said. "It's been a long time, son. I don't have any files or paperwork with me. Remind me...?" "Mark Irving.

Thirty-two years old –" "Ah, yes. Mark Irving. First victim. Multiple stab wounds to the chest." Ethan nodded.
"I spoke with the Chief Superintendent, Jason Gregory.
He said it was believed to be the unsub's first kill." "Yes,
that is what we concluded. It was very messy. Unme-
thodical – hesitant, almost. As if they didn't quite know
what they were doing. An experienced killer wouldn't
have made such a mess. I've seen a lot of murders, kid.
And this one... well, it was overkill. There was anger
and aggression behind it. But this wasn't sexual sadism.
The unsub must have had other motives." "Perhaps he
was gay," Ethan said. "Jason said it's possible that he was
rejected, had problems with a father figure in his life.
So he takes out his anger on these men." Gus shook his
head. "No, this wasn't sexual. In fact, there is no evidence
to suggest that the killer was homosexual at all. I was
certain that we were dealing with a sociopath of sorts.
This guy has little to no social interaction. Terrible social
skills. He works in a lower-class job, doesn't have many
friends, perhaps has a visible or inherent debility, like a
limp, or a stutter. The first victim – Irving – was his first
kill, his first taste of blood. It was overkill because he
was angry, but also because he didn't know what he was
doing. If you look at the rest of the victims, the typology

changes drastically. It was almost as though this unsub was evolving. Each time he killed, he got better and better. Neater, faster, more precise. He had a plan and he executed it thoroughly. Only question that remained was, what did these men ever do to deserve to die?" "Anything more on victimology?" Gus shook his head. "That's the thing – there was no correlation between the victims. Only that they were men. And between the ages of thirty and fifty. Some were married, some weren't. Some had children, some were young bachelors. They all had different careers, eye colour, hair colour." "They could have had their vices," Ethan suggested. "Get some-one into drugs and that's the only thing they need to have in common for someone to target them." "They weren't into drugs," Gus said, matter-of-fact. "You're sure?" "Yes, we went through every single detail of their lives, turned it upside-down. If they were being targeted for a spe-cific reason, I would have found out." Ethan thought about this for a moment. "What about any significance of the dates? Was there anything else that happened on the days of the murders? Any numbers, patterns, signs?" "Nothing substantial. It was all very arbitrary." "Okay, so let's go back to the first victim – Irving," Ethan said. "The unsub uses a knife. What does this tell us?" "A knife is more personal than a gun. As is strangulation. This unsub preferred to get up close and personal with his victims, rather than shooting them from afar. The thing with shootings is that it's very quick and easy, over and done with. An assassination, or a target being taken out. Usually there's no other reasoning behind it other than someone wants that person dead. But the way these men were killed – they weren't just targets, there was more to their deaths. That's why I say this guy was a sadist. He enjoyed the act of killing. Enjoyed it very much." "Do you know what kind of knife was used?" "Geez," Gus exhaled. "It was a pocket knife of some sorts. A trapper or a jack. But that's another thing – the weapon was never found." "You don't say." Gus nodded. "Whoever this guy was, his first kill was well thought out. The doors were all locked, no sign of forced entry. We assumed he must have gotten inside from an open window, perhaps, then closed it when he left." "So we have this unsub," Ethan began. "He's never killed before, but he'd like to. He plans it out meticulously. Picks a time when he knows Irving is home and will be alone. He's not married, doesn't have kids. Perfect time was to strike at night and go unseen. He comes in, confronts Irving...?" "There was no sign of a struggle. No bruises or markings on the skin, no defensive wounds. The unsub might have even talked his way into the house. Or..." Gus paused. "He could have known him." Ethan nodded. "It would be more likely that he used a ruse to get inside. They were talking at close proximity. The unsub lurches forwards and stabs him," Ethan thrust his fist out to portray the motion. "Keeps stabbing him," Gus said. "Seven times." "Then he gets off of him," "Clears the place." "Leaves the word sad," Ethan added. "And exists the home." Gus finished. They both sat there in silence, individually going through the motions in their minds. Finally, Ethan spoke again, breaking the silence. "And what did you make of the word sad? His signature move." "It was interesting, that's for sure. I took it as a sign of remorse. Another reason I suspected this may have been a sociopath who felt that he didn't have a choice. He had to kill – it was his obligation. And leaving the word sad was his way of telling us that he was sorry. That he felt some sort of remorse for them. After all, psychopaths can't feel remorse or empathy. But sociopaths can. Even just the slightest." Ethan nodded, understanding more and more about this killer as the conversation continued. "Not only does the first kill signify high importance," Gus began. "But so does the last – the seventh – Paul Monoghan, The Sad Killer's grand finale. What was so unique about Paul? Why was he the only victim that was shot?" "Right," Ethan nodded. "Blunt force trauma to the head as well, right?" Gus nodded. "Officers found a giant rock beside the body with blood on it. M.E concluded that Monoghan must have been hit with that over the head first, but it didn't kill him. The cause of death was one bullet through the brain." "And this giant rock," Ethan said. "It was at the crime scene already?" "Yeah," Gus said. "It was one of those crystals. An antique looking thing." "So weapon of opportunity, then," Ethan said. Gus nodded. "Mike Darbyshire was weapon of opportunity as well. Suffocated with a pillow found in his home." "So does that mean our unsub was unprepared, or simply preferred to use something that was already readily available to them?" "It was unclear," Gus said. "Because the other five kills were done with weapons brought by the unsub – actually, the last one, Paul Monoghan, died from his own gun." "So the killer brings his own knife for two of the kills, a rope for another two, uses a pillow that was already at the vic's house for two, and for the grand finale, another weapon of opportunity: the victim's own gun." Gus nodded. "Doesn't make a whole lot of sense, does it?" "No," Ethan said. "It doesn't." He thought for a moment, piecing together everything they had just discussed. "I was talking with Martin Gallagher earlier," Ethan said. "He says you had a few suspects at one point. Even made an arrest. But no luck." Gus shook his head. "We had this one guy, I recall. He fit the profile. Was a bit of a loner, lived in his mother's basement, was forty-two years old. He worked at the docks. No alibi for any of the murders. But when it came down to it, there just wasn't enough evidence to prove it was him." "So do you think it was him?" "No," Gus shook his head. "At first I did. But the more we interrogated him, the more it became clear that he wasn't our guy." "What do you think happened to our killer? Why did he stop?" "My guess was that there was only two reasons he would have stopped. He either got what he came for and stopped the killings, or he moved on and changed his M.O. Kept killing in different ways, in different states across the country. He disguised himself, hid in plain sight. And by changing his M.O each time he killed, he was essentially making himself untraceable." "And which option are you leaning towards?" Gus thought about this for a moment. "Seven men within five month, all murdered and left with one word beside the body," he took a break. "With my expertise in this field, I'd have to go with the latter. Serial murderers don't usually go after people they know – so it's unlikely that this was some hit-list he was accomplishing. Especially since there was nothing linking the victims together in any way. I'd say this guy moved on from Briarwood. Graduated to a bigger city and kept killing. Who knows where he is today." "Do you think he's still alive? Out there somewhere?" Gus thought about this again. "Maybe. And if he is, he's likely as old and immobilized as I am," he said. "Or, he's dead. And in that case, we have nothing to worry about." "Yeah," Ethan said. "But I guess we'll never know."

Chapter Eleven

CHAPTER ELEVEN

The first time Ethan saw a dead body, he was seven years old. It was his grandfather. He died from lung cancer. The funeral was a blur and he didn't recall anything from that day. Except for the body.

It was an open-casket. His grandfather had been embalmed; his eyes were closed, his lips were eerily pink. His chest seemed to be inflated, his hands crossed over his stomach. Ethan remembered looking over the casket, staring at this dead human being. It was peculiar to him, how something so evidently deceased could still look so alive. How one minute, this person could be living, breathing, conscious with a soul and a heartbeat, and the next, he was gone, his body empty. As though people are simply host-bodies containing souls, and once they die, what remains is an empty shell.

The second time he saw a dead body was when he was twenty-five, straight out of the academy. The first call he responded to was a woman found dead in her apartment, gunshot to the head. He could recall that day clearly. Following the officers up the stairwell, entering the room and seeing her lying on the floor, her silk robe barely covering her body. Her eyes were open, a hole in the center of her forehead, dark, dried blood oozing down the center of her face and across her cheek.

Her body was lying there so perfectly, as though she had been positioned a certain way. Her name was Amanda Hollands and she was twenty-nine. All Ethan could think was that this beautiful woman was too young to be dead.

It was Monday morning and Ethan was driving back to Briarwood. After he left Gus Fraser's home on Saturday evening, he couldn't get the 1965 case off his mind. He was thinking about many other things simultaneously – Haddie Taylor and her barely pregnant belly; Bentley Carter and Oliver Harris; Oliver with Kiera; Anneka Wilson; what Cloe Wilson had showed him; what Kiera Barnes had told him; all the mixed stories and explanations from the friend group. But his mind was preoccupied by The Sad Killer. The notion that this guy was never caught. That he killed seven men and managed to get away with it. And not only that, but the prospect of not knowing. Not knowing what happened to him. Not knowing if he was still out there to this day. Ethan wished that he knew something. He wished he could solve the case and figure out where the killer went after he left Briarwood. Because surely he left. Surely he continued killing. Someone that deranged doesn't simply stop murdering people once and for all. And Gus Fraser believed that was what happened, so Ethan did as well.

He would look into every single murder that happened after 1965 in the greater area. Maybe he could identify a pattern, follow a trail of bodies eventually leading to The Sad Killer. But The Sad Killer would no longer be sad. He'd have a new M.O and a new signature. Other cities across the country would label him as something different, never quite making the connection that all of these murders were being committed by the same person. And no one would ever catch him.

But Ethan would. He was determined.

Being a detective, you never truly have a day off. But Sunday was technically his allotted day off. Not that he spent much time relaxing, but at least he didn't have to drive into Briarwood and repeat the same process of going in a loop, circling around the same witnesses and getting nowhere.

Today was Monday, the start of a new week. Jordan's birthday was tomorrow and he would leave work early to make it home in time for her. They would go to her parent's place, eat delicious Polish food, and have chocolate cake for dessert – Jordan's favourite.

But as Ethan thought about Jordan and how happy he was to be with her, he couldn't help but think about Olivia. This sometimes happened when he felt that he was getting too happy. It was as though his subconscious had to remind him of the past – that he had something to be depressed about. As though he wasn't allowed to move on from her and have another good thing in his life.

He felt guilty. As though he was betraying Olivia by being happy with Jordan. And no matter how many times he told himself that he was being ridiculous, nothing seemed to change. He knew what kind of person Olivia was. He knew that she would want him to move on and be happy. Yet still, every now and then, she would appear at the forefront of his mind, illuminating there, reminding him of the horrible thing that happened to her.

Ethan arrived at the Briarwood police station a little after ten. Kennedy and Jesse were already inside, talking with Frank and Hal. Ethan was relieved to see that Hal had given up on his cult theory and was finally beginning to take this investigation seriously.

"There you are," Kennedy said when he walked in the room. "O'Riley," Frank stood. "Have a seat. How was your Sunday?" "It was alright. Had brunch with Jordan, then spent the rest of the day racking my brain about this case." Frank laughed. "Join the club." "No rest for the wicked," Hal remarked. Ethan took a seat across from Kennedy. "What are we looking at?" he asked, grabbing the piece of paper that sat on the table. "Toxicology report," Kennedy said. "For Anneka Wilson." "That was quick," Ethan remarked, skimming over the information on the paper. "Frank has friends in high places," Kennedy told him. "Rushed it as fast as he could." "Grand," Ethan said, continuing to read. "She was on Zopiclone," Kennedy said before he could even finish reading the page. "Used to treat insomnia." Ethan placed the sheet back on the table and looked at her. "She was having trouble sleeping. So what?" "That's not all,"

Kennedy said, leaning across the table and pointing her finger at a section of the page. "She was also on sertraline – Zoloft." Ethan stared at her, not saying a word. "She was suffering from depression," Kennedy said, the words piercing Ethan like a knife. "You're back to the suicide theory, then," Ethan remarked, leaning back in his chair. He didn't know how to process this information. "This is good," Kennedy said. "This is solid evidence. We're getting somewhere." "No," Ethan leaned forward once again. "We're not. Those girls were not depressed. And even if Anneka was, the other two weren't. And that just doesn't make sense now, does it? Anneka is depressed and wants to kill herself, so, what...? The girls offer to join her? Best friends till the end, right?" "No," Kennedy said, staring at him defiantly. "But this is more than you've got." "Don't," Ethan said. "Don't do that. You have your tangible evidence, I have my interviews and witness statements. Which one do you think will prove more useful in the end?" "Do you really want me to answer that?" she countered. "Enough," Frank said, looking between the both of them. "Anneka was taking medication for insomnia and depression. Makes logical sense if this was an isolated incident. But O'Riley is right. It still doesn't explain the other two." "Well then

O'Riley better do his job and figure out exactly what was going on in those girls' lives," Kennedy snapped. "What do you think I'm doing?" Ethan snapped back. "Okay!" Jesse interrupted. "Let's all calm down. Ken, get back with forensics. Ethan, go talk to your people. We'll reconvene at five-thirty. Sound good?" Ethan nodded silently. Kennedy made some sort of sound through her nose. Frank stood.

Ethan drove back to where it all began: St. Paul's Catholic School. Ironic that a catholic school could see so much demise and spectacle.

He waited in the lobby for Mrs. Lang. She was in a meeting with a member from the schoolboard. Ethan fiddled with his pen while he waited, observing his sur-roundings.

Finally, the door opened and an older gentleman walked out. Rebecca Lang said her formalities, then turned to Ethan. He stood up and walked into her office. She closed the door behind them, then took a seat at her desk.

"Detective O'Riley," she said. "Pleasure as always. What can I do for you today?" "I need to know if any of the students have been acting differently since the girls' deaths." "Differently?" "Yes. I know you said last week that counselling was setup for students to attend for grieving. Perhaps I could speak with the counsellor, see if she's noticed anything." "Okay," Rebecca said. "What are you hoping to accomplish?" "If those girls were pushed, then whoever did it might be feeling guilty or remorseful. They might have seen the counsellor, tried to talk about how they were feeling." "You think another student did this?" "Well I'm just not sure who else would do something like this, given the means, time, location, and access." "I..." she started, then stopped. "Unless it was a faculty member." "Of course not," Rebecca said quickly. "But a student? It just seems so..." "Unimaginable? Believe me, I know. But the possibility of a triple suicide is growing farther and farther away as the day's progress. In all likelihood, if the girls were pushed, it was someone in this school. Someone who had access to the roof and knew the girls would be there. Apparently they were known to go up there sometimes, to talk and eat their lunch. So it would be a crime of opportunity, throwing out our earlier theory that the girls were somehow lured up there," Ethan explained. "I will also need attendance records to see who was in class and who was absent, considering this happened just before the lunch hour." She closed her eyes and placed her finger and thumb to her forehead. "This is a disaster." Ethan remained quiet. "They should never have been up on that roof," she said. "There's not much we can do about that now," Ethan said. "First, get me in contact with the counsellor. Then, speak with your faculty. See if any of them have noticed any inconsistencies in attendance this past week. Maybe mood or behavioural changes. But something strange and abnormal, not just sad, because of course everyone is grieving. We're looking for someone who is a little less interested than the others. Someone perhaps who has detached themselves from the situation. They know they're guilty and they want to stay as far away from this case as they possibly can. It could have been an accident for all we know. But still, there's a good possibility that someone in this school pushed them. And we need to find out who."

_____

Ethan met with Vanessa Camacho, the school counsellor. She was young – he guessed anywhere between twenty-five and twenty-eight at best. She had dark curly hair and caramel brown eyes. A pleasant smile for a pleasant woman. She was very accommodating, invited him into her office and offered to help as best as she could.

"Many of the students have been seeing me this past week," she told Ethan. "I know a lot of them were friends with the girls, and even those who weren't friends with them are still shaken up by their deaths. Some students have also expressed feelings of fear and anxiety. They think there's a murderer in this school and they don't feel safe." "That's why everyone keeps saying suicide," Ethan said. "It's a coping mechanism, makes them feel safer. It's terrible that these kids have to go through something like this." "It truly is," she said. "What I want to know is whether anyone has come to see you and has seemed a bit odd. Maybe they asked a lot of questions about the investigation. Or they were really eager to talk about themselves?" Vanessa thought about this for a moment. "No one I can think of off the top of my head. The majority of students who have come in here have been girls. I've just seen lots of crying, hyperventilating, and confusion. Some of them just want someone to talk with, to feel that they're not alone. They vent to me. Come in here for one thing, then end up going off about their own problems. You wouldn't believe how many girls come in here and talk about self-esteem issues and bullying. I thought St. Paul's was better than that, but I guess no school is ever safe from those sorts of things." "Did you know the girls? They ever come in here to talk with you?" "No, I didn't know them well. Anneka came in here once or twice last year. Her parents are divorced and she felt that talking with someone helped. It's a difficult situation to be in, with divorced parents." "Did she ever express any signs of distress? Depression?" Vanessa hesitated. Ethan wondered if she was breeching some sort of client-patient confidentiality. But then again, Anneka was dead. "I don't believe so," she finally said. "If she had, I would have come forward sooner. Because of the suicide theory, of course." "Alright," Ethan said. "Well, please, if you remember anything else, or speak to anyone and think something might prove useful, don't hesitate to call me," he handed her his card, stood, then left.

Ethan grabbed a coffee and sat in his car. He wasn't getting anywhere. His leads were proving useless. How was this case so complicated? It was a town of five thousand, for Chris sakes. Why wasn't he getting any answers?

The worst part was not being able to determine whether it was suicide or homicide. Because every time that Ethan convinced himself that it was a murder and that these girls did not kill themselves, he found himself going in circles. Who would want to kill them? And why?

And then there was Kennedy's theory in the back of his mind, making him doubt himself and his certainty. Anneka's sleeping pills, depression, and the discovered bag of marijuana Cloe gave him. She had been acting different these past few months. Quiet, more secluded. Different crowd of people. Perhaps Anneka was suicidal. Maybe they all were and didn't show the signs well enough. Yet still, there was no note. If they did kill themselves, wouldn't they have left a note? He knew that that wasn't always the case. People killed themselves all the time and didn't leave a note. But still, it was peculiar and definitely one of the main factors that kept him on the fence about this whole debacle.

He finished his coffee and threw the empty cup on the seat beside him. He sat up straighter, took out his notepad, and began reading through his notes from the past week. He started with the families. Maybe he should go back there? Talk to them some more, express his urgency to solve this case.

He got to the part about Haddie and her pregnancy. For some reason, out of everything he had gathered, this seemed to be the most important. He wasn't disregarding the fact that Anneka was hiding marijuana and taking Zoloft. Or that Kiera was seeing her best friend's boyfriend behind her back. Those were important, but this was crucial – potentially life altering. People got killed because of unwanted pregnancies. Did someone want Haddie dead because of that baby?

Oliver didn't know about it. But Bentley Carter might have.

Ethan brought Bentley into the station for questioning, along with Oliver Harris. They were kept in separate rooms, unaware of each other's presence. It was the fifth day of the investigation and the interrogation room hadn't been used yet, so it was about time.

All roads led back to these two. Besides Beth Campbell, the girls didn't have any enemies. No one who wanted to hurt them or get revenge that he knew of. So in that case, who would want them dead? These were the only two people that Ethan could think of.

Oliver was up first. Ethan had already gone over most of the questions with him previously, but he had a feeling that Oliver wasn't telling him the whole truth. He sat at the table in the quiet room, hands resting on the table in front of him. He was visibly nervous.

Ethan walked into the room and sat across from him at the table. The video camera was already setup to record their conversation. Ethan brought out his notes and set them in front of him. "Hello, Oliver." He looked up timidly and they met eyes. "Hi." "Do you know why I brought you in today?" Oliver shook his head. "I just need to go over some more questions with you. Alright?" "Okay." Ethan cleared his throat. "When did you first begin suspecting that your girlfriend, Haddie Taylor, was cheating on you?" "Um," Oliver sat up a bit straighter. "I guess around February. Beginning of February." "And why did you believe that she was cheating on you?" "I already told you this," he said. "She was acting different, being strange and distant. Like she didn't have time for me anymore. And the time we did spend together, she was quiet and disconnected." "And you didn't think it was because you did something wrong?" "No," Oliver said. "Because I didn't do anything wrong. And if I did, Haddie would have told me." "Okay," Ethan said, nodding. "So you suspect your girlfriend is cheating on you. What do you do next?" Oliver was quiet for a moment, staring at Ethan. "I did nothing." "You didn't go out looking for this guy? Follow her around? Check her phone and messages?" "I did that," Oliver said. "She wasn't stupid. If there were any messages, she deleted them." "Okay, so then what?" Oliver sighed. "I don't know what you want me to say. My girlfriend was cheating on me. I loved her. There was nothing I could do. I couldn't prove it. I couldn't just leave her." "So you started seeing her best friend. Was that to get back at her?" "I told you, it wasn't like that." "Let's go over it again," Ethan said. Oliver was getting frustrated. "Haddie and I just weren't like how we used to be. And whenever we'd all hang out, Kiera and I just seemed to talk and laugh and get along. I don't know, I guess I looked to her for comfort. Since Haddie wouldn't reciprocate the feelings I was showing, I turned to Kiera. It was nice, just being able to talk with her." "Did Kiera ever express any guilt for what you two were doing?" "Yes. We both did. We felt that it was wrong. Of course we did." "But you didn't stop. Didn't end things." Oliver shook his head. "So you felt guilty, just not guilty enough." "We tried," Oliver said. "Tried to stop seeing each other. But we couldn't." "Did you love her?" "What?"

"Kiera. Did you love her?" He was quiet. "You loved Haddie, yes?" "Of course." "And did you love Kiera?" "I don't know." "Tell me about the weeks leading up to Tuesday May sixteenth." Oliver looked at him again. "What, you mean before they died?" "Yes." He took in a breath. "I don't know, things were fine I guess. I was still seeing Kiera." "But you and Haddie were still together." "Yes." "If Haddie was seeing someone else, and you were seeing Kiera, why did you bother even staying together? Clearly things weren't working." "Because she didn't know that I knew. And she didn't know about Kiera. We were both keeping each other in the dark about things. The only difference was, I knew what she was doing." "Yet you stayed with her anyway. Why? You could have broke things off, ended things for good." "I guess I liked having her around, as my girlfriend. It's what I was used to. And maybe there was a part of me that thought she'd grow out of whatever phase she was going through and realize that we were truly meant to be together." "During the weeks before she died, was Haddie acting like herself again? Wanting to spend more time with you?" Oliver thought about this for a moment. "Yeah, actually. She asked me to go to the mall on the Thursday before. She was also making plans for the spring fair." "And you didn't find this unusual? That she wanted to spend time with you again?" "I don't know. I guess I was so used to her neglect that I didn't realize if she started showing interest in me again." "Were you angry at her, Oliver?" "What?" "It must have made you mad, her cheating on you and such." "What are you implying?" "I'm not implying anything. I'm just saying – if my girlfriend cheated on me –" "You think I pushed her?" Oliver said, exasperated. "I didn't! I would never. I wasn't even near the roof that morning. But I wish I was. I wish I was there so I could have stopped this from ever happening," he began to cry. Ethan sat there in silence. He couldn't help but wonder if Oliver's tears were for Haddie, or for Kiera.

––––––

Bentley Carter sat in the same seat that Oliver Harris had just left. It was ensured that the two would not see each other or have any sort of contact. Bentley Carter was a secret, after all. Oliver didn't know about him. No one did. Except for Kelsey Barnes, that is.

"Mr. Carter," Ethan began. "I'm going to go over some questions with you. Alright?" "Of course," Bentley was sitting straight with his hands folded on top of each other on the table. "When did you and Haddie Taylor first begin seeing each other?" "I met her at a New Year's party. I guess we started seeing each other sometime in January." "And you were aware of the fact that she had a boyfriend?" "I was aware, yes." "Yet you still continued to pursue her." "Well, when you put it like that, it sounds like I'm the bad guy. I'm pretty sure the feelings were mutual." Ethan flipped to the next page of his notepad. "You say Haddie broke up with you a couple weeks before her death," he said. "What day was this, exactly?" "I can't remember the exact day now –" "Give it a little thought," Ethan said. Bentley went quiet. Then he said, "May third." "So thirteen days, then. Not a couple weeks." "I guess." "You guess." "Yes." "Tell me, Bentley, how did you feel when Haddie broke things off with you." "I was confused," he said. "We had been talking for the past four months and things were fine. Then she just says she needs some time and ends things with me. Just like that." "Did you assume she was trying to fix things with her boyfriend, Oliver Harris?" "I didn't really think about that, no. I didn't question her motives. I've had girlfriends before, Detective. Sometimes they simply want to break up. It's a part of life. We all move on." "So you weren't angry after she did this?" "Angry, no. I was confused. A little hurt, maybe. I really liked that girl." "And were you aware of the fact that Haddie was four weeks pregnant when she died?" Just like that, his disposition altered. Eyes wide, face ashen. "What?" "And according to her boyfriend, Oliver Harris, the baby couldn't have been his." "You think it was mine?" "So you weren't aware?" "No! Of course not. God," he looked away, put his fist to his mouth. "She should have told me." Ethan could have said that he wasn't even sure whether Haddie herself knew. But he decided to omit that bit. "Bentley, where were you last Tuesday between 11:30 a.m. to 12:00 p.m.?" "I was in class," he looked up and met Ethan's eyes. "Don't tell me you think I did this, that I had anything to do with those girls' deaths." "Maybe she did tell you," Ethan said. "Maybe you weren't too happy about that. Too young to be a father. Too much responsibility. So what do you do? Maybe you go up there, confront her. Something goes wrong —" "What are you talking about!? I didn't touch her! I would never hurt Haddie," he stopped, breathing heavily through his nostrils. "We'll need to confirm your alibi —" "Alibi? What is this? Am I a suspect or something?" "We need to confirm where everyone was during the time of the deaths. Until we can determine what exactly happened to them, everyone is a suspect."

The principal got back to Ethan with the attendances from Tuesday. There were a few absences and some late's, but Oliver Harris and Bentley Carter were not among them. Both of their teachers confirmed that the boys were in their scheduled classes at the time of the deaths, neither of them left the classroom until the bell rang for lunch. And by that point, the girls were already dead.

Anyone could have been up on that roof. Anyone could have come in contact with the girls and pushed them. But perhaps it wasn't a student as Ethan so quickly predicted. It could have been a teacher or faculty member. Or worse – a parent.

He would need to go back farther, dig deeper into the girls' personal lives and try to pin-point where things went wrong. He was so certain that there was something he was missing – an event or incident that occurred – that was the catalyst to the girls' strange behaviour these last few months.

He decided to return to the Taylor residence. By the cars in the driveway – Beemer and Cadillac – Ethan could see that both George and Renée were home. Renée

answered the door, looking serene and melancholy all
at once.

"Have you found something?" she asked, hope igniting in
her eyes. "Nothing substantial," Ethan said, watching her
face fall. "Can I come inside?" "Please," she stepped back
and let him enter the house. She moved lethargically, as
though all of the life that she once possessed had been
drained from her. She led Ethan through their home
and into the living room, once again. "So," Renée said,
sitting on the couch patiently but anxiously, legs crossed.
George sat next to her. "Sorry to bother you at this
time," Ethan said. "I just feel like I'm still missing a huge
portion of the girls' lives. I need more information. What
am I missing?" "I don't know what more we can tell
you," Renée said. "Do you have any idea of who could
have done this?" She shook her head, tears forming
in her eyes. "We've already told you, we don't know."
Ethan watched her, then turned to George. He seemed
to remain impassive. "Mr. Taylor," Ethan said. "What
do you think happened?" He was quiet for a moment,
thinking. "We live in a good town, Detective," he began.
"Good people. Not many of us, but everyone is kind,
friendly, helpful. We're a community here. We get along,
give each other assistance when we need it," he stopped

again. "Why would someone like that kill my daughter? What could they possibly have accomplished?" "So you can't think of anyone – anyone at all – who would want to hurt Haddie or the girls?" He shook his head. "Unless I'm missing something," he said. "After all, there were things she didn't tell us." Renée turned to her husband, almost as if to say don't. "What do you mean?" Ethan asked, leaning forward in his seat. "It's nothing," Renée said quickly. "Let him speak, please, Mrs. Taylor," Ethan said. She closed her mouth. "Go on," Ethan said to George. "No, my wife is right," George said. "It's nothing disconcerting. I just meant that she's a teenage girl. She has her secrets. Don't they all?" "Yes," Ethan said. "But in this case, it's a matter of life and death. And anything that you might have found odd or conspicuous in the past – well, you need to tell me." It was silent again, as if nobody knew what to say next. "Did the girls seem secretive at all?" Ethan asked. "As though they were sneaking around, doing something they weren't supposed to?" "No," Renée said. "Haddie didn't feel the need to hide things from us. She always asked us whenever she wanted to go to a friend's place or to a party or anything like that." "Did they go out often? To parties?" "Sometimes," Renée said. "Here and there." "Did things ever get out of hand at these parties?" Ethan asked, recalling the party from last month. Haddie getting into the car with Beth's boyfriend, drunk. "I don't believe so," she said. "The kids here are good. Nothing crazy ever happens." "What else did the girls like to do?" "They liked to go exploring," Renée said. "Anneka would take photos and Haddie and Kiera would be her subjects. They were all practicing to get their licences this year. They went to school, did their homework, went to the mall, hung out at our place, or at the Barnes' property," Renée paused. "They were just regular girls, doing regular things. It's not like they were delinquents. I don't know what else you want me to say." "Would you say that Haddie was happy?" Ethan asked. "Of course she was happy," Renée said without hesitation. "Really think about this though – did she truly seem happy, or did it just seem like she was happy?" "Haddie was always smiling and laughing," George said. "She was full of life. She had big plans for her future. She wouldn't have simply killed herself, if that's what you're asking." Ethan nodded, remembering the conversation he had with Oliver the week prior. "Oliver mentioned that Haddie wanted to move away from Briarwood, go to Hollywood, make it big. Is this true?" Renée smiled. "That was Haddie. Obviously we wanted her to go to school and become a lawyer, and that's what she wanted as well. But she also had other dreams, Hollywood was one of them. Ever since she was a little girl, she'd talk about how she wanted to grow up and be famous." "So would you say that Haddie liked it here in Briarwood? Or hated it?" "I wouldn't say hate," George said. "But she didn't want to stay here after she finished school." "Everyone stays here," Renée said. "It's genetic. Families are raised here, and then the kids grow up and repeat the process. No one ever really escapes." "Escapes," Ethan repeated. "You say that as though you're trapped here." "I didn't mean it like that," Renée tried to laugh it off. "I just meant... well –" "You live here and then you die," George finished for her. "But Briarwood's a good place. We all love it here." "But not Haddie," Ethan said. "No," George said. "Not Haddie."

He was in her bedroom again, looking for anything that he might have missed before. Renée and George were with him, going through their daughter's things, looking for a sign, a clue, anything that could help them figure out what happened, what went wrong.

Ethan lifted up a photo album and began flipping through the pages. Pictures of Haddie as a baby, Haddie on her first day of school. Then, to the latter half of the book, photos of her and the girls, smiling, sticking their tongue's out, laughing.

Renée was doing something similar, going through a scrapbook. Ethan looked over and saw the page she was on: photographs, ticket stubs, string bracelets taped to the page.

George had found a bin in her closet full of old papers and receipts. Ethan walked over to see if there was anything useful. Most of the receipts were from clothes and food, some from the movies. Then something caught his eye – mostly because it was purple.

Ethan reached forward and grabbed the piece of paper from the pile, reading it over. It was an appointment confirmation with someone by the name of Esmerelda Fitzgerald.

"What's this?" Ethan said to George. George looked over the page and looked stumped. Renée came over to look as well. "Oh, that," she said, taking it from her husband's hands. "The girls went to see a fortune teller a while back. Just for fun." "When was this?" Ethan asked. Renée thought for a moment. "It must have been in December. Yes, it was just before Christmas actually."

Chapter Twelve

CHAPTER TWELVE

She waltzed around the kitchen as though every movement was sequenced. The place was small but done up to perfection. Ethan sat at the table watching her. She made her way from the counter, walking towards the table where Ethan sat, and placed two mugs of coffee in front of him. She took a seat, crossed one leg on top of the other, and looked at him. Esmeralda Fitzgerald.

He had tracked her down quite easily – she was the only fortune teller in Briarwood. And with a name like that – which he assumed was a pseudonym – well, she wasn't difficult to find.

She told Ethan how she worked out of the mall. Sometimes she would travel around to different events – pubs, bars – set up her stand, do card readings. Sometimes she worked from her house, out of her living room. Today she was going to setup at the farmer's market. Ethan had caught her just before she left.

He didn't believe in fortune tellers. He didn't believe in psychics. Thought they were all bullshit. Most of them just wanted money. They were good, he had to admit that. They knew how to read people, how to work them. They knew what things to look for – jewelry, expensive clothes, a necklace from a deceased parent, perhaps. Fortune tellers were almost like detectives, watching for body language and subtle habits that others didn't pick up on. Except detectives didn't exploit people for money.

They spoke to you as though they were your friend. Then, slowly, they eased the information out of you before you could even realize you were saying it, telling them everything they needed to know. So when they presented you with your fortune, open-palmed on a silver platter, you just gobbled it right up and accepted whatever fate they handed to you.

"Do you recognize these girls?" Ethan held up a photograph of Kiera, Haddie, and Anneka. The woman took the photo from him and studied it. "They look familiar," she said, then stared at the photo longer. "Aren't those the three that jumped off the roof?" Ethan took the photo back and placed it in his pocket. "That is undetermined right now. If it was suicide, that is." "Such a shame," she said. "So young and beautiful." "I believe they came to see you a few months back," Ethan said, putting the appointment sheet down on the table and sliding it towards her. "In December." Esmeralda took the sheet and looked at it. "Ah," she said, her eyes lighting up once she read the page. "Haddie Taylor. That was her name!" she handed Ethan the piece of paper and looked at him. "I remember now. Lovely girl. All three of them." "What did they want?" "To have their fortune told, of course." "Who went first?" Esmeralda thought for a moment. "The other blonde one." "Anneka Wilson?" "Yes. She went first. Then the brunette." "Kiera Barnes." "And Haddie went last," Esmeralda said. "I remember her specifically. She was endearing." "What makes you say that?" Ethan asked. "What made her stand apart from the others?" "I'm not sure what it was exactly. Something about her. She had charm and charisma, knew how to hold a conversation." "What did you say to them?" She smiled secretively. "I can't tell you that." "Ma'am, these girls are dead. I need to know what you said to them." Her smile fell and she nodded solemnly in agreement.

"The first one, I believe I told her that she would meet a boy. She was meek, a cute little thing. Perhaps she just wanted some company." "What else did you say to her?" Ethan asked. Esmeralda made a face, trying to think back. "I might have said something along the lines of going to school for the arts. She was creative. Hipster, they call it now. I think I told her that good things were coming for her. That was pretty much it." "And what about Kiera?" "The second one," Esmeralda said, "Was so eager and full of energy. She was laughing and smiling. We had a good chat. I told her there was an opportunity on the horizon – a high ranking position either at school or of employment. Maybe an offer from a place she applied to." Ethan stared at her. "Do you bullshit all of your clients, or just the teenaged girls?" Esmeralda stared back. "I give them what they want: hope. Nobody wants to hear that they will be stuck in a rut for the rest of their lives. So I listen to them as they speak. I tell them what they need to hear. Something to be hopeful for." "Okay, let's skip to Haddie Taylor," Ethan said. "What did you say to her?" "We talked for a little bit. She told me about herself and I got a sense of what kind of person she was. I told her that I saw big things coming for her. She would graduate school, get married, start a family, and make a life for herself." "In Briarwood?" "Well, yes. She was a small-town girl. I assumed that's what she wanted." "And how did she seem after that?" Esmeralda thought for a moment. "I'm not too sure. She was kind of quiet. Smiled, thanked me for everything, was very polite. And then that was it. They left." "Did you ever see any of them again after that?" "No," Esmeralda said. "Never saw them again."

Ethan left Esmeralda's place thinking about everything she had just told him. Haddie had gone to a fortune teller hoping to hear good things. And while Esmeralda might have believed that she was helping Haddie, in reality, she had just made things worse. Because while most would have thought that a fortune such as that would be exciting for Haddie, it was in fact the opposite of what she wanted to hear. The idea that she would be stuck in this town forever, caught in the loop, unable to break free. Her biggest fear coming to life.

_ _ _ _ _

It was nearing five o'clock. Ethan would need to get back to the station to regroup and discuss the investigation with the others. He wouldn't have time to speak with the

Wilson's and the Barnes' today. He would need to put it on the agenda for tomorrow.

He was trying to think about what he could gather from today's events. It was a bit of a longshot going to see the fortune teller. It was, after all, a thrown away ticket at the back of Haddie's closet. Did he expect to get anything useful from this woman? Not particularly.

But then Esmeralda explained what she had said to the girls. More specifically, Haddie. Ethan was thinking about it from every angle, trying to link this back to the disconcerting behaviour over the past few months. His previous suspicions entailed there being some sort of event or incident that happened in the girls' lives that was the catalyst for their sudden change in behaviour. Given the timeline, he predicted that this would have happened sometime around January, since it was around this time that Oliver began noticing the change in Haddie, and Cloe began noticing changes in Anneka. Initially he thought that they had gotten themselves into some sort of trouble. Perhaps they went to a party and something went wrong. Perhaps they saw something they shouldn't have. Perhaps they did something to someone.

But what if this was it? The event that began to change things for them – well, Haddie at least. Ethan began to speculate: Esmeralda tells Haddie that she will be happy and content here in Briarwood. She'll get married, start a family, and create a good life for herself.

Haddie didn't want to hear that. In fact, it probably frightened her. She had big plans for her future – move away from this small town, go to Hollywood, make it big and have the fame and fortune. Who knows if she even wanted a husband and a child?

So what does Haddie do? She panics. She thinks that her normal life with Oliver isn't quite satisfactory enough. She meets Bentley at the New Year's party, decides to go out on a limb and try something new. She wanted to be bold and daring. She wanted to know how it felt to be with someone who wasn't Oliver, someone she hadn't grown up with and was expected to marry. It was audacious, branching out the way she did. Leaving a life of comfort for a life of risk and thrill.

And with Haddie secretly seeing Bentley, Oliver, in turn, began seeing Kiera. And the rest is just a chain reaction of events, tumbling together from that very moment that they saw the fortune teller.

This had to be it, Ethan thought. It made sense. There was no way to prove it, seeing as though the girls were dead, and it was simply a theory. A thought. A single thought planted into Haddie Taylor's head. But it was possible. This could be it. This could be what started it all.

Everyone met back at the station for their end-of-day debrief, then headed down to the local pub afterwards for a few drinks. Ethan debated going straight home to Jordan, but ultimately decided to stick around to have a quick visit with the team.

He showed up at the pub where Jesse, Kennedy, Frank, and Hal were all seated at a booth in the far back corner. Frank was ordering drinks for everyone. Ethan slid into the booth and took off his jacket.

"There he is," Kennedy remarked, taking a sip from her beer. "This case is making my head spin," Ethan said. "No talk about the case," Jesse said. "We're off duty tonight." Ethan looked to Frank. He didn't protest. Ethan complied. He was fine with that. Besides, he needed a break anyway. He was spending too much of his time thinking about the minds of teenagers. He needed to be having drinks with people his age, in his field of work. "And this woman," Kennedy explained as she told her story. "Was insane. Never have I seen anyone behave that way. She was screaming, yelling, threatening me and the other officers," Kennedy rolled her eyes and took another sip of her beer. "She needed to be sedated." "So what did you end up doing?" Jesse asked. "Nothing. We had to leave her and let it be. But oh boy, if I had it my way," Kennedy smirked. "This one guy I was dealing with a couple years back," Frank said. "He was good. Smart. You know the type, think they're superior to you. So anyway, we know it's him. Only problem was, we couldn't prove it." "Don't you just hate that?" Hal said. "The worst. So we have him in the interrogation room. And one of my best men is trying to get a confession out of him. Psyche him out, make him slip up. But he doesn't budge. He just sits there playing all innocent. But then, as the conversation progressed, the guy said something, which, at the time, seemed irrelEthant. But later we discovered that the only way he could have known that little piece of information was if he was there, at one of the crime scenes. He knew this specific detail that no one else could have possibly known." "So what happened?" Kennedy asked, intrigued. "We got him. Nailed him."

They all laughed. "I'm sure he wasn't too happy about that," Hal said. "Oh, he wasn't," Frank said. "Kept asking for his lawyer. We said, fine, here's your lawyer. Good luck mate." "And you charged him?" Frank nodded. "We did." "Cheers to that, then," Jesse lifted his beer. They all clinked their glasses together and drank. "What about the ones that don't get solved?" Ethan asked, placing his glass back on the table. "Well," Frank took in a breath. "Those are tough. But as an officer, it's something you have to live with. It's going to happen sometimes. There will be crooks and thieves and murderers out there who get away with it. But we don't focus on that. We focus on the ones we do catch. The ones we rid society of and bring justice to. That's what matters." Ethan nodded, trying to accept this answer. "You're thinking about that case, aren't you, O'Riley?" Frank asked. "Yeah. I've been looking into it a bit. Talked to a reporter on the case. And the constable in charge all those years ago." Frank stared at him. "And when did you have time to do this?" "Saturday," Ethan said. "After the funeral." "As long as you don't let this take your time and focus away from the current case." "I won't, sir." "Good," Frank said. "We need to solve this thing soon. It's driving everyone in this town mad." Hal nodded. "They just want answers. People hate not knowing. Especially when the idea of a potential murderer is on everyone's minds." "But we still don't know that for sure," Kennedy said. "I'm sticking with suicide." "Could have been cult related," Jesse sipped his beer. "Or they were pushed," Ethan said. "Either way, it's our job to find out. This town – and those girls' families – are depending on it."

CHAPTER THIRTEEN

It was Tuesday May twenty-third, which meant two things. The first was that it was Jordan's birthday. Ethan was up early making banana pancakes and leaving her a bouquet of flowers before he was out the door again, on his way back to Briarwood. The second thing was that it had been exactly one week since Haddie, Kiera, and Anneka ended up dead on the pavement at St. Paul's.

The phone records from the girls cellphone's were finally in. Ethan headed over to the police station and met with Tony Cruz, who was responsible for everything from digital crime and cyberbullying, to identity-fraud and theft, to obtaining phone records and computer warrants.

First up was Kiera. Just as Ethan predicted, there were copious amounts of texts and calls, both outgoing and incoming, to a phone number registered to Oliver Harris.

There was the usual stuff; calls and texts from mom, dad, Kelsey, Haddie, Anneka, and a few other numbers that he traced to the girls from the school. Other than that, there was nothing conspicuous or out of the ordinary.

Next he looked through Anneka's. Similar to her Facebook, there was nothing out of the ordinary. Regular texts to and from Haddie and Kiera. Lots to her sister. Mom, dad, Pamela, even. Hardly any calls. A few numbers Ethan didn't recognize, but Anneka didn't have enough contact with them for him to be concerned.

Finally he looked at Haddie's. She had enough cellphone records to make up for the entire town of Briarwood. Calls, texts, data. The most reoccurring numbers were Kiera and Anneka's. He skimmed over the past few months, identifying which number belonged to Bentley Carter. And Bentley didn't lie – the texts and calls between the two of them began in January, and ceased around the third of May. Did something happen that Bentley omitted? What made Haddie decide to break things off with him so suddenly? And then not thirteen days later, end up dead with her two best friends.

There were other numbers in Haddie's records as well. The girl seemed to be in contact with almost everybody.

Fortunately for Ethan, there was another section of the records that listed the actual data contained in the text messages. It felt like an invasion of privacy, but Ethan could read everything those girls had said over the past six months. But going through every single text would take weeks.

Instead, he jumped to the day it happened, May sixteenth. The last text messages the girls had ever sent were in a group-chat between the three of them. The first one from Haddie.

+12126243821(Haddie Taylor): Meet @ our spot for lunch. Things to discuss.   +19146739564(Anneka Wilson): I left. Stomach hurts. +12126243821(Haddie Taylor): Where r u? +19146739564(Anneka Wilson): Library.   +12126243821(Haddie Taylor): Don't leave yet. +19146739564(Anneka Wilson): Why? +12126243821(Haddie Taylor): Need to talk. +19146739564(Anneka Wilson): U in class? Where's K? +3158297433(Kiera Barnes): I'm in math.   +12126243821(Haddie Taylor): meet now. +3158297433(Kiera Barnes): where? +12126243821(Haddie Taylor): roof. +19146739564(Anneka Wilson): When? +12126243821(Haddie Taylor): ten minutes.

That last message was sent at 11:07 a.m. And Ethan already knew what would ensue after that. So it was Haddie's idea to meet on the roof during class. Anneka had left with a stomach ache, and Kiera was in math. Yet whatever Haddie had to say was urgent enough to constitute skipping class.

Ethan remembered what one of the girls had said at the service. Haddie and Kiera are usually lab partners. But on Tuesday morning, Haddie asked to switch. So Ethan was possibly right after all. Haddie must have found out about Kiera and Oliver – what other explanation was there? Then she asked both girls to meet on the roof. And from there, it was a mystery. A fill-in-the-blank that needed to be solved.

But why ask both girls to meet if it was just Kiera that she wanted to confront? Could there have been something else going on, something that Ethan wasn't even aware of? And how did all three of them end up dead?

Ethan flipped through the pages, skimming the sheets, his eyes scanning for key words, names or numbers. Anything that might stand out and mean something.

Then he saw a number he recognized. It belonged to Bethany Campbell. The text message from her was sent

April 21 – just last month – to Haddie's phone at 2:06 a.m. The message was short and simple:

Stay away from Corey. Or else.

_____

Ethan told Kennedy about the text messages and she offered to pick up Beth and bring her into the station. Perhaps this day wouldn't prove to be useless after all.

Bethany was sitting in the interrogation room looking ever so complacent. Her white blonde hair was falling slightly over her shoulders. Her posture was straight, both of her hands folded in front of her on the table. Ethan walked into the room and took a seat across from her.

"Hi, Beth." "Why am I here?" was the first thing she asked. "No one will tell me anything." Ethan stared at her, matching her gaze. "I came across something of concern. I thought I'd bring you in to see if you could help me out with it." Her eyes flickered to the paperwork in Ethan's hands, then returned to his. "What is it?" Ethan laid the single sheet of paper on the table, then slid it towards Beth so that she could read it. She picked up the paper and read the text message. She maintained her composure, her face barely faltering. She put the paper back down on the table and looked at Ethan. "So?" "That to me looks like a threat," Ethan said. "Oh my God, you're not serious?" Ethan remained silent. "You think I killed Haddie? Is that why I'm here?" "I don't know, Beth. Why don't you tell me?" "This is ridiculous," she laughed. "You think I would kill someone because she talked to my boyfriend?" Ethan remained silent. "Listen," Bethany said, leaning in close. "I was drunk. It was stupid, really. The night of Wren Kreigler's party. Haddie was being obnoxious, blatantly flirting with Corey right in front of me. Not only did she do that, but she had the audacity to get a ride home with home. In his car." "Why would your boyfriend offer her a ride in the first place?" "He was drunk!" she said. "Boys do stupid things when they're drunk." "You two still together?" "Yes," she fidgeted in her chair. "I wouldn't stay with someone like that," Ethan said. "Flirting with other girls, giving them rides." "It's not like that!" Beth said. "Our relationship is fine. And none of your business, by the way." "So let's go back to Haddie for a minute." Beth made a sound. "This looks bad. Okay, I admit that. I shouldn't have texted her. I can see why you might think this looks like a threat." "You said or else, Beth. That is a threat." "But I wasn't serious!

It was just a warning. So that she'd stay away from my boyfriend." "And what did you plan to do if she didn't?" Beth shrugged. "I don't know. It never came to that." "So you're used to making idle threats?" "I guess. Haven't you ever said something you didn't mean?" Ethan didn't respond. "Detective, I can assure you that I had nothing to do with Haddie or the other girls' deaths. You can ask anyone! I'm not a murderer! And besides, even if I did want to push Haddie off a roof, why the hell would I push Kiera and Anneka off as well? It just doesn't make sense." "Good logic," Ethan said. "But who knows what you're capable of." Her mouth fell open. "I may have had my issues with Haddie, but I can assure you, I would never kill someone! Over a boy, especially. That's just insane. Do you think I'm insane? They must have jumped. Everybody already believes that. Those three did everything together. Everything. Live together – die together." Beth paused for a moment. "Maybe they were the insane ones." Ethan stared at her, allowing his silence to speak for itself. "Do I need to call a lawyer?" she finally asked. "Depends," Ethan said. "Do you think you'll need one?"

———————

Only a short hour later and Beth Campbell was free to go. Ethan had only needed to make a quick call to the principal to check the attendance to see that Beth was in class and well accounted for at the time of the deaths.

That settled things. Beth had nothing to do with this. Unfortunate, really. Ethan believed he was finally onto something.

Now what was there to do? He had made note to return to the Wilson's and the Barnes' today to speak with them, yet again. The only question was, what else was there to say?

There was a question in the back of his mind that had been there for a few days now. It was formed when he was speaking to the principal, Rebecca Lang. He was thinking about possible suspects, who would want the girls dead, who could be capable of killing them. They must have known that the girls would be up on that roof. It was a common meeting place of theirs. So was this an opportunistic kill? Was it an accident? A confrontation taken too far? Was the killer after one girl and the other two were simply witnesses? Collateral damage? What possible motive would one have? Did the girls do something to someone? Were they planning to do something? Did they know something they shouldn't have?

Suspects. That's what he was thinking about. Who could it be? It was limited to three categories: students, faculty, and other. Students included their close-knit group of girlfriends, as well as the boys, such as Oliver Harris and Bentley Carter. Faculty wasn't far-fetched either. Could a teacher have gone up there? A janitor? Someone looking for the girls?

And then there was other. This included anyone from Briarwood. Strangers, neighbors, parents. The last one was what got to him. Most of the time when there were murders such as this, it's someone close to the family. Boyfriend and secret boyfriend were both ruled out. The other girls had alibis and no motive. So could it have been a parent? There were seven of them, each with their own opinions and perceptions of the girls. Perhaps one of them went up there to find the girls – their daughter, perhaps. Something happens, there's an argument, something goes wrong.

Did the parents like their daughter's friends? Far as he could tell, they all seemed to get along fine with each other. But there was one thing that Ethan noticed, and it was that nearly everyone in this community that he had spoken to had something to say about one of the girls' in particular. And that was Haddie Taylor.

What was so different about her? What made her stand out from the other two? Cloe Wilson had said that Kiera was Haddie's shadow. Hyper, bubbly, full of energy, but always in the ranks with Haddie, struggling to keep up with Queen B.

Then there was Anneka. Sweet, quiet Anneka. It wasn't a wonder why she didn't stand out. The girl probably did her best to blend in, stray away from attention and hide in the crowds. Odd, seeing that she was friends with Haddie and Kiera. Two dominant personalities and one passive. But clearly the three of them bonded like no other. One of the girls – either Maya or Rachel – had mentioned that Anneka wasn't like that when she was with the girls. She let loose, had fun. Maybe it was only an illusion, this other side of Anneka. Or maybe her outgoing side was the illusion, put on to conform to societal norms and blend in with Kiera and Haddie.

The case was complicated when it should have been straight-forward. Three girls turn up dead. Is it suicide or homicide? Why was it proving so difficult to rule out one or the other? Ethan couldn't help but feel that he was going through all this work, all of these interviews and interrogations, trying to find a killer, when in all honesty, a killer may not even exist. What if it really was suicide?

It was thoughts such as those that made it difficult. Doubting himself, unsure of what to think. Just when he was sure of one idea, he was brought back to another.

Did they jump off that building or were they pushed? The answer lied somewhere in this town. Ethan just needed to try harder to locate it.

Vivian Barnes sat on the couch across from Ethan. Patrick was at work, expectedly, so the conversation would be left to the two of them. Ethan assumed that speaking to the mother of a teenage girl would prove beneficial enough as a separate entity. Mother's always know more.

"How are you holding up?" Ethan asked. "I'm okay," Vivian said. "It's an ache that will never stop hurting. But I'm managing." Ethan nodded. "Did you think of anyone who might have done something like this?" She shook her head. "I tried, but I just can't think of anyone. Kiera was such a good girl. And so were Anneka and Haddie. I can't imagine why anyone would ever do such a thing. They were innocent —" she began to cry. Ethan handed her the tissue box and waited for her to collect herself. "People are talking," Vivian said. "They're still saying that it was suicide." "We don't know that for sure," Ethan said. She looked at him. "What do you think, Detective?" He didn't know how to answer her. "It doesn't matter what I think. It matters what I can prove." "It does matter," Vivian said. "It matters. Do you think the girls did this? You think they jumped?" He hesitated. "I'm impartial," he said. "I follow the evidence, find the facts. That's what matters." She nodded her head, accepting his answer. "How did you get along with the other parents?" Ethan asked. "The Taylor's and the Wilson's?" "We got along well. I went to school with Renée Taylor. Known her since we were young." "Were you two close?" "No particularly. Just friendly. We reconnected once the girls became friends." "And what about the other parents? You all get along, you would say?" "Yes. I communicate more with Renée and Mary-Ella. Jason and George, no. And Jason's wife, Pamela, not at all. Perhaps Patrick could be of more help there." "No, that's fine," Ethan said. "I just wanted to know how the overall relationship was." She nodded. "What did you think of Haddie?" Ethan asked. Vivian seemed caught off guard. "What do you mean?" "Did you like her? Were you happy that she and Kiera were friends?" "Yes," she said. "They always got along splendidly. Haddie was a sweet girl." "I know that some people have certain thoughts about Haddie." "What kind of thoughts?" "Maybe she wasn't the best influence all of the time?" "I don't know," Vivian said. "The girls are not the passive types. They can stand up for themselves and make their own choices. If Haddie ever pressured the girls into doing anything, I'm sure Kiera and Anneka wouldn't have stood for it. Well, Kiera at least. I can't speak for Anneka." "What makes you say that?" "Anneka's the quiet one. The pushover. I can't be certain that if Haddie told that girl to do something that she wouldn't just comply." "But Kiera wouldn't?" "No, Kiera is independent," Vivian said, and Ethan noticed that she continual referred to the girls in present tense. "That's why she and Haddie would butt heads sometimes." "Do you know if anyone in Briarwood had a problem with Haddie?" "Not that I'm aware of. She's a sixteen-year-old girl, how many people could she have a problem with?" "Did Kiera have a boyfriend?" Ethan asked suddenly. Vivian's face changed. "A boyfriend? No. No she didn't. Why?" "Haddie had a boyfriend, correct?" "Yes, Oliver Harris." "Right," Ethan said, trying to pick up on any indication that Vivian knew about her daughter's secret love affair. "What about Anneka? Any boys there?" "I wouldn't know.

You'd have to ask her parents." "I will," Ethan nodded. "I will do just that."

He visited Mary-Ella Wilson next. She was rushing around her house, trying to tidy things up. To Ethan, everything looked fine. But of course, he wasn't a woman. Or a mother.

"Sorry to see you again under such short notice," Ethan said. "No need to apologize," Mary-Ella said once she finally took a seat. "Has something happened? A break in the case?" Ethan shook his head. "I just wanted to talk to you again. Go over a few more things." "Of course," Mary-Ella nodded. "What can I do?" "How would you describe the relationship between the parents? You, the Barnes' and the Taylor's?" "Well, we see each other from time to time. Have a few chats whenever we were dropping off or picking up the girls' from one another's place. But other than that, there's not much else to it." "Were the girls close with any of the other parents?" Mary-Ella thought for a moment. "I know Anneka always loved going to Kiera's place. I think it's because they have a big house and lots of property. They're well-off, have a lot of money. And they have a stable family environment. Anneka was accustomed to switching back and forth between here and her dad's place. And as you can see, I don't have the nicest home." "So Anneka enjoyed being there," Ethan said. "Did she get along with Vivian and Patrick?" "I believe so. They're nice people. Always very accommodating and welcoming." Ethan nodded. Then he said, "Were you aware of the fact that Anneka was taking Zopiclone and Zoloft?" Mary-Ella's face changed. "What?" "Medication for insomnia and –" "I know what they're taken for," Mary-Ella said. "But I didn't know Anneka was taking them. How do you know this?" "Tox-screen came back. Both medications were in her system when she..." "Oh." "She never said anything to you?" Ethan asked. Mary-Ella shook her head. "No. She didn't." Ethan wanted to ask her if she knew her daughter was also smoking marijuana, but he decided it was better to omit that part. "Did Anneka have a boyfriend? Or have any boyfriends in the past?" "She didn't have a boyfriend, no," Mary-Ella paused. "Now that I think about it, I don't recall her ever really having boyfriends." "Perhaps she didn't tell you?" Mary-Ella shook her head. "No, if Anneka had a boyfriend, she would have told me. I think she just preferred to be alone. She was very studious – always focused on her schoolwork and extracurriculars."

"Is there anything else you can think of, Mrs. Wilson? Anything you'd like to add before I get going?" "Not that I can think of. But I have your card. I will contact you if I have any questions or anything else I think is important." They both stood. "Thank you," Ethan said. "And again, I'm so very sorry."

It was four o'clock: time to head back to Riverton.

By the time he got home, Jordan was just coming down the stairs, ready to leave for her parent's place.

"You're late," she said to Ethan as he walked through the door. He looked at his watch. It was four-fifty-three. He was actually ahead of time. Jordan met him at the bottom of the stairs and gave him a kiss before turning around again to grab her shoes. Ethan hurried up the stairs, changed into something dressy-but-casual, then met Jordan by the front door. "Ready?" he smiled. "Yes," she kissed him again. "Thank you for breakfast and flowers." "Of course. Happy birthday."

Dinner at the Hopkins' was extravagant, as always. Jordan's mother was Polish and was constantly introducing Ethan to new dishes. The whole family was in attendance, from Jordan's sister, Ella, to her brother, Tom and his wife, Krista. Jordan's parents – Katherine and Tom Senior. And then there was Jordan's grandmother.

Ethan enjoyed visits with Jordan's family. They were the type of people who could laugh at themselves. Ethan had grown up in a household that was strict and conservative. His parents had high expectations of him and his sister. And while McKayla proved herself worthy and lived up to their parent's idealized perceptions of her, Ethan always saw himself as lesser.

Ethan's father was diagnosed with early on-set Alzheimer's a few years back. When things got bad, they had to move him to a home where he would have round-the-clock care. His mother lived alone. Ethan tried to visit them once in a while, but it was never a priority. The relationship simply wasn't what it used to be.

Seeing his father was a bit easier because at least they could have a conversation without all his father's preconceived judgments. Sometimes he recognized his own son – other times, he did not. When he wasn't lucid, they could talk about almost anything. Sports, the weather, politics. It was easier this way, Ethan thought.

Visiting with his mother was a different story. She had always favoured McKayla and Ethan knew that. There was a tension in the air that Ethan couldn't quite get passed. As though his mother was still judging him for every single detail of his life.

But at least here, with the Hopkins', there was no judgment – just love and laugher. Ethan surveyed the room and watched as everyone chatted and enjoyed themselves. Tom Jr. and Krista were pregnant and expecting their first child soon. It was a girl. They would have a daughter. Jordan would have a niece. It was an exciting time.

Jordan loved babies. Ethan knew that she probably thought about it quite often – having children, that is. But Jordan knew better than to talk about it with Ethan. It would come up eventually. But they would cross that bridge when the time came.

"Oh, Gran," Jordan said suddenly, looking across the table to her grandmother. "I've been meaning to tell you – Ethan is working a case in Briarwood right now." Jordan's grandmother – who everyone called Gran Susie – turned to him. "You are? What on earth are you doing there?" "Investigating a triple death, unfortunately."

"Oh, goodness. What happened?" she asked. The room quieted as everyone else began to listen in. "Three girls were found dead at their school. Plunged off the roof. It's still unclear whether it was suicide or a homicide." "Westley or St. Paul's?" Susie asked. "St. Paul's." Susie nodded. "I was telling Ethan how you grew up there," Jordan said. "Any tips you have for him in terms of navigating around?" Susie laughed. "Stay away from Chi Chi's." "What's Chi Chi's?" "It's an old Italian restaurant by the lake," she said. "Terrible produce. Always gave people food poisoning. I believe it's still around. Gosh, I haven't been for some time." "I'll make a note to stay away," Ethan laughed. "I lived on Hazel Street," Susie said. "You know where that is?" "I believe I've passed it a few times. It's so small there, I feel like I'm going in circles most of the time." "I lived in the corner house. The one with the giant tree out front." "When did you leave?" Ethan inquired. "A very long time ago," she laughed. "I only stayed in Briarwood until I was about twenty-five. Then I knew I had to get out. Riverton was calling my name. And so was my Jack." "My grandfather," Jordan said to Ethan. "He passed away a few years ago." "I'm sorry," Ethan said. "He was a good man," Susie said. "Very smart. He could tell you anything," Jordan's father added.

"Like a human calculator," Ella said. "If I hadn't have left Briarwood, I never would have met Jack. And then none of these ones would be here," Susie laughed. "Thank you for leaving, then, Gran," Jordan teased. "Speaking of Briarwood," Ethan said to Susie. "You must know of The Sad Killer?" "Oh, Christ, here we go," Jordan rolled her eyes. "You told me I could ask her." "Of course I know The Sad Killer!" Susie exclaimed. "Well, not personally." "How old were you at the time?" Ethan asked. "Young, I bet." "Oh, yes. I was about twenty-three, twenty-four I believe. But I remember like it was yesterday." "What's this talk about killers?" Tom Sr. asked his mother. "Did I never tell you about that?" "No." "Huh," Susie said. "Well, I'll let Ethan here explain it to you. He's the detective." "Oh, no, you go ahead. You were there," Ethan insisted. She smiled at him. "Oh, alright. Well," she folded her hands in front of her. Everyone was finished eating now and was paying attention to Susie. "It was the summer of '65. A hot one. Before we knew it, bodies were piling up. All young men in Briarwood." "The only serial murders the town's ever seen," Ethan added. Susie nodded. "Such a small place, small population. Makes me wonder who it could have been." "Wait," Tom Jr. said. "They never caught the guy?" Susie shook her head. "Never caught him. He got away." "That's why Ethan is so interested in it," Jordan play-punched his shoulder. "He loves a good cold-case." "I bet," Tom Jr. said. "Got any suspects?" "No," Ethan laughed. "I'm afraid not. But I've been talking with people from that time. Reporters, officers. Awfully kind of them to let me pick their brain. I just find the whole thing so intriguing. Jordan says that's sick," he looked to her. "I just mean intriguing in the way that the guy was never caught. And I find psychology and the criminal-mind so interesting. The mechanics of it all." "So, what," Tom Jr. said. "You're going to solve this thing now? Fifty years later?" Ethan laughed. "I don't know. It would be cool to at least have a few leads. I'm sure the guy is long gone by now. Could be dead, even. They predicted he was anywhere between thirty and fifty in 1965. So he could be in the ground already." "Then what's the point?" Tom asked Ethan. "I guess it's just something to do," Ethan said. "No it's not," Jordan said to him. "You have another case to solve. One that's in this time period. You should be focusing on what happened to those girls, rather than running around playing detective on a cold-case from fifty years ago." "You sound like Frank," Ethan told her. "Good," she smirked. "This one will keep you in line," Jordan's father winked. Ethan laughed. "I have this thing," he said to Tom. "I can't accept a closed-case. It's tempting, this one. It's as though I'm drawn to it. I need to solve it." "Well, I hope you do. That would be satisfactory for you." "And all of Briarwood, I'm sure," Tom Sr., added. "Do you remember anything from back then?" Ethan said to Susie. "Did you know any of the victims or their families?" "I don't believe so," Susie said, thinking back. "It was so long ago. But I don't recall knowing any of them personally. I think they were all older than me anyways." "Yeah, I think the youngest was twenty-seven," Ethan said. She nodded. "Is there anything else you remember from that time? Any suspects or witnesses?" Ethan asked. "Oh, leave her alone, Ev," Jordan said. "It's fine, dear, really," Susie said to Jordan. "I love chatting with Ethan." "Yes, Gran," Jordan continued. "But you could talk about something other than serial killers." "Jordan's right," Ethan smiled at her. "It's her birthday, after all. We'll cut this talk about murder for the night. Sound good, love?" "Sounds more than good," she said. "How about some cake?" Jordan's mother was standing up, already on her way back to the kitchen.

- - - - -

They got home shortly after eleven. Jordan was full of energy and Ethan was exhausted. He had enjoyed himself at the Hopkins' place, laughing and talking for hours. He was glad that Jordan had a good birthday.

At least he was able to get a bit of reprieve from the case, even if only temporarily. But as he entered the quietness of the house, Briarwood and its inhabitants were slowly seeping back into his mind. Haddie, Anneka, and Kiera staring back at him, pleading with him for answers.

Don't you know I'm trying, he wanted to say to them. If only he could get some answers. There was still so much that he didn't know, so many unanswered questions. If only he could speak to them, what would he even say? Did you jump? Did someone push you? Why?

And to Haddie: did you know? About the baby?

It was a task that felt impossible. When he first arrived in Briarwood one week ago, he believed it would be cut and dry. But as the days progressed, and the situation grew more complex, Ethan began to question whether he'd ever get to the bottom of this.

Why was it so complicated? He had solved dozens of murders and homicide investigations in the past. What was so difficult about determining the deaths of three teenage girls?

He needed to get some rest. That was the best course of action. He would go to sleep, stop thinking about Briarwood – both the girls and The Sad Killer – and he would reconvene in the morning. It would be a new day. Perhaps he'd get lucky and discover something new.

Or maybe he wouldn't.

CHAPTER FOURTEEN

Ethan had a late start to the day. He slept in, took longer than usual to get ready, and by the time he drove to Briarwood and arrived at the station, the rest of the team were already long gone.

He stood there for a moment, thinking, debating what to do. Where else could he go? Who else could he speak with? He felt as though he was chasing his tail, going in circles. He couldn't find one person who would want to hurt those girls, and simultaneously, could not conclude whether they jumped or not. Could they really have done this? Could they have ended their own lives? Killed themselves, simply by jumping off the building?

But then he thought back to the lack of suicide note. That fact alone was odd, but still, it didn't mean the notion of suicide was impossible.

Perhaps a break from the case would be beneficial to him. He could come back with a clear mind, a fresh perspective.

Ethan's mind was already made up before he could stop himself. Before he knew it, he was following the secretary back to the evidence room.

"You know," she said to Ethan as she unlocked the door. "If you want more information on this case, you should speak with Gus Fraser. He was the constable in charge back then." "I have, actually," Ethan smiled at her. "He was very helpful." "That's great," she said. "You could also speak with Gil Vanhorn. He wrote the book on The Sad Killer. Literally." "He's an author?" She nodded. "The Sad Summer, it's called. Look him up. Maybe he can help you." "I will. Do you know if he's still in Briarwood?" "No," she shook her head. "I don't believe so. I think he moved away years ago." "I'll look into it. Thanks, Nancy."

Ethan was in the vacant office at the Briarwood station, skimming over the files. In particular, he was reading over the first victim's file, Mark Irving. Why was Mark the first?

He was thirty-two, a charming bachelor, a pillar of the community, was well-liked and respected by everyone.

Perhaps the unsub knew him personally. Or had an attraction to him. Felt threatened by him? There had to have been a reason why this man was murdered, why this man was the first of seven.

Ethan wished he could get a better idea of what Briarwood was like in 1965. What the community was like and how the people interacted with each other. He decided to take Nancy up on her recommendation and look up Gil Vanhorn. A quick Google search informed him that Mr. Vanhorn was the author of four non-fiction crime novels. The Sad Summer was his first, published in 1967.

After searching through his website, phoning a plethora of different numbers, and talking to his editor, Ethan was finally able to reach a number connected directly to Gil Vanhorn.

"Hello," a man's voice answered on the third ring. "Mr. Vanhorn?" "Speaking." "This is Ethan O'Riley. I'm a detective from Riverton working on a case in Briarwood," he paused a moment. "I was wondering if I could ask you some questions about The Sad Killer." "Ah, I see you've stumbled across Briarwood's most well-known case." "I have. And I hear you're the man to speak to." Gil Vanhorn gave a slight laugh. "How is Briarwood today?"

"Fine, I guess. I wouldn't really know. It's my first time here. Well, this past week." "You get lost in it," Gil said. "I haven't been there for about twenty years now." "Where are you currently?" "Seattle. But everything's always up in the air. I've traveled all over. Lived in Thailand for a year, wrote a book about the tourist murders there." "Why did you decide to write a book on The Sad Killer?" Ethan asked. "Well," Gil inhaled deeply. "Crime had always interested me. And so had writing. I was going to school to become a journalist. The murders happened at a time in my life where I needed something to do. So, I started investigating. I would camp out in front of the police station, nag them for details on the case. I was invested. As if solving the case and finding the killer was somehow my duty." "Did you always plan to write the book? Or did that decision come afterwards?" "I guess it came afterwards. I mean, as I said, I was focused on catching a killer," he laughed. "It's funny, really, how ridiculous I was. I was a writer for crying out loud! What did I know about crime and murder?" "But you did discover a lot, yes?" "I did. The police found me a nuisance in the beginning. But they knew I wasn't going to relent. Eventually the officers began to work with me in a sense. Accepting ideas I threw at them, sharing key pieces of information they found." "I spoke with Gus Fraser," Ethan said. "The constable at the time. Are you familiar with him?" "Oh yes," Gil said. "Gus hated my guts. Thought I was getting in the way of the investigation. But eventually they caved. Let me follow them around with my notepad and tape recorder." "Okay," Ethan said. "So what can you tell me then?" "I have one question for you, son," Gil said. "What is it?" "Why are you looking into this now? I mean, it's been fifty-one years." Ethan thought about this for a moment. "I guess the same reason as you," Ethan said. "I only heard about it last week, but it's been at the back of my mind ever since. And I think being here in Briarwood is making the case even more alluring. Because they never caught the guy, and that really bothers me." "Trust me, kid, me too," Gil said. "So you have some questions?" "Yes," Ethan opened the file in front of him. "I guess let's start with Mark Irving." "Ah," Gil said. "Victim number one." "What was he like? Did you know him personally?" "I didn't, no. I only knew one of the men, and that was David Hill, the sixth," he paused for a moment. "But Mark Irving – he was a good guy. When I went around doing interviews for the book, everyone had only good things to say about him. How nice he was, helpful. The kind of man who would help an old lady get her cat down from a tree. "He was an electrician, made a fair bit of money. He was good-looking, I recall. Had a knack for golf. He flourished for thirty-two years in Briarwood. And then ended up dead on his living room floor, stabbed to death." "Did you have any ideas on who could have done it?" "Around the time – and remember, this was the very first – the police were looking at friends and family, members of the country club – anyone who he associated with. They brought a few people in for questioning. Now, what I can tell you, as a writer, is that police have a biased opinion when interrogating people. They're desperate. They want to catch a killer, so they treat every suspect as though they're guilty. And you can't do it like that," he paused. "No offence. But really. I mean, they brought in about a dozen or so people, desperate to solve this singular, isolated murder and bring Mark Irving justice. Little did they know, Mark was simply number one on a list of seven." "And there was no other correlation between the men?" "I mean, correlation? Of course. Briarwood was miniscule. Everyone knew each other in one way or another. My buddy's sister dated my cousin. My boss was related to my neighbor. But concrete correlations? No. Nothing that would explain why this guy killed seven of

Briarwood's brightest men." "What did you say?" "Which part?" "The last part. About Briarwood's brightest?" Gil laughed. "That could be the name of my next book." "Why did you say that? What was so special about those men?" The line was quiet for a moment. "Listen, kid – they were good men. All of em. That's what doesn't make sense about this case. My buddy, Dave – he was a good guy. Had a family, a six-year-old girl. His wife, Melinda, was devastated. No one could understand what was happening in Briarwood. Why all of these men were dropping off, being eliminated. We were all worried, wondering who was next. David was the sixth, and by then, even I had my concerns. I was a man, in the same age group as the victims. Hell, I convinced myself at one point that I was next! That's how arbitrary these murders were. Any one of us could be next. And then there was the seventh – Paul Monoghan – and seven dead bodies was enough to drive that city into mayhem. But we waited and we waited. Months passed and no more men died. No more bodies turned up. We were finally safe. The killer had finally finished with Briarwood. No one ever heard from him again." "What about you," Ethan said. "Who do you think did it?" "God, that's a difficult question," Gil said. "I wrote the book and still don't have a definite answer," he was quiet again. "I mean, I had my suspicions back in the day, but nothing ever progressed. There was this one guy. Larry, I believe his name was. A real creep. I thought it might be him, just from his look and disposition. Obviously I knew better than to judge a book by its cover, but I mean, detective – if you had a look at this guy. And he was always watching things. People, buildings, observing everything. Didn't talk to many people, didn't socialize or have many friends. I think the police might have brought him in for questioning, but he had a solid alibi for one of the murders. That's the thing with serial murders – they all have to add up and make sense. It's one person doing it all and somehow getting away with it." "No one ever thought it might have been a group thing? Gang related, even?" "A gang? In Briarwood," he laughed. "But no, that's a valid question. I don't think the police ever suspected a group, or even a partner, for that matter. It was always one guy. One sociopath behind all of the madness." "But the M.O's were so different," Ethan said. "A group or a cult would have made sense." "Maybe," Gil said. "What about drugs?" Ethan asked. "Or gambling. What if the seven men were into some trouble? Couldn't pay off a debt or something." "You're thinking a hitman angle?"

"Yeah. It's a possibility, right?" Gil made a sound. "It's a good theory, but the police disproved any drug theories back then. They looked into everything. Money, bank accounts, family history. The men were clean." Ethan nodded silently. "Tell me about his signature. The thing that made him so infamous." "Sad. That's all he put – sad. The police took it as an apology of sorts. I mean, what kind of killer murders someone, then writes sad beside the body. Was this an apology? A sign of remorse? No one was sure. They had a behavioural analyst come in. She said something about feelings of empathy and guilt being portrayed through this last, final act. The killer might have felt forced to kill. That's the thing with psychopaths and sociopaths – they don't have a choice, it's their obligation. And it's sad. It truly is. That these people have an inherent problem in their brains. They were born with it. They can't help it. Killing is in their DNA. No matter how many times we arrest them and attempt to rehabilitate them, it doesn't do any good. Because they are intrinsically good at this one thing – killing. It's what makes them whole, what they do to survive," he took a moment. "So that's why he left the word sad. Not only as a type of apology or sign of remorse, but it became his signature. A way to let us know that it was him. Because you know serial murderers have to do that, right?" "Do what?" "Let everyone know it's them who is doing the killing. Psychopaths are narcissists. They thrive off attention. The notoriety is what they live for. They want people knowing it was them. It's like the murder is their artwork, and they have to take responsibility. Another compulsion of theirs, much like the killing. It's all very artistic. Not the killing, I mean. The act around it." "I see," Ethan said. "This is very helpful, thank you." "Of course. Anything I can do to help. It sure would be great to finally solve this thing. After all these years." "It would be, but I highly doubt I'll be able to." "Why not? You got all the tools, you're talking to the right people. Hey, I bet it would help if you bought my book," Gil said. "No promo or nothing, just saying. There's a lot of good information in there." "Maybe I will. Thanks." "And you should also try to contact the families if you can." "The families of the victims? You think they're still around?" "Probably. You're a cop – look em up. I bet most of them are still in Briarwood for God's sake. People never leave that place. And those who did leave, like me, well, I'm sure you can track em down. Give em a call or something." "If they're still around," Ethan said. "Or alive." "Fifty one years," Gil said. "Some of them would be. The children, definitely. A few of the victims had kids, so you could try starting with them. That might prove useful. Although, a few of them were young at the time, so don't expect too much. I'd also try the wives or girlfriends of some of the victims. Like Mark Irving. I'm sure you could track down a whole list of women who dated him back in the day. I'm sure they're old geezers now, like me, but still worth a shot." "Alright, I'll look into it. Thank you, Gil." "My pleasure, kid. Hey, give me a call if you ever crack this thing, alright? I'm dying to know." "Will do."

Tracking down the surviving families of the deceased wasn't difficult. As Gil Vanhorn said, most of them would likely still be in Briarwood.

The first was a seventy-nine year old woman named Flora Whittaker. Married to Robert Baldwin in 1948, Flora remarried twice since the death of her husband on June 16, 1965.

Robert Baldwin was victim number four. Cause of death was a single stab wound through the heart. A mature step-up from the first murder, Ethan thought, thinking back to Mark Irving.

Flora Whittaker was living on Appleton Crescent, just a six minute drive from the station. Ethan packed up his things and headed over to her house.

A petite elderly woman greeted him. Her hair was dyed dark brown and she had bright green eyes. She looked significantly younger than seventy-nine.

"Flora Whittaker?" Ethan said. "Yes?" "I'm Detective O'Riley," he began. "I was wondering if I could talk to you. Maybe ask you a few questions." "What is this regarding?" "Your first husband. Robert Baldwin."

They sat in her living room, Flora continuously offering him tea or coffee. Finally, Ethan caved and allowed the woman to get him a tea.

She came back into the room holding two small tea cups and placed them on the coffee table in the center of the room. Flora took a seat in an old rocking chair and nursed the cup between her palms.

"That's a name I haven't heard in quite some time," Flora said. "It was a long time ago." "Fifty-one years now," Flora said. "How did you and Robert meet?" "He was older," Flora admitted. "He worked with my father, was always dropping by the house, paying us little visits. My father adored Robert. He was like a friend and a son to him. He was so charming. I fell head over heels for that man," Flora said, taking a sip from her tea. "We married when I was twenty-two. He was thirty-four." "And what was your relationship like?" "It was grand," Flora said. "We were married six years when he was murdered. I remember that day as if it were yesterday." "Why don't you tell me about it? If you're up to it, of course." "Yes, well," she paused. "It was fifty-one years ago. I've been married twice since then. But I will tell you, Detective, it was one of the most traumatizing experiences of my life." She placed her cup on the table and exhaled deeply. "I had gone with some of my girlfriends to the beach that day. It was beautiful out, just another hot June day. On our way home, the car broke down. We were stranded on the side of the road for hours, waving down cars and begging old men to help us out or give us a lift. We ended up hitching a ride home and making it back just shortly after sundown. The man who gave us a ride dropped me off at mine and Robert's house. I unlocked the door and walked inside. The house was awfully quiet. I remember calling out his name, but there was no response. I assumed he was out, busy doing other things. "I went to the kitchen, got myself a drink, and spent some time tidying up and getting dinner prepared. It must have been an hour after being home that I went to the bedroom to fetch something. And that's when I saw him. He was lying on the floor, covered in blood," she stopped. "Are you alright?" Ethan asked. Flora stared blankly ahead, taking a moment to herself. Then she nodded quickly and returned her gaze to Ethan. "Apologies," she said. "It's always difficult, re-living it." "Of course, no need to apologize," Ethan said. "Are you okay to continue?" She nodded. "I ran out of there and phoned the police. They came right away, taped off the bedroom and the house. I was so shaken up, could hardly breathe or think straight. Here I was, having fun at the beach. Meanwhile, my husband was being murdered in our home." "You were aware of The Sad Killer though, yes? He had killed three men before your husband." "I'd heard of the other murders, yes. It was very unfortunate. I don't know whether Robert and I knew there was a madman on the loose in Briarwood at the time of his death. I don't believe we thought much of it. We tried to stay away from the news – it's only filled with negativity. I never kept up with it. But after Robert died, well, I followed the case closely. I witnessed each victim's death after my husband. Three more men, just like my Bobby, all murdered in their homes. No traces of the culprit anywhere. It's as though it were a ghost who simply disappeared into thin air." "Did you or Robert know any of the other victims?" She thought for a moment. "Not particularly. I'd seen them around before, here and there. The grocery store, the beach. Everyone went to the beach in the summer. But we didn't know any of them personally." "Did any of the family members of the deceased ever reach out to you? Maybe there was a support group or something of that sorts?" She shook her head. "Everyone kept to themselves after that. I know I did. Once Robert died, it was like I went into a depression. Well, can you blame me? I had lost my husband. At only twenty-eight years old! I could hardly leave the house, buy groceries, live my life. It wasn't until a few months later that I met Carl, my second husband. He brought out my sunshine once again. I have to be honest with you, Detective, after Robert died, I didn't think it would be possible to ever find happiness again. But I did. I found it with Carl." Ethan could attest to this. He did, after all, find happiness after Olivia. "Unfortunately, that didn't work out in the end," Flora continued. "We divorced five years later. And then I met Arnold Whittaker," she smiled softly. "Now that was the man of my dreams. Third times a charm, right? The other two were trials, I suppose. Simply a pathway that eventually led me to Arnold. But he passed four years ago. My heart was broken all over again." "I'm so sorry," Ethan said. The poor woman had been through enough hardships in her lifetime. "Yes, well," she paused. "I have six children and fifteen grandchildren. They bring me joy and happiness when I need it the most." "Do you they live in Briarwood?" "Some do," Flora said. "Others have moved on. Farthest one is only two hours out, so they make sure to come visit as much as they can." "Did you ever have any suspicions on who killed your husband, Flora? Anyone at all?" She was quiet a moment. "No," she admitted. "The police were always saying one thing. Then there was the reporters, always gabbing on, blaming someone or other. But Briarwood was so small back then. Everyone was getting backlash for those murders. And everyone became a suspect. I don't even know if this person – the person who killed my husband – was even from Briarwood." "What makes you say that?" "It just didn't make sense," Flora said. "Everyone got along here. We were a good community. Why would somebody from here have such rage and aggression towards others in the community? I believed it was an outsider. Someone from out of town, perhaps. They could have been visiting for the summer. That would explain why the murders began at the end of April and ceased in August. A summer thing." "That's interesting," Ethan said. "I never thought about that before." Flora nodded and took another sip of tea. "Anyway," she said. "Why the sudden interest? Don't tell me they're re-opening the case." "No, no," Ethan said. "I'm actually in town for another case. I'm from Riverton, actually. I heard about The Sad Killer last week. It hasn't left my mind since." "It definitely is one for the history books," Flora said. "We had never seen murders like that before, and we never saw them again after. It was all very strange." "Yes, well," Ethan said. "I'm doing my best to get the big picture here. I've been contacting old reporters and officers from that summer. I spoke to an author just this morning. He's the one who suggested I speak with some of the family members." "Oh, don't tell me it's that Vanhorn character." Ethan laughed. "You're not a fan?" "Heavens no," Flora said. "He is a havoc, I tell you. Just a God awful man." "What happened?" "Oh, just the type of person he is. I can spot the bad ones from a mile away. He didn't care about the murders or the victims. He just wanted to make a buck. Turn a profit from all of our tragedies." Ethan nodded but didn't respond. "Well, I don't want to take up any more of your time, ma'am."

"Oh, nothing of the sorts," Flora said. "My family is so busy now a days, I hardly get any visitors. I love a good chat once in a while. I just never expected to be talking about Bobby Baldwin again." "I will try to keep you in the loop and let you know if I find anything." She smiled and they both stood. "I hope you do."

The sun was shining. It was a gorgeous day out in Briarwood and Ethan was driving around the small town with his windows down. He knew he had more pressing matters to attend to. He still needed to figure out what happened to Haddie, Anneka, and Kiera. But he was on a roll. He was obtaining new information today that was proving useful to the Sad case.

He would visit one last person then call it a day. Once he spoke to Angela Ramaro, he would return to the current case. That would be his main focus. He couldn't lose track of that. But just this one last visit.

Angela Ramaro, (née, Brooks), was Patrick Brooks – victim number three's – daughter. Patrick had a son named Joe, but he had moved out of town many years ago. Fortunately for Ethan, Angela was still here, living just around the corner, and only sixty-one years old.

That would have made her ten or eleven at the time of her father's murder. Ethan wasn't sure how much she would remember, or how useful this visit would be, but he had to give it a shot.

She had dark red hair, curly beyond belief. Her face was older, but her voice was young. She spoke with cadence and poise, but also had a sense of humour. They sat in her dining room, Angela's three small dogs running in circles around their feet.

"Don't mind them," she said to Ethan. "They all have ADHD." Ethan laughed. "Is your husband home?" "He's at the grandkids soccer tournament today." "You didn't go?" She shook her head. "We usually take turns. I went last week." Ethan smiled then cleared his throat. "So, to get into things." "My father," Angela replied. "Yes. Are you comfortable talking about this? I understand if you're not." "No, no," Angela held up a hand. "I'm a big girl. I can handle it." "You were, what, eleven at the time?" "Ten turning eleven in November that year." "Do you remember much from that summer?" "More than you'd think," Angela said. "I have so many memories from back then. So many that I still surprise myself on how much my old mind has retained." "What can you tell me?" "Well," she said. "I was ten, my brother was eight. It was summer time. Everything was normal. One day my father was there. The next, he was gone." "Can you recall the day?" "May twenty-eighth. I won't ever forget that date," she took in a deep breath. "It happened in the night. We were all asleep. My parents were separated at the time, so Joey and I were staying at our father's place. He said good-night to us, we went to sleep. The next morning, we got up, went about our morning routine. It was a Saturday, so we didn't have school or any other responsibilities. We were waiting in the kitchen for my father to get up and make us breakfast, but he wasn't in there. We went all around the house, calling for him, but we couldn't find him. I guess we finally decided to look in his bedroom. There he was, in the bed, sleeping. Or so we believed. He was just lying there, so still," she paused. "I still remember the look on his face. That moment will haunt me forever. His eyes were open, staring up at the ceiling. So vacant and empty. "We thought he was sleeping, so we jumped on his bed and began to shake him. That's when we noticed his eyes were open. We were calling him, daddy, daddy, daddy, but he wasn't responding. At some point it clicked in my ten-year-old brain and I knew something was wrong. I ran back into the kitchen, grabbed the landline, and called our neighbor. He came over and called the police. My father had been dead for more than seven hours at that point. Sometime in the night." "That's horrible," Ethan said. "It was terrifying. The very thought that we were in the next room, sleeping silently, while my father was being strangled to death. That's how he did it, you know. The killer. He strangled him with a cord of some sort. That was the cause of death." "You were so young back then," Ethan said. "Were you aware of the other deaths that were going on at the time? Your father was the third victim. Did that mean anything to you?" She shook her head. "No. You're right, I was so young. I hardly had a concept of what death was at the time. All I knew in that moment was that my dad was gone and he wouldn't be coming back," Angela said. "My mother was horrified. She changed after that. Never let us out of her sight. Doctors said she developed PTSD. She held herself accountable for my father's death. As though if she were there, she would have somehow been able to prevent it." "Do you believe that's true?" Angela shook her head. "Maybe I believed it at the time. All she wanted to do was protect us. But now I know the whole story. That killer didn't come into our house at random. And he wouldn't have come if my mother was around. And he wouldn't have touched my brother or me. Because we weren't his targets. My father was. From the beginning, that was who he had his eye on. It was never about us, or my mother. It was always about him." "You think the killer targeted your father specifically, as opposed to an arbitrary kill?" "Yes." "Why's that?" Angela stared at him for what felt like hours. Then finally, she spoke. "Listen, Detective. I'm going to tell you something. Something I never told the police back then." Ethan sat up straighter. "I'm listening." "My father," she said. "He wasn't the good man that everyone believed he was." "How so?" She took a moment, folding one hand on top of the other. "He... he would sometimes," she paused. "Hit us." "He was abusive to you?" She nodded. "Not only me, but my brother as well. And my mother. I think that's why she left us. She's never told me anything, but I can only assume. Looking back, what he did to us – it was wrong. But as a kid, I always took the blame, believed it was my fault. How terrible is that? That a child takes responsibility for her father's actions?" "Why didn't you ever tell anyone?" "Have you ever been abused, Detective?" He was quiet, then shook his head. "Then you don't know what it's like. Especially being a child. Like I said, I believed it was my fault. My brother and I, we stuck together. We took it, handled it the best we could. We still loved my father because he was a nice man. It was like he had this entirely different persona, and he could bring it out whenever he pleased. Some days we'd get the kind, happy man that I knew and loved. Other times, a different side would come out. Usually after a few drinks. "I'm guessing things weren't good between my mother and him. That's why she left. But little did she know, she was abandoning us with him. She never knew what he did to us." "I'm so sorry you went through that, Angela." "Please, don't apologize," she said. "It was a long time ago. And it made me stronger, taught me hard lessons that helped me later in life. Of course, I would never wish that upon anyone. Any child. But it was something that I had to live with. I survived. And I persevered." "What happened after your father's murder?" "It was hard, of course, but there was always this small part of me that felt relieved. Because I knew he couldn't hurt us anymore. And I condemn whoever did this to all of those men from the bottom of my heart. Because I know it wasn't just my father that fell victim. It was six other innocent men. And yet, there was still this small part inside of me that felt glad. As if whoever did this was doing me a favor." "Did you ever have any suspicions of who it might have been? Anyone in Briarwood that could have done such a thing?" Angela shook her head. "If it was a single murder, sure, it could have been anyone. I might have even believed it was someone he knew. Someone who knew us and was doing it to protect us. Hell, I might have even thought it was my mother. But of course, she didn't know what was going on. And this wasn't an isolated incident. This was just one in several other murders. And whoever did this," she paused. "Well, like I said to you before, were they doing it for a reason? Was it arbitrary? Why did this person kill seven men in Briarwood that summer?" Ethan stared at her for a moment, taking in everything she had just said. "That's a good question. A question I intend on finding the answer to."

Chapter Fifteen

CHAPTER FIFTEEN

It was a new day: Thursday. Ten days since the deaths and Ethan was still no farther ahead. It was infuriating him beyond belief. How was it that they still didn't have any new information? They had interviewed everyone involved in those girls' lives. He had brought people into the interrogation room, checked out witness statements and any possible leads there might be. But still, nothing.

He was reviewing everything they had gathered over the past ten days. There was the basic information about the girl's lives. The teachers and counsellor at school had nothing but positive things to say. The friend group revealed some drama in their inner circle. The frenemies – Beth, Audrey, and Megan – had revealed new information that led Ethan to believe Haddie Taylor wasn't as perfect as everyone made her out to be. She was, after all, four weeks pregnant with a baby that didn't belong

272   SECRETS AND MURDERS

to her boyfriend. She was cheating on Oliver Harris with Bentley Carter. She was caught flirting with Beth's boyfriend, Corey Gibbons. Dramatic. Attention-seeking. Compulsive liar. Contrasted against words from her family: kind, loving, enthusiastic.

Haddie hated Briarwood and wanted to leave it behind. She wanted to move to Hollywood and become famous. She saw the fortune teller who crushed those dreams, and in Ethan's opinion, made her stray from her normal life of comfort and began experimenting with new things.

She started up a relationship with Bentley Carter. But then ended things on the third of May. Bentley admitted this, and it was confirmed to Ethan when he went through her phone records. What happened around that time? What changed Haddie's mind about Bentley all of a sudden? And why did she stay with Oliver Harris during all of that?

Could Haddie have found out about her pregnancy? But if so, why end things with Bentley?

He thought about what he had gathered on Kiera Barnes. Funny, energetic, and loud was how everyone described her. A shadow of Haddie, Cloe Wilson had said. If those two were as close as everyone said, why would Kiera date Haddie's boyfriend behind her back? Was she jealous of Haddie? Wanted everything that she had? Did she feel the constant competition, just as Beth Campbell once did? It was difficult being friends with Haddie Taylor, Rachel Dunn had said. Could Kiera have felt the difficulties? The constant sense of rivalry? The need to prove herself?

When speaking to her parent's that first day, Vivian and Patrick Barnes were stumped with the question of whether Kiera had other friends or not. Odd, was it not? The girls clearly had other friends. Why did Kiera's parents not know this? Why did Kiera never talk about them?

They were also very quick to dismiss any mental illness. Could Kiera have been suffering from her own demons? Kelsey and her sister were close. Surely Kiera would have confided in her sister and told her if anything was wrong. But then again, she didn't even tell her about Oliver. Kelsey figured that one out on her own.

Then there was Anneka Wilson. The quiet one. The introvert. The sweet, pleasant one. The girl no one could understand yet somehow remained friends with girls like Haddie and Kiera.

Her sister revealed to Ethan that she had been acting strange the last few months. Zopiclone and Zoloft were found in her system at the time of her death, which meant that she was depressed and suffering from insomnia. Cloe found the bag of marijuana in her art room. Rachel Dunn admitted to seeing Anneka smoking pot but was sworn not to tell anyone. The guidance counsellor at school said that Anneka had come in two or three times over the last year, but nothing too serious. Just to talk about family problems, her parent's divorce. Could there have been more to the story? An underlying problem that no one suspected? Anneka was depressed – but was she also suicidal? And how would the other two have reacted to that?

There was the Beth Campbell theory – rivals, enemies, competitors – but that never panned out. Beth couldn't have pushed Haddie or the other girls. And while Bentley Carter could have been a good suspect with a more-than-probable motive, he, too, had an alibi.

There was the information he gathered after the funeral at the reception at the Barnes' residence. Gabriella remembered Haddie's behavior from the day before the deaths. Said that she was in a bit of a mood, cancelled their lunch plans. And then there was that bit of information that Gemma had shared with Ethan. First period biology, Haddie asking to switch partners from Kiera. There must have been internal problems occurring in their tight-knit group of three. Seemingly perfect to the world, but trouble in paradise deep down. Ethan was convinced that Haddie would only put Kiera on the outs for one reason. She must have found out about her and Oliver.

Ethan played it out in his mind, trying to get a better understanding of it all. Haddie breaks things off with Bentley. She wants to try and fix things with Oliver, work everything out and continue on with their pleasant, mundane relationship. Graduate high school, get married, just as everyone said they would. But something happens. Haddie finds out about Oliver and Kiera somehow. Did one of them tell her? Did Oliver break up with Haddie for Kiera? Or did Kiera admit her guilt in a fit of desperation?

Haddie must have found out about them somehow; the method of how she found out was irrelEthant. Or perhaps Ethan was wrong. Because when Haddie asked to meet on the roof that day, she needed Anneka to be there as well. Perhaps there was something he was missing. They were girls, after all. Haddie and Kiera could have been on the outs for a number of reasons.

Ethan wasn't there that day. He didn't know what was happening in the girl's lives. And no matter how hard he tried – no matter how many people he interviewed, no matter how many diary and phone records he read – he might never truly know what happened up on that rooftop. Perhaps no one would.

–––––

Ethan arrived at the Briarwood police station later that day, only to find Kennedy standing there, awaiting his arrival.

"KC," he said once he saw her. "Where is everyone?" "Major and Tanner got called back to Riverton," she said. "More pressing matters to attend to." "Crime doesn't stop for us," Ethan remarked. They walked into the vacant office they'd been using as a meeting place for the case. "You know," Kennedy said. "You can end this thing whenever, Ev. Call it a suicide and close this case." Ethan looked at her. "Why would I do that?" "It's been ten days," she said. "And we have zero leads. Nada. And well, the little bit that we do have all points to one thing: suicide."

Ethan pictured them on the roof: Anneka Wilson, taking Zoloft, isolating herself from the world, smoking pot in seclusion, feeling as though jumping is her only way out.

Haddie Taylor: willing and daring, reckless and determined. Pregnant with an unwanted baby. Unsure of what to do next. Feeling the pressure. Scared, as though her life is over. Would jumping solve that?

And that left Kiera. Would Kiera have jumped? Live together, die together.

It would be so simple, closing the case, determining the deaths a triple suicide. Everyone would believe it. Everyone already did believe it. The mayor, the principal, and Jason Gregory would all feel relieved. They were in luck – there wasn't a potential murderer looming the streets of Briarwood. The girls were simply suicidal. Problem solved. Case solved. Over and done with.

But Ethan knew he couldn't do that. Not only did he owe it to those girls, but he owed it to their families. He needed to find out what really happened to them. Because knowing that there was even the slightest possibility that it wasn't suicide was enough to make him keep trying.

"I can't do that, Ken," he said to her. "It's not that simple." "What do you mean?" she seemed surprised by his answer. "I'm telling you, there isn't much more we're going to find. But, oh, apologies – you're the detective here, not me." "There's more that we don't know," he said. "Yeah, you're right. It could be suicide. But what if it's not? We don't know." "Think about that killer you're onto now," Kennedy said. "It's been fifty-one years and still, no one has solved it. People had to stop looking for him eventually and just give up. And that's fine. Cases get like that sometimes. We can't solve them all, Ev." "I don't know if they ever did," he said. "Did what?" "Give up. It may have been fifty-one years, but people are still looking for him. I'm not going to give up on those girls."

Ethan knew he was doing the right thing, even if Kennedy didn't agree. Resources were wearing thin. Frank and Jesse would have to return to their regular duties back in Riverton. How much longer could he keep doing this? How many more days would he drive into

Briarwood and wander around the town aimlessly, trying to determine what happened?

There were only so many people he could talk to, so many scenarios he could think of. But when it came down to it, he had no idea why those girls were on the roof that Tuesday. And he had no idea if they were pushed, or if they truly did jump.

He was between a rock and a hard place. Give up, go back to Riverton, and continue on with his life. It would be so easy. But how could he live with himself knowing that he let those girls down? That he was potentially leaving a killer in Briarwood?

The other option was to stay. To return to Briarwood each day until he figured this thing out and closed the case for good. But how long would that take? Would he ever truly know what happened? Or would fifty-one years go by until some young detective from out of town stumbled upon the case and took it upon himself to solve it?

Ethan gathered up his things and headed over to Gus Fraser's house, once again. The PSW let him inside and he made himself comfortable on the couch. Gus looked well today. Perhaps it was the warm weather that was doing him justice. And he was happy to see Ethan, of course. These days he didn't do much. Having a young detective here to keep him company was doing him well, even if the topic of their discussions happened to be murder.

Ethan was taking a break, he decided. He needed to clear his head for a bit. If he was going to solve the triple deaths of the girls, he needed to get into the mind of a killer. Perhaps talking with Gus and discussing The Sad Killer would help him with that.

"Let's go to the second victim," Ethan said. "Mike Darbyshire." "Mike was a good kid," Gus started. "And the youngest of the victims. Cause of death was asphyxiation, most likely something placed over his mouth that prevented him from breathing. It was a change up from the M.O of the first victim." "Right," Ethan said. "He went from overkill of seven stab wounds to the chest, to something completely different." "If it wasn't for the signature, we might not have linked the two murders together. But because of the signature – the sad – we knew it was the same guy," Gus said. "We actually had a theory in the beginning. Victim one and two's names both started with an M. We weren't sure if it was a coincidence or if the unsub was going after men with M names." "But after Patrick Brooks..." "Our theory was disproven." "And Brooks was strangled," Ethan said. "Yes," Gus said. "Ligature marks around the neck indicated a thin wire or cable of some sort." "How do you explain this constant change of M.O?" Ethan asked. Gus took in a breath. "It's very strange. I've never seen anything like it before. I mean, there are cases where a serial murderer kills his victims differently once or twice, but it's very rare. They usually stick to their regulated method. It helps keep order and balance in their world." "So why did our unsub change so drastically each time? And not just evolving his M.O, but doing one thing, and then going back to another?" "Only thing I thought of back then was that he was experimenting. This was a game for him and he wanted to try out new things. If this was his first time killing, he was probably on cloud nine. Brainstorming all the possibilities that existed out there. So he stabs the first vic, suffocates the second, strangles the third, then returns to stabbing the fourth. And repeat." Ethan nodded, going through the motions in his mind to get a better understanding. "What was Darbyshire like?" "He was a good guy, just like the others. His pop owned the local pizza shop off Hazel Street, so he rotated between running the place and going back to school to get his

PhD. He'd go fishing at the docks, drive his ATV around town. I believe he was seeing a woman named Holly at the time. Nice fella, he was." "What did everyone think when he was murdered?" "Everyone was shocked. Briarwood was in a state of panic, you see, because after Mark Irving, they thought it was over. And then Darbyshire turns up dead with the same word written next to his body. We didn't know what to think." "I can't imagine. Must have been terrifying, especially being a man." "No one was safe. Husbands and father's feared that they were next." Ethan nodded. "Anything else? On Darbyshire, I mean." Gus thought about it. "Not that I can think of off the top of my head. If you want more info on the vic's, you could always head down to the station, go through all their records and personal files. I'm assuming that's what you're doing, digging your way through their lives, trying to determine what caused them to fall victim." Ethan nodded. "It's the only thing I can think of. Since I don't know the killer, the only thing I can do is know the victims. Find out why they died, why they were chosen." Gus gave a hearty laugh. "You're a smart one, kid. You're doing exactly what I did fifty-one years ago."

Ethan was back at the station, sitting in the vacant room, going over the array of files. Gus was right – he really did have everything on these seven men, from how long they'd lived in Briarwood, to where their parents had emigrated from. Ethan knew their occupations, where they lived, their children's names, what they did for fun, everyone they had dated, who they interacted with. In the files there were multiple witness testimonies and interviews from each of the victim's family members and friends from their inner circles. Everyone saying similar things: "He was a good man." "I don't know who would do this."

Was there some sort of link between them that Ethan was missing? He knew there didn't need to be a link. Serial murderers tended to kill arbitrarily, simply choosing their victims based on look, preference, or convenience. But still – if there was something, anything, that could help him solve this case, he needed to find it.

Ethan traced back over his initial theories – that these men were connected somehow, not necessarily to each other personally, but through their social circles and life patterns. Could they have been into drugs? Gambling? In debt? Owed money to the wrong person? And perhaps whoever this person was that they all owed something to came back for more.

He tried focusing on the dates of the murders, as though these might hold some significance. Mark Irving, April 23 – stabbed. Mike Darbyshire, May 7 – suffocated. Patrick Brooks, May 28 – strangled. Robert Baldwin, June 16 – stabbed. Jason Morgan, July 1 – stabbed. David Hill, July 23 – strangled. And finally, Paul Monoghan, August 14 – shot in the head.

It was definitely a peculiar case, that was for sure. With nearly all of the victims being killed in a different manner, it was hard to pinpoint exactly what the unsub was doing or thinking. Gus' theory was that the killer was experimenting, getting into the hang of it. He was trying out different methods to see which one best suited his liking.

The first victim was killed on April twenty-third. What happened on that date that made the unsub decide to start killing? Did he plan this out? Or was it spur-of-the-moment? The next victim was killed fifteen days later. And after that one, three weeks. There was no common pattern between the dates of the murders. As far as Ethan could tell, they were arbitrary.

He began searching each of the dates, seeing if anything important happened on those days. The only thing that came up was the annual Briarwood fair that took place on the seventh of May. Perhaps Ethan would need to speak with Gus to see if he remembered anything more specific. It could be anything – a full moon, economic recession, days of scheduled appointments. Hell, this guy could have been an alcoholic and he killed each time he ran out of alcohol.

Ethan grabbed the file of the second victim, Mike Darbyshire. He scanned through the testimonies, reading what kind of man Mike was. Ethan flipped through the pages. His medical records were good. Lung cancer ran in the family, but he was clear. No criminal record, priors, or arrests of any sorts. This guy was clean as a whistle.

Then Ethan got to his driving record. Darbyshire got his licence in 1954, right when he turned sixteen. He purchased his first car – a 1950's Coupe de Ville – a year later. And then, six months after that, the car was totalled and written off. Ethan flipped the page to continue reading, but there was no record as to why. No incident number or details of an accident. So the question begged: what happened to Darbyshire's car?

There was nothing in the files that elaborated on this information further. Fortunately Ethan had one tool that they didn't back then – the internet. He opened his browser again and began searching for 1950's Cadillacs; any information regarding recalls or vehicle malfunctions. Nothing.

He racked his brain. If Darbyshire totalled his car, it must have been from an accident. Ethan searched for all news reports in 1955, Briarwood.

There was a few articles that came up, but one in particular that stood out to Ethan. He clicked it and began to read.

On May 7, 1955, a drunk driver t-boned a family of four, killing them instantly. The driver was not named due to legalities, but the family killed was. Craig and Karen Weller, along with their two young children, Joanie and Kyle.

Ethan didn't need to look at Mike Darbyshire's file to recall the day of his murder. It was May 7, 1965. Exactly ten years later to the date. And that couldn't be a coincidence.

What did this mean? And what did this have to do with The Sad Killer?

The killer must have somehow known about this incident from Mike's past. It was clearly a cover up. Darbyshire killed four people and somehow got away with it scot-free, the accident wiped completely from his record. He must have had friends – or family – in high places.

Did the police know about this back then when they were investigating the serial murders? This was potentially a huge lead.

If the unsub was someone from Mike's past – more specifically, someone related to that incident – then this would make sense. They came back ten years later to kill Darbyshire and get revenge.

But then how did that explain the other six men who were murdered? If Mike's cover up was the catalyst to the killing spree, he would have been murdered first. But instead, Mark Irving was the first victim. And then three weeks later, Mike Darbyshire turned up dead.

Perhaps the unsub was saving Mike for another time, waiting to perfect his kill method before going for him.

That would make sense, especially given the multiple M.O's. The unsub kills Irving first as practice. It's his first kill. He's still learning, getting the hang of it. It's messy and a bit over the top, but when it's finished, he knows he'll be able to kill Mike. For three weeks he plots it out, and then finally, on May 7 – the anniversary of the deaths – he murders him.

This had to be someone from Mike's past, Ethan was sure of it now. Someone connected to the Weller's in some way. Someone who knew the family and wanted vengeance for what Mike did to them. Ethan knew what he had to do. He gathered up the files and headed back to Gus's house.

Gus was surprised to see him back so soon, but he invited him in nonetheless, eager to hear what he had discovered.

"It has to be someone connected to the Weller's," Ethan said, speaking so quickly he could barely catch his breath. "You didn't know about the accident, did you?" "I don't believe so. How did you connect the dots?" "I was going over Mike's records. Saw that his car was totalled in 1955, but there was no further information.

Thought it was a bit odd. So I started looking it up on the internet. That's when I saw the news article from May seventh. Darbyshire wasn't named because he was only seventeen at the time – still a minor. There must have been a cover up. He was never charged or penalized for that accident. Someone must have helped him sweep it under the rug." Gus was nodding, trying to follow along. "His father must have had connections. An accident like that wouldn't be easy to cover up. No, they went through great lengths to hide this." "But clearly someone else knew. And I believe that person is our unsub. We need to start looking at all people connected to the Weller's. Friends of Karen and Craig, family members – someone that was out for vengeance." Gus looked at Ethan. "This is good. You could really be onto something here." "I think I'm more than onto something," Ethan said. "If I'm right about this, then it won't be long before we finally figure out who The Sad Killer really is."

Chapter Sixteen

CHAPTER SIXTEEN

They went through everything: traced family-trees all the way back to the early 1900's; read files upon files of obituaries and tributes about the Weller's; tried to pin-point who was close to the family that could be capable of something like this.

Ethan began making a list in his head. There was, of course, Craig Weller's brother, Steve. Ethan would need to track him down, and, if he was still alive, have a talk with him. That was the most difficult part about this case. Everything took place over fifty years ago. Anyone involved in that incident or the murders of 1965 were either far too old, or long gone.

Jacqueline and Peter Jones were a couple that was close with Karen and Craig all those years ago. Could one of them be capable of murder?

Karen had two sisters – one was dead, and the other was eighty-nine, still living in Briarwood. Ethan could speak with her, but he had a feeling that she wasn't The Sad Killer.

The only possible suspect Ethan could see as being re-alistic was the brother, Steve. Ethan looked him up to see if he was still in Briarwood, and sure enough, he was listed as living in a small cottage down by the lake. He was twenty-five at the time of his brother's death – which would make him eighty-seven years old today. Could he be The Sad Killer?

Ethan located the small cottage and parked his car out front. He took in his surroundings. The cottage was right on the waterfront and Ethan could see the blue water shimmering underneath the brightness of the sun. It was a good location, quiet and isolated from the center of town. He made his way up the pathway and knocked on the door.

An older woman answered the door, looking caught off guard, as though she was not expecting any visitors. "Hello," Ethan said hesitantly. "Is Steve Weller here by any chance?" The woman looked at him, her face falter-ing slightly. "What is this regarding?" "It's a case from a long time ago actually. Involving his brother, Craig, and his family." The woman was quiet for a moment, staring at Ethan intently. "I'm afraid that won't be possible," she said. "Steven passed away six months ago." Ethan could feel his heart sink in his chest. This was his opportunity. His one chance to potentially come face-to-face with The Sad Killer. And he was no longer living. This was bound to happen, he had to realize that. The murders were fifty-one years ago. Most of the people from that time would unfortunately be dead. Ethan tried to hide his disappointment. "Is there anything I can do to help?" the woman asked. "I'm Mary, his widow." Ethan refocused and looked at the woman. Perhaps she could be of some assistance. "Yes, actually," Ethan said. "I'm a detective from Riverton. Ethan O'Riley. Perhaps I could ask you some questions?" "Pleasure to meet you," she stuck out her hand. "Would you like to come inside?" They made their way into the small living room of the cottage. There was a giant window that took up the majority of the north wall, allowing a full view of the lake. It was magnificent. "You mentioned Craig," Mary said once they were both seated on the couch. "I'm assuming you're here about the accident." "Yes." Mary closed her eyes, nodding. "It was tragic. The children were so young. We were all devastated." "Do you remember what happened?" Mary was silent for a moment, gathering her thoughts. "It was summer-time," she began. "Craig and Karen had went out for dinner that night with the kids. Steve and I were supposed to meet them at their place later for a visit. They were on their way home when the car hit them. The paramedics told us they died on impact." "Do you remember anything else about that night? The driver of the other car, perhaps?" She nodded slowly. "He was young, I remember that. And he was drunk. That was the main thing. He had too many drinks, thought he could drive, and it cost that family their life." "Did you or your husband know the driver at all?" "We never found out who he was. They told us that because he was underage, his name wasn't permitted to be released. A shame, really. All this time and it's still a mystery to me who killed them." "Mary," Ethan said. "Do you ever recall your husband fixating about the accident? Of course it was his brother that died, but does anything stand out to you at all? The date? The driver of the car? Anything?" "I'm not sure what you mean. We were all so devastated after the passing. It changed Steven, it truly did. He and Craig were always very close. It was just the two of them growing up and they did everything together. Having his only brother and best friend ripped away from him – especially at such a young age – was very difficult. There were times when I didn't think he'd ever truly recover. But eventually he did. Death is hard, but we all have to move on at some point or another. We can't allow ourselves to get stuck in the past. Because that's not a life. And the ones who perished wouldn't want us living that way." "I'm so sorry that you and your husband had to go through that," Ethan said. "I'm sure it was devastating," he hesitated a moment, unsure of what to say next. "Were there many other people close to the Weller's? Others who were affected by their deaths?" "Oh, of course," Mary said. "Craig and Karen had so many friends. Everyone adored them. And those children – they were darlings. Everyone took their deaths exceptionally hard. It truly was a loss in Briarwood." Ethan needed to think. Steve was no longer alive. If he was The Sad Killer, or if he had indeed killed Mike Darbyshire, would his wife had even known? Was his visit here proving useless after all? "I won't keep you," Ethan said. "But I just wanted to verify something you said. You and your husband did not know the name of the driver, is that correct?" "That's right. The police wouldn't release it. It's something that always haunted the both of us." Ethan nodded, feeling even more disappointed than he did as he stood at the door. "Alright, well," he stood, tucking his notepad back into his pocket. "Thank you for taking the time to speak with me, Mary. I really do appreciate it." "Of course," she gave him a warm smile. "Anything you need."

It was almost three o'clock. Ethan was back at Gus's house, sitting on the couch in silence as the both of them thought.

"It couldn't have been him," Ethan finally said. "Unless Mary is lying, her husband couldn't have killed Mike Darbyshire. They never even knew his name." "It was a long-shot, anyway," Gus said. "Besides, why would he kill six other men if Darbyshire was the one he was after? I get what you're saying, kid. And you're right, it's definitely not just a coincidence that Darbyshire was murdered on May seventh. But there has to be more to this. Something we're not seeing." Ethan was thinking, scanning through his memory of all the case files, witness statements, interviews, records. Then something hit him. "He killed those seven men for a reason," Ethan said. "Mike wasn't the main victim. He was just one of six, but he was killed for a reason – the car accident cover-up," he looked at Gus. "What if each of them was killed for a reason?" He stood up from his seat on the couch as the plethora of information flooded his brain, fitting together like a puzzle. "What if the victims have more in common than we initially believed? What if they all had something hidden in their pasts? A sin that nobody knew about?" Ethan looked around the room, trying to make sense of it all, then looked at Gus. "What if those men weren't so good after all?"

––––––

Before he could stop himself, Ethan was out the door and back in his car. He was onto something – he knew it this time. The last lead proved fruitless, but perhaps this one wouldn't. His mind was racing and his was pulse beating feverishly. He had to figure this out. He had to find The Sad Killer.

He pulled up in front of Flora Whittaker's house, recalling their conversation from just the day prior. How she relayed her life with Robert, as well as life afterwards. Remarried, twice. Finally happy and content. And now here he was to intrude on her life and ask more questions.

"Detective O'Riley," she said as she opened the door. "What a pleasant surprise." "Can I talk to you?" he asked. "Of course," she opened the door further and took a step backwards into the house. "Sounds urgent. Is everything alright?" "Yes, sorry," Ethan laughed. "Everything's fine." They walked into her kitchen and took a seat at the table. She poured him a glass of water and he chugged it back in one gulp. "My my," Flora said, filling his empty cup once again. "What's gotten into you?" "I've been running around all morning." "Chasing the killer, are you now?" "Trying to. I've been putting together the pieces, trying to figure this whole thing out. I need you to tell me more about Robert." She stared at him, blinked once. "If you're not up to it, that's fine," he said. "Apologies." "No no," she said. "I just thought we covered everything yesterday." "It's just," he started. "I've come across some new information about the victim's today. So I need to know more about Robert. Well, everything about Robert, actually. Can you tell me about him?" Flora inhaled deeply. "As I told you yesterday, we met through my father. Robert was a very charming man. Very friendly and courteous. All of the woman adored him. Fortunately for me, I was the one he chose." "What were some of his hobbies? What did he like to do?" "He fished sometimes," Flora said. "He spent most of his days working. He was a very career-driven, hard-working man. He loved to take me on dates. We'd go for dinner, to the cinema, the fair when it was in town. On weekends we'd drive to the beach with the windows rolled down, listening to music and basking in the sun. It was wonderful. Six years with him, but we did so much." This wasn't helping. Ethan needed to know one thing and one thing only. He had to ask her flat out. "Flora," Ethan said as politely as he could. "I need you to tell me if Robert had any secrets. Anything from his past that he kept concealed or hidden." Flora gave him a strange look. "I don't know what you mean." "Perhaps he did some things before he met you," Ethan suggested. "Or maybe even while you two were together. It could be nothing, but perhaps little things. Petty crime, drinking and driving..." "Are you asking me if Robert was a criminal? A delinquent?" "No, I just mean –" Ethan paused. "I'm sorry, Flora. I'm just trying to figure this out and find out why your husband and the other six men died." "You think it was their fault that they were murdered?" "I don't know what to think." She stared at him and the room was silent. He almost didn't think she was going to answer until she spoke again. "You want to know if he had secrets. If he ever did anything bad?" Ethan looked at her. There was something about the tone of her voice. "Do you know something?" he leaned forward in his chair. Flora pursed her lips together, hesitating. "I didn't mention it before because, quite frankly, I didn't think it was relEthant. And because it was so long ago. I pushed it so far back in my mind that I forgot it ever happened. All these years and I never thought about it. Because after Robert was gone, I no longer had to worry. I was safe. And it never crossed my mind again." "Flora, what happened?" She closed her eyes and her lips parted. "He would hit me," she said slowly. She opened her eyes and looked at him. "Robert had a... temper. What I said to you before was all true. He was a very kind, charming man. He bought me anything I needed, would bend over backwards for me. But unfortunately, my Robert had another side to him – a side he didn't like to showcase often. And that was his abusive side," she stopped, tucked a stray curl behind her ear. "It was very difficult for me, you see. Because I was so young when we married. And he was ten years older, and so experienced in this world. He was this somebody, and I was a nobody. I felt special when I was with him. As though I finally meant something. And he was so good to me, don't get me wrong. But he would hurt me. And

I believed it was my fault. As though I were the one doing something wrong. "It took me a long time to move past that mindset. To finally realize that I was the victim, and blaming myself was not fair. It was only after his death that I was finally able to move on and find myself again. Because for so long, I was lost. Sure, I was happy and smiling and in love with him, so in love with him. But during that time, I was someone else. I wasn't Flora anymore, and I think people were beginning to notice. Our marriage was a sham. I would put on a fake smile every day and I'd endure it. I'd survive and get through each day, just to live to see another. "He never hit me where it was noticeable. Always on the stomach, or back, or legs. If he bruised my arms, he'd make me wear long sleeve shirts, even when it was scorching out," she stopped. Ethan stared at her, analyzing everything she had just said. "What you did was very brave, Flora." "No," she looked up at him. "It wasn't. I was a coward. I hid away and ignored the truth. Because I couldn't handle it. I wanted to continue living in this perfect bubble that I called life. I was ignorant to it all. And if he wasn't murdered –" she stopped. "Then... I'd probably still be with him, taking his abuse." Ethan empathized with this woman. Empathized for what she had gone through all those years ago. And how long she kept it a secret. "Let me ask you one thing," Ethan said to her. "If it wasn't for me coming around asking you these questions today, would you ever have told anyone?" She stared at him, her green eyes glossy with tears. She said one word. "No."

It was six o'clock. Ethan should have been on his way back home to Riverton, but he couldn't leave, not when he was this close. He was definitely on the right path now and he knew it.

He sat in front of Gus Fraser and told him everything he knew, everything he believed was happening. "Mark Darbyshire," Ethan said. "Victim two. Killed four people in 1955 in a drunk driving accident. It was covered up and he was never penalized," he took another breath. "Patrick Brooks, victim three. Was abusing his two children, Angela and her younger brother. I spoke with her and she revealed to me that he had a drinking problem. Would come home and beat the kids," Ethan stopped again, gathering his thoughts. "Robert Baldwin, victim four. Charming, friendly, and kind. Pilar of the community. Seemingly perfect marriage to Flora Whittaker. But behind closed doors, he abused her. Gave her bruises and forced her to cover them. Maintained their perfect marriage for everyone to see, but no one ever knew the truth. Not until today, when she admitted to me what Robert was really like." Gus stared at Ethan, his mind racing, processing everything Ethan had just said. "So what are you saying, son? What are we dealing with here?" "So far we have evidence that three of the seven men had secrets," Ethan started. "Very troubling secrets. And I'm sure willing to bet that if we keep digging, we'll find something on the other four. Here's the thing with this case," Ethan said. "Everybody said the same thing about all seven victims: they were good men. Well, now I have proof that contradicts that claim. These men were not good. They were bad," he took in a quick breath, preparing himself for what he was about to say next. "I believe The Sad Killer was a vigilante."

Chapter Seventeen

CHAPTER SEVENTEEN

It was after 10 p.m. and Ethan was lying in bed next to Jordan. She was telling him about something, but he wasn't paying attention. His mind was fixated on one thing and one thing only.

"So she goes around and hands us these tiny dolls," Jordan said. "Who did?" She gave him a look. "The meditation instructor. Were you not listening to me at all?" "I was, sorry. Continue." She made a sound of irritation. "So she gives us these tiny dolls, and they have straggly looking hair and minuscule faces, barely even a doll. And we're supposed to yell at them, swear at them, take our anger out." "At the doll?" "Yes." "This is what you do at meditation?" Ethan asked. "No. This was before class started." "Who handed out the dolls?" "The instructor! I just told you!" "Okay, so then what?" "So all of these women were screaming at these tiny little dolls, swearing at them, throwing them. I just sat there staring at its tiny face. I couldn't yell at it. I felt so bad." "Jor, it's a doll." "I know, but still. Anyways, it was hilarious! We were killing ourselves laughing. Grown women giving hell to these dolls." "Is it like a voo-doo doll or something?" "No. It's just... a tiny doll – I don't know, Madeline gave them to us and said it will help." "Help with what?" "I don't know – anger management?" "Where is this doll now?" Jordan reached over to nightstand and grabbed the doll. "It's cute," he said. "Right? I couldn't hurt the poor thing." Ethan stared at it for a moment, then took it from her hands and threw it across the room. They both laughed. "How's the case going?" she asked. "What case," he said with irritation. "That bad?" "It's not going anywhere. I'm honestly stuck. Kennedy tells me I should give up and throw in the towel. Call it a suicide and close the case." "But you know there's a chance it could not be," Jordan said, finishing his thought for him. He nodded. She sighed and rolled closer to him. "What do you think happened, Ethan? No biases or other opinions. No pressure from the Major or Kennedy. What do you believe happened to those girls?" He thought for a moment, then looked at Jordan. "There's evidence suggesting –" "Ev," she said. "Forget the evidence. What do you think?" "I think they were pushed." "Good," she rolled onto her back. "Then go from there." "I have been. I've talked to everyone. Everyone. And Briarwood's not that big. If those girls were murdered, I've most likely spoken to the culprit by now. But there's also evidence indicating that one of the girls was depressed. The other girl might have had a likely reason to jump. But that leaves the third girl, and unless I can find a reason as to why Kiera Barnes would jump off the roof of her school with the other two, then I can't close this case. I can't call it a suicide until I've ruled out all other possibilities." "Then it looks to me like you're on the right track," Jordan said. "Yeah, it's harder than it seems." "Maybe it was a dare," Jordan said suddenly. "Maybe they were playing a game like Risk. You know how kids do that thing where they run across the freeway?" "Yeah." "Kids are always doing stupid things, risking their lives. What if they were up there and something like that happened? They were standing at the edge of the roof, and then they fell?" "All three of them?" "I don't know," Jordan said. "Maybe. Or maybe you were right – one of them did jump. Did you think of that?" "Anneka Wilson," Ethan said. "Then what would cause the other two?" "Maybe they were trying to help her, and they fell off too. Or maybe one of them slipped, and the other two were trying to help her, and they all got pulled down as well." "I don't know," Ethan said. "Kennedy was saying from day one that it could have been an accident, but I wasn't buying it. You don't know what it's like at that school. There were so many secrets. So many lies." "Okay, so we're back to murder then. Who would want them dead?" "That's the thing," Ethan said. "The only suspects I brought in for questioning that would have likely motive had an alibi during the time. Everyone was in class – it happened right before lunch. So everyone is accounted for." "Then who does that leave?" "A faculty member. A parent." Jordan was quiet a moment. Then she said, "Go back there. Interrogate all of the adults. Grill them hard, Ev. Get to the bottom of this. If someone did push those girls, you're going to find out who." He nodded his head in silence, taking everything Jordan said with caution. It was easy for her to spew out advice; harder for him to actually follow through with it. "I made a big breakthrough on the other case," he told her. "The one from the 60's?" "Yeah. The Sad Killer." "Oh God," Jordan rolled her eyes. "You're still on that?" "I figured it out today. The killer was a vigilante." "Is this big news?" "Yes," Ethan said. "We're one step closer to finding this guy. Once the motive is figured out, the rest could come just as easily." "You don't know that," Jordan said. "Listen, Ev, I think it's great that you're so interested in this case. And sure, it can be thrilling to be on the tail of a famous serial killer. But it was fifty years ago. You're chasing a guy who might not even be alive anymore." "But what if he is?" "And what if he isn't?" She had a point. What if he continued down this road, only to reach a dead end, yet again, like he did with Steve Weller: Deceased, unable to make a statement or tell his side of the story. "Even if the killer is dead," Ethan said. "Even if I can just find out who it was, it would be ground-breaking." She turned towards him and smiled through the darkness of the room. "I just think you need to focus on one case at a time, not get swept up in the past. Because the past is great, but it's not the present. And those girls, Ethan – they're in the present. And they need you."

It was Friday morning and the weather was dreary. Dark clouds covered the sky and rain was pouring down onto his windshield. Ethan arrived at the Briarwood station expecting to find it vacant of his team since Kennedy had told him they were called back to Riverton. But lo and behold – Major Frank Connolly was there, awaiting Ethan's arrival.

"Updates?" he said as Ethan walked through the doors, shaking the rain off his umbrella. "Nothing concrete, sir," Ethan said. "What did you do yesterday?" Frank asked. Ethan hesitated. "I was going over the case files, looking over the interview transcripts –" "Don't bullshit me, O'Riley. You've been looking into that other case." Ethan didn't know how to respond. "Do you want me to take you off this case?" Frank said. "Because I can find another detective just as willing and able." "No –" Ethan said quickly. "No, I will solve this. I will. I just need more time." "Time is the one thing we don't have," Frank said. "Kennedy tells me it's suicide, but she says you won't comply with this." "Because, sir, I do not believe that Officer Cross is correct." Frank stared at him. "Yes, there is evidence pointing to suicide –" "Then why are we not following where the evidence points us?" "Because it's not that simple. There are other factors to be considered. For one, the family members expressed no concerns of suicidal thoughts or depression in the girls. The friends that I interviewed said that the girls would never kill themselves. With the exception of few testimonies that stated Haddie Taylor was reckless and crazy," Ethan said the word with air quotations. "No one else seemed to concur with this notion." "The pregnant one?" Frank asked. "Yes." "Who said she would jump?" "Two girls at the school made a comment. One saw her getting into a car with a drunk driver about a month ago. Said she thought she had a death wish." "And the other one?" "Just said that she was unpredictable," Ethan said. Oliver's words echoed through his mind. She wouldn't have jumped to prove a point. Or would she? How far would Haddie Taylor go to get the attention that she so desperately required? "Did she know about the pregnancy?" Frank asked. "That is unknown." "And the boyfriend didn't know?" "Said it wasn't his." "Right," Frank said. "There was the Carter kid you interrogated. He didn't know either?" "No, sir." Frank thought for a moment. "Then perhaps she really did jump." Ethan was dumbfounded. Here was his major, standing in front of him, agreeing with everyone else. Like sheep being sent to slaughter. "Sir —" "Unless you can find solid evidence that those girls didn't jump, then we're going to have to call it," Frank said. "Understood?" Ethan nodded. "So get back out there and determine whether or not those girls jumped or not."

There was only one missing piece to this equation, Ethan knew, and that was Kiera Barnes. He had probable cause to believe that both Haddie Taylor and Anneka Wilson could have jumped off that building, but not Kiera. He needed more information. And the only place he could go was back to the parents.

Patrick Barnes was at work, of course, but Vivian was there. She let Ethan back into their home, leading him into the living room to sit and talk where they had all those times before.

"I'm sorry to return with nothing new," Ethan said. "Truly, Mrs. Barnes, I wish I had more." "You don't have to apologize," Vivian said. "I understand how difficult it is." Ethan was quiet. "How is your family doing? How's Kelsey holding up?" "Kelsey's alright," Vivian said. "The last eleven days have been misery. Everyone's been very quiet and out of it, as though we can't believe she's really gone. I keep thinking that she's going to walk through those doors and everything will go back to normal. As though this was one big nightmare," she paused, looking at her hands in her lap. "But that's not going to happen. And I need to stop thinking that way." Ethan nodded sympathetically. "I need more information about your daughter. There has to be something I'm missing here."

Vivian looked taken back. "About Kiera? I've already told you everything." "Yes, I know," Ethan said, crafting his next words carefully as not to offend her. "But there still remains the possibility that your daughter jumped, Mrs. Barnes." She opened her mouth to interject but Ethan held up his hand. "I know it's something no parent wants to hear – that their child committed suicide. But I've explored many avenues. I've talked to everyone involved. And there is evidence to suggest that Anneka was depressed. Haddie had some personal issues that we believe might have caused her to jump. And that leaves Kiera." Vivian Barnes stared at him, eyes wide. "You're asking me if my daughter jumped off that roof? If she killed herself along with her two best friends?" Ethan was silent. "That would be an easy and convenient answer, wouldn't it, Detective?" she said. "Because that would mean you could stop looking, stop investigating this possible murder that this fucking town has such a problem admitting exists. Why is it so difficult for everyone to realize this? Kiera didn't jump. Those girls didn't jumped. Somebody did this to them." "With all due respect, ma'am, you don't know that. I don't know that. Nobody knows what happened on the roof that day. I know you want to protect Kiera. You want to protect her name and her legacy, what she left behind. But if there is even the slightest possibility that Kiera would have jumped – if she had any mental illnesses, if she was going through personal struggles in her life – then it is imperative that I know." Vivian continued to stare at him, not saying a word. Finally, she spoke. "I will tell you this once more, and my husband will tell you the same thing: Kiera was not suicidal. She would not kill herself. There's more to this story that you're clearly not seeing."

Ethan didn't know where else to turn, so he ended up at Gus's house. Right now, he didn't care what Frank wanted. He was getting nowhere with the triple deaths, the families refusing to even entertain the notion of suicide, and to be quite frank, his mind was preoccupied with The Sad Killer. He was onto something here.

Figuring out the motive had opened multiple doors for Ethan. Previously, they were looking at the situation all wrong. This changed things drastically. This wasn't a demonic sociopath who felt the need to kill his victims. This was someone killing with a purpose.

Vigilantes feel as though they are helping society, doing what no one else can. The unsub was careful and meticulous. They did their research, handpicked their victims individually based on their own personal histories and deviances. The unsub believed that each of these men deserved what was going to happen to them, and that it was his job to bring justice.

If Ethan was going to find this guy, he needed to know how the unsub got started. And in order to do that, he needed to know everything he could about the first victim, Mark Irving. Why was Irving first? How did the unsub find him? Did the unsub know him personally? Or did he witness whatever wrongdoings Irving was committing and realized he needed to put an end to it?

As far as Ethan could tell, Mark Irving was a good guy. Everyone had only positive things to say about him. Even Gus could vouch for Irving. So what were they missing? What was Irving doing behind closed doors that no one knew about? That's what Ethan needed to find out. Because the key to the killer's identity lied there.

"We need to look at everyone who knew Mark Irving," Ethan said to Gus. "Friends, co-workers, neighbors." "You think the unsub knew him personally?" "It's hard to tell," Ethan said. "But if we can start there and get a better idea of what his life was like, we may be able to build from there. I wouldn't say family members. I think our killer might have either known Irving, or known of him. But not anyone too close to him, because he went on and killed six others afterwards. If it was someone too close to Irving, perhaps they would have solely killed him and been done with it." "Unless Irving was a realization for them," Gus said. "Killing him led to something bigger. The unsub realized that he enjoyed the act of killing, as well as taking down the so-called bad men. Irving was the catalyst." "Okay," Ethan said. "So what makes the unsub start killing? A trigger, something in his early life? We see injustice happening every day, but our unsub must have seen injustice on another scale. Perhaps they were a victim themselves. A child of divorced parents, a victim of abuse. We know that both Patrick Brooks and Robert Baldwin were abusers. We could start there?" "Yes," Gus said. "Sons, brothers, father's. These are all possible individuals who could have been victim to an unjust situation – such as abuse – and they wanted to right the wrongs. They discovered whatever it was that Irving was doing and they needed to make things right again, bring justice to the people." "Exactly," Ethan said. "Our unsub might not have known Irving personally, but he recognized the aberrant behaviour. So we go back.

We look at all of the people in Irving's life. Where he went to school, what car he drove, which girls he dated. I want to know everything there is to know about this guy, because he was hiding something. And it's our job to find out what."

So that is exactly what they did. Ethan pulled the files on Irving and got to work reading through everything. Gus could recall witness testimonies and statements from 1965, but if they were going to get anything concrete, they would need to speak with these people in person. The only problem was, how many of them would still be in Briarwood?

Mark Irving was notorious for being the town bachelor. He had plenty of girlfriends, and Ethan believed that if he could speak with one of them, perhaps they would reveal something significant, such as abuse or violent tendencies, similar to Flora Whittaker.

He began with Kristen Bretwiser. (née: Frost) She was one of the only few women that he could track down that were a) still living, and b) still in Briarwood. Ethan had read her statement from 1965. She had dated Irving the year before and they maintained an on-and-off again relationship. Ethan drove to her place, hoping this visit would prove beneficial.

He knocked on the door and waited. An elderly woman answered moments later. She would have to be in her late seventies by now. "Kristen Bretwiser?" Ethan asked. "Yes?" "My name's Ethan O'Riley. I'm a detective with the Riverton PD and I'm looking into an old case, one that you might be familiar with." She stared at him, her eyes focused on his. "You're here about The Sad Killer, aren't you?" He nodded. The poor woman had probably been harassed about this case for years, all because she simply dated victim number one. "Well, come on in then," she opened the door and he stepped inside. Her place was quaint and small, the aroma of baked-goods filling the air. He didn't know if she was still married or whether she lived alone. "Would you like to sit in here?" Kristen asked, motioning to the living room. She was tiny and frail and moved at a steady pace. "Sure, that would be great." They walked into the room and Kristen motioned for him to sit on the couch. She sat on the chair adjacent from him. "So what made you start looking for him again?" she asked. "The Sad Killer?" She nodded. "I'm here working another case, actually," Ethan admitted. "I heard about The Sad Killer and have been hooked ever since. I'm kind of determined to solve this thing, figure out who he is." "And I'm assuming you're here because of Mark." "Yes," Ethan said. "What can you tell me about him?" "It was a long time ago," she said. "Mark and I were never serious. We dated for a few months. He wasn't one for commitment. Then he turned up murdered. Nobody knew what happened to him. I believe it wasn't until the second or third man turned up dead that we began to understand there was a pattern here." "That must have been scary." "Oh, it was, especially knowing the men personally. I knew David as well. David Hill. He was friends with my older brothers." Ethan recalled what Gil Vanhorn had said about David Hill. He had known him as well. Said he had a wife and a young daughter. What did you do, David? Ethan thought. All of these men were hiding something. "What can you tell me about Mark as a person?" Ethan asked. "Anything about his personality, how he treated people, how he treated you?" "He was a good man," Kristen said. "Mark was very kind, outgoing. He'd do anything, really. A jack of all trades. He was charming and endearing, had a way with words – knew how to make the girls swoon," she laughed. "That's why no one could understand why he was murdered. It was a shock to us all. Even if Mark and

I weren't together anymore, I still cared for him. It was devastating." "Did Mark have any secrets? Anything you know that he hid from the world? Maybe he was a smoker and didn't tell anyone. Perhaps he liked to get away and have weekends to himself somewhere." She thought for a moment. "I don't recall anything of the sorts. He wasn't a secretive person. There was nothing inherently bad about him. He was honest and kind. That's all." "Mrs. Bretwiser," Ethan said. "I'm going to be honest with you – I've noticed a pattern in a few of the victims. Each of them were harboring a well-hidden secret to some degree, something from their past. Another woman I spoke to recently revealed that her husband, one of the victims, was abusive to her. She had never told anyone for fifty-one years. What I'm looking for," Ethan said. "Is anything like that. Was Mark ever abusive to you? Was he ever violent or had a temper?" She shook her head feverishly. "No, not at all! Mark was a very gentle, caring man. He never laid a finger on me. And I never witnessed anger or aggression of the sorts. I mean," she paused. "As I told you, we only dated for a short period of time before his death. But from what I could tell, he was a good man. However," she said. "If you want details such as the ones you're evidently looking for, I'd advise speaking to any friends of his from that time. They'd know more than I would."

Ethan looked through Irving's file. The detective on the case back then had interviewed nearly everyone in Irving's life, similar to what Ethan was doing now with the Anneka, Haddie, and Kiera. Of all the friends, family members, co-workers, and neighbors on that list, there were only a select few that were still alive and in Briarwood.

One had died in a motorcycle accident a few years after Irving's murder. Another had passed away of a heart attack. His family members were long gone. So that left a few friends, neighbors, and coworkers.

Ethan began speaking to them one-by-one, starting with an elderly man by the name of Henry Williams. Henry had worked with Irving for five years before the murder. They became close friends through their job. Henry said that the two would get together on weekends, have a drink or two, and hangout with some of their friends. This included other co-workers as well as the townspeople of Briarwood. Everyone was close, Henry had said, describing the quaint, tight-knit community that Ethan had become so familiar with these past eleven days.

Henry told him stories. Work disasters gone wrong, double dates ending in failures. He talked about fishing trips and canoe rides, drunken nights and hangovers that lasted days. He told Ethan about their dreams and aspirations. Both Mark and Henry had family roots here in Briarwood, and while they both dreamed and imagined themselves elsewhere – living in the big city even – they both knew that they would remain in Briarwood. For it was their home. It was what they were accustomed to. And they loved it there.

"Was Mark ever violent? Did he show any signs of aggression?" Ethan asked. "Not at all," Henry said, taking a drag from his cigarette. They were sitting on his front porch, watching the rain pour from the sky. "I knew some mean men in my time, but Mark Irving was not one of them. He was a hilarious fella. Always crackin' jokes and entertainin' the guys at work." "And what about when he drank?" Ethan asked. "Maybe he had a different side to him? Got violent or angry? Maybe acted stupid?" Again, Henry was shaking his head. "Not Mark. I can assure you, Detective, Mark was a good guy. Wouldn't hurt a fly."

There had to be something he was missing. Ethan was certain that he was onto something. There was a pattern. The victims were bad men. The unsub was a vigilante. He was killing for a reason. But perhaps he was getting it wrong. Perhaps Mark Irving wasn't angry or violent. Two of the victim's may have been abusive, but then there was Mike Darbyshire, who wasn't abusive, but rather, accidently killed a family of four and got away with it.

Ethan might have been looking for the wrong signs. What everyone was saying about Mark might have been true. He was a good guy – a nice man. Friendly, charming, helpful. But underneath it all, there was a secret he was hiding, something that nobody knew about. And while that idea proved useful in Ethan's head, it had made this case even more difficult to solve. Because if Irving was as good at keeping secrets as Ethan thought, then how was he ever supposed to find out what it was exactly that he was hiding?

He needed to find out. It was the cipher to cracking this whole thing. Mark Irving was significant for a reason. He was the first victim. Overkill. Seven stab wounds to the chest. What did that mean? Why did the unsub choose him?

Ethan was back at Gus's place. It was approaching three o'clock and Ethan was going over everything he had gathered today: His talk with Kristen Bretwiser, his visit with Henry Williams and a few other's that were friends with Irving. And still there was nothing conclusive.

Ethan was looking at the photos of the crime scenes again, going over anything he might have missed. He was looking at Irving: the bloody mess, the stab wounds, the word written beside the body in black marker: sad. Suddenly, Ethan sat up straight, looking closer at the photo.

"Gus," Ethan said. "The signature," he handed him the photo. "What about it?" Gus asked, taking the photo and examining it. "We had it all wrong," Ethan said. "I mean, you guys did. Back then. What reason did the unsub write 'sad' beside the victim's bodies?" "Remorse," Gus said. "We concluded that the unsub was a sociopath who felt obligated to kill. Leaving this one word was his way of telling us that he was sorry, that he didn't have a choice. That he in fact did feel some sort of empathy to-wards the victim's. And it was also his signature to let us know that this was all him. He might have felt bad, but he still wanted credit for those murders." Ethan nodded as a smile began to form on his face. "Exactly," he said. "You guys had his M.O all wrong. We now know that he wasn't a sadistic sociopath who felt obligated to kill. This was a vigilante. He was killing for the good of society." Gus was nodding, following along. "You're right. We didn't have the circumstances correct, and therefore, we concluded the signature was something completely off." "So what does the signature mean then?" Ethan asked. "He's not sad. Unless he's sad that it had to come to this. That these men were corrupt in some way." "No," Gus said. "It has to be more than that. Sad isn't an emotion – it means some-thing else, something more personal to the unsub. There is no sadness here. He is bragging, showing off what he has done. Look, I took down the bad guys." "It could be short for something," Ethan suggested. "Sad," Gus said aloud. "Short for sadism?" "But he wasn't a sadist," Ethan said. "He didn't receive pleasure or gratification from the kills. He did it because he believed they deserved it. The killer believed that since the law wasn't convicting these men, it was up to him." Gus nodded. "So if not sadism, what else could it be short for?" "Maybe not short for something," Ethan said. "What about an abbreviation.

What does sad stand for?" "Seasonal Affective Disorder?" Gus suggested. "But it was summer when the murders happened." Gus thought. "There are many abbreviations for SAD." "Singles Awareness Day," Ethan said. They both laughed. "Social Anxiety Disorder," Gus suggested. "Perhaps," Ethan said. "But what is the relEthance?" "The unsub could have been suffering from anxiety and other mental illnesses." Ethan thought about this but wasn't convinced. "What about the modes of killing? Stabbing, suffocation, strangulation, and shooting. They all begin with the letter S. Could that be significant?" "Perhaps," Gus said. "Asphyxiation, maybe. Stabbing, asphyxiation..." "S and A," Ethan said. "But no D." Gus shook his head. "Unless you can come up with another word for suffocation or shooting." "Dismembering?" Ethan suggested. "Drowning? No..." "It's not the modes," Gus said. "But maybe something to do with the deaths. Seven men dead. Seven starts with an S." "Seven Are Dead," Ethan said. Gus made a face. "But would he have known that from the beginning? With the first victim?" "If he had the hit-list all along," Ethan said. They sat there in silence, thinking. "Search and Destroy," Gus suggested. Ethan turned to him, intrigued. "That makes more sense. Search and Destroy. SAD." "It's a military term," Gus said.

"The victims are his targets. And it's his duty to seek them out and annihilate them." "He could be a soldier then?" Ethan said. "Special ops?" "It could make sense," Gus said. "Given the subject matter. Although, it would be more likely he was a solider or a seal, not special ops. The level of killing would be more advanced, more meticulous and precise. Now, the latter six were that exactly. It's the first one that was messy and hesitant." "Right," Ethan said. "Okay, this is good. This is progress." "We don't even know if that's what sad means," Gus said. "It's speculation." "Yes," Ethan said. "But right now, speculation is all we got."

They had been researching Briarwood's populace and going through files upon files. They were looking for victims, children of abuse, someone with a military background – anyone who might have had a motive to murder seven men in cold blood.

So far the search had come up empty. Only three men from Briarwood were in the army, and two of them were dead. The third wasn't even residing in Briarwood during the times of the murders. Ethan couldn't even be sure that the unsub was military. Every lead they followed was guesswork, and nothing was guaranteed.

"I don't know who else I can talk to," Ethan said. "What about that reporter?" Gus suggested. "Maybe give him an update and see if he knows anything."

Since there was nothing else that he could do, Ethan grabbed his cellphone and dialed Gil Vanhorn's phone number. He picked up after the fourth ring.

"Hello," he said. "Gil," Ethan said. "It's Detective O'Riley." "Ah, good to hear from you son. You crack the case yet?" "Not yet, I'm afraid. That's actually why I'm calling. I wanted to bounce a few ideas off of you." "Go for it." "So we made a bit of a break through," Ethan said. "We figured out that the unsub was a vigilante." "A vigilante? Don't they go after criminals of sorts?" "Yes," Ethan said. "Vigilante killers tend to watch from the fringes of society. They see injustices happening and decide to take matters into their own hands." "So how do you figure your guy was a vigilante then?" "Well, it turns out that Briarwood's Best and Brightest weren't as good as everyone made them out to be," Ethan said. "I found things that they were hiding – secrets and vices that no one else knew about. So far I've got stuff on three of them, but I bet if I keep digging, I can find more." "What kind of stuff are we talking about here?" Gil asked. "Two were abusive to their wives and kids. The other, Darbyshire, was involved in a cover-up back in '54. Drunk driving accident where he killed a family of four." "You don't say..." "It's definitely not what I expected," Ethan said. The line was quiet for a moment. "You speak to anyone from that family that was killed? Could it be connected somehow?" "That's what we thought too, but no luck there. I was trying to track down more people with a direct correlation to Darbyshire, but the family of the brother that died didn't even know Darbyshire's name." "Okay," Gil said. "So where are you at now?" "Now, we're on the signature. Tell me again – what was the purpose of leaving 'sad' behind at the crime scenes?" "A sign of remorse. His signature." "Right," Ethan said. "Well, now that we know we're dealing with a vigilante, that means nothing. No remorse here." "Interesting," Gil remarked. "So what does 'sad' mean then?" "That's what we're try-ing to figure out. Could be short for something. Or an abbreviation. Any ideas?" Gil exhaled. "I have no idea." "Gus Fraser thinks it could be an abbreviation for Search and Destroy. Our guy could be military." "Could be," Gil said. "You'll need to go through all the old records." "We have been," Ethan said. "No luck. That's why I thought I'd give you a ring. Did you know anyone in Briarwood during that time that was in the army? Or maybe not even that, but anyone that was a good, upstanding citizen? Someone who may have wanted to bring justice to the people?" "It was so long ago, kid. Gus would have more answers than I would." Ethan was quiet. "I'm sorry," Gil said. "That I couldn't be more help. I'll give you a call if I remember anything." "Thanks Gil."

Ethan ended the call and looked at his watch. It was nearing six o'clock. He had gotten so caught up going through case files and talking with Gus that he had completely lost track of time. He hadn't even made an attempt to work on the current case at all today. Frank was going to kill him.

Chapter Eighteen

CHAPTER EIGHTEEN

Day twelve: Saturday.

Ethan had avoided going back to the Briarwood station last night. He really didn't feel like getting an earful from Frank. Ethan had spoken with Vivian Barnes yesterday, hoping to find anything useful, but that didn't lead anywhere. So, he resorted to working on the other case with Gus. There was no harm in that. At least he was doing something, rather than just sitting around idly, waiting for answers.

The dreary weather from the day prior had cleared up and the sun was trying to break through the clouds. Ethan had a new idea. He wasn't sure where this would lead him, but he had to at least try.

He gathered them all at the Taylor's home. Although it was Saturday, George wasn't there. He was out somewhere, keeping himself busy. On the couch in front of him sat Renée Taylor, Vivian Barnes, and Mary-Ella Wilson.

"I thought it would be best if we all got together in person," Ethan said. "That way we can discuss the girls and all say what we need to." "You still haven't found who did this?" Vivian asked. Mary-Ella looked at her. Ethan took in a breath, preparing himself for how this conversation would go. "Mrs. Barnes," he began. "I know you don't want to hear this, but right now, we need to discuss the elephant in the room. And that is the notion that the girls jumped." Vivian visibly shuttered. "Now, I know it's difficult to hear," Ethan said. "Especially for a mother. Nobody wants to believe that their child would commit suicide. But in all likelihood, and given the circumstances, I'd say it's still a possibility." "But we already told you everything," Renée said. "The girls weren't depressed or suicidal. Why on earth would they jump?" "Sometimes kids hide things from their parents," Ethan said. "We like to think we know everything that is happening in our children's lives, but that's not necessarily true. All three girls could have been suffering. And they could have been good at hiding it." "Why are you pushing this suicide route?" Vivian cried. "Is it because everyone else is? Because the Chief thinks it will make Briarwood a better place? Can none of you accept the fact that someone pushed our babies off a roof?" she broke down and started sobbing. Mary-Ella handed her the tissue box, but somehow remained composed. "As I was saying," Ethan continued. "Kids – especially teenage girls – are good at hiding things. For instance," he looked at Renée. "I'm sure I don't need to mention Haddie's secrets." Renée scowled at him. He turned to Mary-Ella. "And there is evidence indicating that Anneka was suffering from depression." Mary-Ella's face fell. "Not only was she on Zoloft and Zopiclone, but Cloe confided to me that Anneka had been acting differently the last few months. Sequestering herself away from others, getting into drugs –" "Anneka did not do drugs," Mary-Ella snapped. "Again," Ethan said. "We have evidence. And like I said before, your daughters did not tell you everything." He truly didn't mean to turn this into a witch-hunt and expose the girls to the other mother's, but they weren't really leaving him with any other options. "People have said that Haddie was acting differently these last few months as well," Ethan said. "Different," Renée echoed. "What does that even mean?" "I'm not exactly sure," Ethan said. "It's just what

I've gathered from a number of people." The room was quiet. Ethan looked at all three of the women. "Now, I've spoken with you all regarding the topic of mental illness, and I know you all say the same thing: that the girls didn't suffer from any –" Mary-Ella turned to Vivian again and made a face. The two exchanged a look in silence that Ethan couldn't decipher. "What is it?" Ethan said to Mary-Ella. She turned to Ethan. "That's not true." "What's not true?" Ethan asked. "That none of the girls had a mental illness," Mary-Ella stated. "Kiera did." Vivian's head snapped towards Mary-Ella. "How dare you? Your girl was the one taking anti-depressants!" "He needs to know," Mary-Ella retaliated. "Tell him or I will." Vivian stared at Mary-Ella, a grimace on her face. None of them faced Ethan. Finally, Mary-Ella turned back to him and said, "Kiera had an eating disorder. That's a mental illness." "How could you?" Vivian cried. "Is this true?" Ethan said to Vivian. She closed her eyes and waited a moment before answering. "Yes," she finally said. "But just because she had some issues in the past does not mean that she was suicidal. The two things aren't even correlated!" "Why was this not in her medical file?" Ethan asked. "Because she was never clinically treated for one. We were dealing with it ourselves."

"Was it serious?" Ethan asked. Vivian pursed her lips but didn't respond. "The poor girl was starving herself," Mary-Ella said. "It was devastating." "Like I said," Vivian gave Mary-Ella another look of disgust. "Just because Kiera had an eating disorder, does not mean that she killed herself." "You are aware of the fact that eating disorders are often associated with depression and anxiety, right?" Ethan said to her. "There's a direct correlation." And that's when Vivian broke down.

Ethan sat in Jason Gregory's office, Jason and Frank on one side of the desk, Kennedy, Jesse, and Ethan on the other. The room was silent, not one of them saying a word. Jason was flipping through the file in front of him.

"So you're declaring it a triple suicide?" he finally said, breaking the unbearable silence. Ethan hesitated a moment, then nodded. "How did you come to this conclusion?" Jason asked. Ethan cleared his throat. "I spoke with all three mothers today. We discussed mental illnesses and the possibility that their daughter's jumped. I already had probable cause to believe that Haddie Taylor and Anneka Wilson jumped. The one that left doubt in my mind was Kiera Barnes. It was revealed today that

Kiera had been struggling with an eating disorder for the past two years. There is a direct correlation between anorexia nervosa and depression. Once the cat was out of the bag, Vivian Barnes came to terms with reality – that her daughter might have been struggling and never told anyone. That the three of them had talked about it and decided to end their lives together. It's very tragic," Ethan said. "That all three were suffering and did not seek help. I wish I had a better answer for you. And I wish that this case turned out differently, despite the popular opinion that this was suicide. I explored all avenues. There were no solid suspects, no evidence of foul play. Any leads that we did acquire proved fruitless. Everyone was accounted for in class which meant that no one else was on the roof that day. Just the three girls." It was quiet in the room as all five of them took in this information. Finally, Jason closed the file and placed it on his desk. "Well done then," he said. "It is very tragic, yes. I am deeply saddened that it had to come to this. But at least we can all sleep well tonight knowing that there is no killer in Briarwood."

Ethan, Kennedy, and Jesse were sitting in the coffee shop, going over the last twelve days. From the moment that they were called to Briarwood: going door-to-door, interviewing neighbors and students, discovering Haddie's pregnancy, talking with Bethany Campbell, Oliver Harris, and Bentley Carter.

They went over all the possible theories, even the far-fetched devil worship idea implemented by Hal Davis. They compared notes, went over things twice, three times, just to be sure. When they finally finished, nearly two hours had gone by and the answer was conclusive. The girls killed themselves.

"It's depressing," Kennedy said. "Part of me hoped that they were pushed simply because the other option is almost too much to bear." "Suicide is worse than homicide then?" Jesse asked her. "Well, yeah," Kennedy said. "It's one thing to kill somebody else. But to kill yourself — with your two best friends? That's horrible." It was silent again. They sipped their coffees.

Ethan was going over everything in his head. The look on the mother's faces when they finally realized the truth. All the people he had spoken to over the past week. The fortune teller, the teachers, Dr. Meredith Kepler. He accepted the fact that he would never truly find out what happened around the third of May – why Haddie broke things off with Bentley Carter.

He figured she must have found out about the pregnancy around then. It scared her. She broke it off with Bentley and retreated to the comfort of Oliver. But even that wasn't enough for her. She was driven to the edge – literally.

Ethan thought about Cloe Wilson and Kelsey Barnes – how they would never see their sisters again. How Cloe picked up on the small details. The way Kelsey had noticed her sister's change in behaviour and discovered her secret relationship with Oliver. He thought about the bag of marijuana in Anneka's art room. Kiera's diary, kept hidden in her bookshelf. The fortune teller ticket in Haddie's closet.

It was as he was thinking about his search through Haddie's room that he remembered one specific detail: her walls – covered in hearts.

"She loved love or something?" he had asked Renée. "Oh, that," she took the book from Ethan's hands. "Her initials are HART, so she puts it everywhere, metaphorically. As though she is the heart. HART. Haddie Anne

Renée Taylor." Ethan nodded his head. "I see." She handed him the book and he placed it back on her desk.

HART. It was a symbol and it was her name. It all clicked together for him at once. SAD wasn't short for something and it wasn't an abbreviation. It was a name. The Sad Killer was leaving behind his initials.

Chapter Nineteen

CHAPTER NINETEEN

ONE MONTH LATER

Ethan had been busy all week. There were a series of bank robberies happening throughout the downtown core of Riverton. The three masked men caught on security footage were smart and vigilant. They were in and out in under sixty seconds each time, not leaving a hair particle or a finger print behind.

On top of that, there was a stabbing in the north end of the city. A nineteen-year-old male was found dead on the corner of McQuay and Lawrence two nights prior, no money or identification on him. A Jason Doe. Once fingerprints were taken, it was discovered that the identity of the kid was Holden Scott. His family had reported him missing four months prior. But because he was nineteen and a legal adult, on top of the fact that he was into drugs and dealing, the police didn't take his disappearance seriously. And now he was dead.

It had to be gang related, Ethan thought. Either that, or he was working the black market in Riverton. This ranged from drugs, to illegal tobacco, to human trafficking.

Ethan and his team had arrested a guy earlier this year who was believed to be running one of the operations. He was bringing in illegal immigrants and selling them off to the highest bidder. Perhaps Ethan would start with him. Pay Reagan Knight a little visit in prison and see if he knew anything about the kid.

It couldn't have just been a random stabbing – not after he'd been missing for four months. Either he ran away and got himself involved in that business, or they took him and threatened his life if he tried to leave. Kids these days feel hopeless, as though they don't have a choice. They turn to the streets in hope of something new – a better life, perhaps. But the streets don't do them any good. It swallows them whole and only spits them out again when they either can't take it any longer, or they're dead. In Holden Scott's case, it cost him his life.

Despite being kept busy with the plethora of cases he was currently working, there were still remnants of the previous month lingering in Ethan's mind. Haddie, Kiera, and Anneka. How he felt so uneasy about concluding their deaths and closing the case. And then there was The Sad Killer – a man who was never caught, another cold case added to the collection that would probably never be solved.

Following that afternoon in the coffee shop when Ethan had his sudden realization, he rushed back over to Gus Fraser's place to tell him about the initials. It was a good theory, Gus had told him. They went through everything. Files, records, phone books, data, surveys, medical records. They scoured through it all in search for their needle in a haystack. For that one person with the initials SAD that fit their profile.

There were a few contenders that they checked out. First was a man named Samuel Archer Duncan. He was even a war-vet who fought in WW2. But as it turned out, Samuel was in Denmark visiting family for the summer when the murders took place.

Then there was Stanley Arthur Douglas. He would have been forty-three at the time, a husband and father of three. But there was no correlation to any of the victims. And he had died twenty-five years ago, so even if he was the unsub, they would never be able to prove it.

One of the other men of consideration was Stephen Alexander Davis, Officer Hal Davis's father. Not only did Hal swear up and down that his father wasn't the infamous Sad Killer, but it wouldn't have logically made sense anyway. Stephen Davis was only fourteen in 1965.

Their last lead was Shane Anthony Darbyshire – Mike Darbyshire's younger brother. Ethan and Gus had thought it was a good lead. Perhaps the unsub was hiding under their noses all along. The brother of one of the victims – why didn't they think of it before? But when they tracked Shane down and spoke with him, they realized why he could never be the killer. Besides the fact that he expressed his sincerest love and devotion to his late brother, Shane had been wheelchair-bound since he was sixteen. There was no possible way he could have committed any of the murders.

Ethan and Gus investigated for as long as they could. Ethan drove into Briarwood as often as he was able, permitted his caseload wasn't too busy in Riverton. Frank had told him several times to drop it and let it be, but Ethan refused to give up. Not when they were so close.

But eventually, after another seven days of searching with barely anything else to go on, he needed to call it quits. Not because he necessarily wanted to, but because things were getting busy in Riverton. They needed Ethan's full attention. And with no other leads to follow, and no outstanding information that would take them any further, he couldn't justify his time there any longer. He packed up the files, said farewell to Gus Fraser, and headed back to Riverton.

It had been three weeks since then and the case was hardly on his mind anymore. Although it would be a lie to say any thoughts of The Sad Killer had been eradicated completely. He still thought about it every now and then. The what ifs and could haves. He wondered to himself if anyone out there would ever solve the case. If justice would be brought to Briarwood. Or if The Sad Killer would remain a mystery forever, going down in the history books with none other than the likes of The Zodiac Killer and Jack the Ripper.

Other than the multiple cases that were currently on his plate, things in Ethan's life were getting back to normal. Jordan had spent the past week shopping, filling the house with new furniture. They had been talking about re-doing the place for a while, but it was never a good time. Then again, when was it ever a good time for renovations?

With Ethan's busy work schedule and Jordan's hectic life with the magazine, neither of them could find time to settle this thing and begin organizing. But it was almost July now, and with the nice weather would come the renovations.

Jordan had taken charge and Ethan was okay with that. Yes, she was bossy and controlling, but someone had to do it. She had picked out a beige colour for the living room, the kitchen would need new tiles and a marble counter top for the island, and the old cabinets would be ripped out and replaced with new ones.

She had been on a shopping spree that week. She found everything either on discount or thrifted. She brought home a new couch for the living room, a coffee table, and new curtains. For the bedroom, she found a mahogany stained dresser and two matching night stands to go on each side of the bed. The room looked great and everything was coming along smoothly. There were even some nights when Ethan could go to sleep and not be haunted by the faces of the three dead girls.

It was Thursday evening. Jordan had taken the day off from work and Ethan, surprisingly, had finished early. They were set up at the kitchen table, sipping red wine and going through old pictures. Jordan had bought three new photo albums and was in the process of transferring all of her photos from the past twenty-nine years into them.

Ethan was assisting her, sorting through the photographs by date and organizing them into sections. Not only did Jordan have every single photograph from her own childhood, but she had kept photos from her parent's generations as well. There were tons of her siblings, her parents, and her father when he was a kid.

Ethan especially enjoyed nights like these, simply staying in and spending time with Jordan. There was never that expectation for them to go out and do spectacular things. Sure, they'd go out on occasion, dress up nice, see their friends. But the majority of their time spent together was quite mundane, and that's how Ethan liked it. Jordan didn't require fancy things or have expensive tastes – she was a simple girl, minimalistic at best.

He watched her as she sorted through the albums, eyes cast downwards, focused. She reached for her wine glass and took a sip. She was so beautiful, he thought, without even trying. Effortlessly.

Ethan was flipping through the pages, occasionally laughing at photos of Jordan as a baby, an empty bucket on her head. Another of her and her siblings, standing naked together with the chicken pocks.

"We thought they were cute," Jordan said, snatching the photo from Ethan. "Clearly so did my mother." Ethan laughed. "What is inherently cute about red bumps covering your entire body?" Jordan shrugged. "We called them Chicken Farms. Mommy, mommy, we all have the Chicken Farms!" Ethan laughed again. "I don't think I've ever had the chicken pox." "You're not safe then. You could still get them you know." "I have all my vaccinations," he winked. She rolled her eyes and flipped to another page. Ethan did the same and came across an old black and white photo. "Who's this?" he asked, holding up the photo. Jordan glanced over at it. "That's Gran and the kids. Look how funny my dad looked." Ethan examined the photo closely. "You look just like her here." "Who, Gran?" "Yeah, she was beautiful." "She was. Still is." "Your dad kind of looks like you did when you were a kid," Ethan remarked. "Are you saying I looked like a boy? Or he looked like a girl?" "You looked like a boy." Jordan punched him in the arm. "You know," she started. "People always thought that Tommy and I were twins. But they thought I was a boy. One time my mom had me and Tommy out, before Ella was born, and Tommy was in his little shirt and shorts, and I was in a little dress with a bow in my hair. Mind you, I barely had any hair, but still. A woman walking by said to my mother, 'awe, he's so adorable.' She was referring to me." Ethan laughed. "I told you." She rolled her eyes. "Whatever. Do I still look like a boy now?" "No," he said, staring into her eyes. "You most certainly don't." "Then that's all that matters."

Ethan flipped the page and found more photos of Jordan's father and his siblings, along with their mother, Gran Susie. She truly was stunning back in the day. It was difficult to believe that this was the same frail old woman they had dinner with last month.

He took the photo out of the seal and flipped it over to put into the pile of photos being transferred into the new album. That's when he saw the names written on the back.

Susie, Tommy, Lily, and Dave. 1978

"Why is her name written like that?" Ethan said to Jordan as he held up the photo for her to see. "With the A capitalized?" Jordan looked at it and shrugged. "She always wrote her name like that."

Ethan nodded, placing the photo back in the pile. He continued going through the photos. He was in Susie territory now. All of the photos in this section were black and white, from the 1960's onward. Ethan was trying to look for small details, seeing if there was any sign of Briarwood. But then he remembered what Susie had said previously – that she had left town when she was young and met her husband, Jack.

Something was churning in Ethan's mind that he couldn't quite put his finger on. He began flipping through the pages feverishly, scanning over each photograph. He took the photos out of their seals and read the backs of every single one, seeing the same thing over and over again. His pulse quickened. He looked up and faced Jordan.

"Jordan," he said, grabbing her attention. "What's Gran Susie's last name?" "Same as mine," she said nonchalantly as she flipped to another page. "Hopkins." "No," Ethan said, staring at her intently. "Her maiden name." Jordan put the photo album down and thought for a moment. Then she turned and looked at Ethan. "Dennicker. Her maiden name was Dennicker."

CHAPTER TWENTY

Ethan was driving down the main strip of Riverton, his foot on the gas, his mind racing. He had left behind a dazed and perplexed Jordan, sitting at the kitchen table calling after him as he dropped everything and raced out the front door. He didn't know what any of this meant. All he knew was that he needed to see Susie Dennicker – now.

As he was driving, he got a call through his Bluetooth. The screen read Kennedy Cross. "O'Riley," he said, keeping both hands on the wheel. "Ev, its KC. Where are you?" "Driving." "Can you come to the station?" "Uh, I'm a little busy right now. Is it urgent?" The line was quiet for a moment. "It's about the triple suicides from last month," Kennedy said. "New information has been brought to my attention," she paused. "I'm not so sure that it was suicide after all." Ethan's pulse quickened. What did she find?

"I'll be there in half an hour. I just need to take care of something first."

He arrived at Susie's apartment building. He had been there with Jordan a couple times in the past, visiting Gran, helping her move furniture. He entered the lobby and found her name on the wall: S. Hopkins. He checked his watch – it was quarter to nine. He rang the buzzer and prayed that she answered.

Sure enough, her raspy voice echoed through the speaker. "Hello?" "Gran," Ethan said, nearly out of breath. "It's me, Ethan. Can I come up?" "Oh, hello Ethan. Is Jordan with you?" "No, she's uh," he paused. "She's at home." "Oh," she sounded caught off guard. "Is everything alright?" "Everything's fine," Ethan said. "I just wanted to talk with you, if that's okay." "Of course," Susie said. "Come on up." The buzzer sounded and the door unlocked.

Ethan went inside and headed straight for the elevator. He waited and waited as each number lit up, taking it's time coming back down to the main floor.

Finally it arrived and Ethan ran in, pressing the number eight, Susie's floor. Another man was in the elevator with him. The silence was unconformable as Ethan tapped his foot on the ground and stared at the numbers above, moving slower than ever. The elevator stopped at the fifth floor and the man exited. Ethan gave him a slight nod and felt relief as the doors closed again.

The eighth floor, finally. The doors opened and he rushed into the hallway, down to Susie's door. He knocked twice and waited.

"Come in," he heard her voice call from inside. He turned the handle – it was unlocked. He opened the door and slowly entered the apartment. He closed the door behind him and scanned the room. Susie was sitting in her wheelchair over by the window. A candle was burning – it smelt like vanilla – and leftovers from dinner were sitting on the counter. "Ethan," she smiled, taking in his appearance. "What a surprise." "Hi Susie," he said as he took a few steps closer. She remained in her wheelchair, not making an attempt to come over and greet him in any way. He stopped in the center of the room and stared at her. Analyzing her face, her expression, her old hands resting on the wheelchair. It was silent, neither one of them making an effort to say anything. Finally, Susie spoke and broke the silence. "What do I owe the pleasure?" Ethan cleared his throat, a thousand thoughts racing through his mind. "Was it you?" She stared at him defiantly, her eyes flickering to his. An eternity passed between them before she spoke. Finally, she said, "I've been waiting for this day. I've been waiting a very long time." Something inside of Ethan broke at that moment. He could feel his heart physically sink in his chest, a pit growing in his stomach. "I didn't expect you to figure it out," Susie said cautiously. "When you mentioned it back at Jordan's birthday dinner, I figured you were just playing around, trying to distract yourself from other cases. No one has solved that mystery for over fifty-one years. Why would you be any different?" Ethan didn't say anything. He didn't move, didn't breathe. "But here you are," she said enthusiastically. "Congratulations, Detective. You finally cracked the case. You solved something that no one else ever could. You unveiled the true identity of the infamous Sad Killer." "It's you," he said the words aloud, testing them in his mouth, seeing how they would sound. "You're The Sad Killer." She smiled and he could see how old she truly was. Her dyed hair was graying at the roots, the lines on her face evident. Yet still, she was only seventy-five. And she looked good for her age. "Are you proud of yourself?" she said to him. Ethan didn't respond. He stared at her. She stared back. "Why did you do it?" he finally said. "Kill all those men?" "You know why," she said. "You must have figured it out or else you wouldn't be here." "Actually," Ethan said. "I forgot about the case. I let it be, just like those girls. I figured some things would never be solved. But it was you," he said. "You gave yourself away, signing your name like that on the pictures. Did you think that no one would put the pieces together? Why would you leave a trail like that?" "You mean the capitalized A?" she asked. Ethan nodded. She laughed. "How clever of you. What were you doing – going through Jordan's things?" "We're renovating," Ethan said. "She had me sorting through the photo albums." "And I'm assuming you figured it out before then. What SAD stood for." "A name. We tried everything. Short forms, abbreviations – none of it made sense. And then it all clicked for me. Because of Haddie Taylor and those hearts. It all came to me," he said. "But of course, I couldn't be sure. Just like many things, it was up in the air, unverified, pure speculation. I assumed it was a name, a signature of sorts. The killer leaving a bit of themselves behind. We found a couple of people with those initials, but nothing panned out. Why did you do it? Leave your initials?" "As a little reminder, not only to them, but to myself. For what I did. What I accomplished." "Why did you do it?" he asked again. "You know why." "I want you to tell me. I want you to say it." She stared at him and took in a deep breath. "They were bad men, Ethan. They deserved to die." "I know what they did," Ethan said. "But what did they do to you?"

Chapter Twenty-One

CHAPTER TWENTY ONE

I was born and raised in Briarwood. My family had lived there for many years after my mother emigrated from Germany. It was a quaint town, far enough away from the rest of civilization to go undetected, but still within enough proximity to get where you needed to.

As far as I could tell, there was nothing wrong with Briarwood. It had about three restaurants and two grocery stores during my time there. It was right on the lake, which brought in a lot of attraction during the summer months. Fishing was big there. Water-skiing and tubing too. When we were kids, we'd swim out as far as we could go, which didn't prove to be all that far in the end. They kept the buoys out there so that we knew our limits. The lake froze over in the winter and people would go skating, play hockey, ride their snowmobiles. Only once or twice did someone fall through the ice and perish.

Speaking of deaths, there wasn't all that much. The leading cause of death in Briarwood was old-age. People lived there, they grew old there, and then they died there. It was a safe town, a good community. We all worked together, got along, went to school together. If you needed help with something, you asked your neighbor. Everyone was like that in Briarwood. Kind and willing to lend a hand.

I attended Briarwood Public School. There were only six other girls in my first-grade class, so from the beginning I was used to being a minority. As I grew older, I came to realize what my role in the world would be: wife and mother. There weren't that many job opportunities in Briarwood, especially for women. Not unless you wanted to travel far and commute to cities like Riverton or Oakville. So that meant that people stayed where they were. The men owned the shops, worked in the factories, created their own businesses. The women attended school, but then after graduating, they began their role as a woman. It was almost as if it were a prerequisite to a happy life. Find a suitable man, get married, and start a family. All in that order. As if it were so easy – neat and organized into this tiny, pre-prepared package.

My parents were not well-off like some of the families in Briarwood. They divorced when I was only ten, which was a rare thing back then. My father had girlfriends throughout the years, but nothing permanent. My mother remarried two years later to a man named Paul Monoghan. Ah, a name you might be familiar with. We'll get into that later.

Due to the fact that my parents were separated, money was sparse. I had to drop out of school in the eleventh grade and get a job in order to contribute to the household. My brothers and sisters had to follow suit and get jobs as well. None of us graduated from secondary school.

Yet still, I had high hopes for Briarwood. It was a beautiful place. Tourists often missed it because it was so small and off the map, but those who did find it were mesmerized. I can't describe to you the exact novelties that Briarwood possessed, for one would need to see it for themselves to realize the true beauty. Whether it be the lake, the small cottages, the poppy fields, or Hazel Street. I was in love with my town.

When I was young, a close friend of my father was killed in a car accident. His wife and two children died as well. It was a drunk driver who was going far above the speed limit and t-boned them while running a stop sign. My father was haunted by their deaths, tortured by how instantaneous it was. How in a split second, four lives were ended, and one continued on.

I was thirteen. My youngest sister was eight, the same age as the boy, Kyle Weller. My father was angered by the injustice of it all. How four innocent people lost their lives, and the one person responsible managed to walk free with just a head wound, a stained conscious, and a totalled car. No handcuffs, no criminal record, nothing.

When I was sixteen, the house across the street from mine burnt down. It was no accident. A man named Jason Morgan got drunk and set it ablaze, his two sons still inside.

Fortunately, Adam and Jason Jr. were able to escape the flames and make it out alive. However, their mother was not so lucky. She perished that day, and it will be a day I will never forget. I remember looking out my bedroom window that faced the street, seeing the smoke and the flames, calling for my mother and running down the front steps of our house.

Jason Jr. and Adam were lying on their front lawn, coughing, gasping for air. My mother called the police and the firetrucks and ambulance arrived shortly after.

Jason Morgan was never charged or penalized for what he did. He burnt down his house for no apparent reason and was responsible for the death of his wife.

But we will get to that eventually. You're clearly here for a reason, and I believe that reason is the catalyst to the killings. Let us begin then, shall we?

I was twenty-one when I first encountered Mark Irving. I'd been working as a waitress for the past few years, following my job as a cashier at the laundromat. The diner was nice. It was the place to be for people my age. We served everything from milkshakes and burgers, to steak and sandwiches. The music was hip, the scenery was inviting. Everyone loved coming there. Mark Irving loved coming there.

He came in on one night in particular. It was a Tuesday, I believe. I was wearing a yellow top with my apron tied around the front. He smiled at me and I recall that it was a charming smile, a flirtatious smile. He was attractive. And everything about Mark Irving was inviting.

I served him and his friends. They had all ordered burgers and shakes. I smiled as I took their orders, laughed with them as I brought them their food. They tipped me well. He winked at me before leaving.

It became a routine of his, coming into the diner. Part of me believed that it was to see me. But while I hoped that this was true, I also didn't want to be naïve. He was Mark Irving, after all. I knew who he was – everyone did. He was gorgeous, charming, wonderful. A real man.

One night, he struck up a conversation, had me laughing and twirling my fingers through my hair. He made me feel special, as though I mattered. Looking back now, I realize that I did matter. I always mattered, with or without Mark Irving.

Finally he made his move. Took him long enough. He asked me to dinner. I happily obliged. We met that Saturday at a restaurant called Polly's, which was one step up from the diner. It had a mellow vibe, classy and jazzy all at once.

We ordered our food and chatted the night away, laughing and confiding in each other. He paid for dinner. We left the restaurant. We got to his car and he offered me a drive home. Of course I accepted; why on earth would I walk home – at night – after an exceptional date with an exceptional man? Well, that is where things took a turn for the worst.

If I could go back in time, perhaps I would have declined that ride. Perhaps I would have avoided meeting Mark Irving altogether. That would have certainly changed the course of things to come. And then there would have been no killings and you wouldn't be here listening to this story.

But there is no time machine, and I cannot go back and change what happened that night. Rather, I can only look back and reflect upon these events that subsequently led to one catastrophic encounter that would alter not only my life forever, but the lives of many to follow.

I didn't see Mark Irving for a while after that night. I wasn't sure if he was avoiding me or not. Perhaps it was I who was avoiding everything. I didn't leave my bed for a week. My boss nearly fired me for not showing up to work for five consecutive days. I didn't know how to re-immerse myself into the world. Everything I had known and loved was damaged, shattered, nothing like before. I couldn't go back to that. I couldn't face myself, let alone anyone else.

Life was different after that night. There was a constant aching in my head. The pain only ceased when I closed my eyes and stopped breathing. And I was afraid. Not only of Mark Irving, but of everyone, everything. Any man who passed me on the street had my heart racing. A stranger, accidently bumping me in line at the grocery store. I would hear my own cries of protest, echoing throughout his car. His hands on my arms, my chest, my back. Strong hands. Willing hands. Threatening hands.

My own body became a strange and unfamiliar place that not even I could recognize. I became delirious. I didn't know what was reality and what was fiction. I developed dark bags underneath my eyes. I stopped going to work. Eventually I was fired. But that was okay. As long as I didn't have to leave my bed or see anybody, then it would all be okay.

Three years passed. I was twenty-four-years-old. I didn't know what I wanted to do with my life. My best friends were marrying off and having children. My father was getting ill with heart disease. My eldest brother was moving out of Briarwood with his new bride, ready to start a family. And then there was me, standing still, going through the motions of everyday life, but never really going anywhere. I was stuck. Trapped. I couldn't breathe, couldn't live. I didn't know how I was going to go on living a life like this.

And that's when he resurfaced – Mark Irving. When I saw him, all of the fear and anguish from my past came rushing back, full forced. He was thirty-two at the time, still not married, and still known as the town bachelor.

He was walking down the street by the grocery store I was in, his arm looped through another woman's. She was beautiful. Raven black hair, porcelain skin, bright blue eyes, a birth mark above her lip. She was the embodiment of everything I wished I was, everything I knew I could never be. Because no matter what I told myself or how hard I tried to turn my life around and become someone new, I couldn't. That part of me was ruined. The damage was irreversible. I was broken. He broke me. Mark Irving broke me.

I became envious of that woman, and not because her arm was linked through Mark's, but because her arm was linked through Mark's and she was so happy. Smiling, her lips parted. Her eyes wide and turned to him. How was she not aware of the evil he possessed? How could she walk with him, so care-free and effortless, and not realize what he was capable of? What he had done?

It was in that moment that I knew something had to change. I guess you could call this the catalyst moment – the moment I knew. I didn't know what I would do initially, but it became clear to me, there in that moment, that I needed to make a change. Something needed to be done.

I believe the desire to murder Mark Irving was always inside of me, from that very night in his car. But the ambition and the actuality of it all wasn't there. It was always subconscious, subtly in the back of my mind. Slowly brewing and manifesting, becoming something bigger than itself. I took one more look at him and my desires were confirmed. In order to end his tirade, I would need to end his life. I would need to kill Mark Irving.

And thus began the planning. The months and months of meticulous planning. The doubts and second thoughts, the worries and anxieties of what would happen, the thought of getting caught, the fear of what would happen to me afterwards. Would I be changed forever? Would it damage me more than I already was? How would I be able to live with myself knowing that I took another person's life?

I pushed those thoughts and worries away. My life wouldn't get any worse than it already was. I needed to focus. With one goal on my mind, it became easier to deal with. It would be simple, I convinced myself. I would need to watch him, study his moves. Memorize his frequent locations, determine when would be the best time to strike. And this is how I would do it: I would doll myself up, spray a bit of perfume on my neck, and knock on his door. He would smile at me, perhaps say, hey, don't I know you from somewhere? And I would lavish in saying the words, why yes, Mark. You raped me in the back of your car three years ago. Do you remember me now?

I felt giddy with anticipation. I was really going to do it. I was going to kill him. And it wasn't necessarily the act of killing that excited me, rather, the finality of ending his life once and for all. The realization that what I was doing was just. And when I was finished, he wouldn't be able to hurt anyone else ever again. It would finally be over. And perhaps then I could finally get some sleep at night.

But let me fast forward to the good part. It was April 23, 1965. I knew from my studies that Mark would be out at the bar with a few of his friends before returning to his home around eleven or twelve. I waited.

I wore a dress that sat just below my knees, a spring jacket overtop since it was still cool out. I had done my hair and makeup, sprayed some perfume on my neck. I slipped on a pair of flats and placed the knife in my purse. I had taken it from my father's work bench. He never noticed it was missing.

Mark stumbled home around quarter after eleven. He was slightly buzzed, and by the looks of things, tired. Because if he wasn't tired, he wouldn't have been coming home alone.

He unlocked his door and hobbled inside. The coast was clear. It was my opportunity to strike.

I strutted across his front lawn with poise and confidence. Any onlookers watching would simply see a pretty young woman going to see Mark Irving. No surprise there. I knocked twice and waited. He answered after a moment.

"Hi there," he breathed, a haze in his eyes. "Hi," I smiled at him. "May I come inside?" He looked me up and down, heel to head. "Course you can, miss," he took a step backwards and welcomed me into his home without hesitation. He locked the door behind us. "Do I know you from somewhere?" he asked, a sly grin on his face. I blushed. "I don't believe so," I said. "But I saw you at the bar tonight. I wanted to come introduce myself. I'm Suzanna," I stuck out my hand. He shook it. "Mark," he said. "Mark Irving."

He led me to his living room. The television was buzzing quietly in the background. One of the windows on the main floor was open, allowing a cool breeze to enter the house. It provided a tranquil feeling of relief over my body that had become hot and fuzzy with anxiousness and anticipation. It would also become my escape route.

He offered me a drink and I declined. I needed to stay clear-headed. He shrugged and got himself a beer. I was unsure if Mark Irving was seeing a lady at this time, but that night, it didn't matter. She didn't matter. Because that was the type of man that Mark was. He only cared about himself, his own needs.

I didn't want to be there too long. He was taking his time, sipping his drink, making small talk. I slid towards him, closer to his seat on the couch. He smiled at this, invited me closer. And that's when I knew it was time. I reached my hand into my purse as slowly and carefully as I could. He didn't notice, of course. His eyes were locked on mine. And that's when I said it.

"You don't remember me at all, do you?" He turned his head slightly, trying to focus on my face. "I thought you looked familiar," he said. I smiled. "But you don't remember that night, do you?" He laughed. "Oh, don't tell me we've hooked up. And I've forgotten?" "Even worse," I said, keeping my eyes locked on his. "Three years ago you took me out on a date," I said. He lowered his beer from his lips. "It was wonderful, actually. You were quite the gentlemen. That was, until we got to your car." His expression changed then. A slow recognition finally settling upon his face.

And that's when I did it. I drew my hand backwards and shoved the knife into his chest with full force. He jolted backwards, his hand releasing the bottle of beer instinctively at the shock. I knew I had to act quickly. He was bigger than I was, and stronger. If I didn't weaken him soon, he would overpower me.

So I withdrew the knife from his chest and stabbed him again. And again. I stabbed him seven times until I felt it was safe to stop.

He was gasping for air, trying to say my name. Reaching for my face, my hands, anything. Grabbing at me, trying to stop me. I felt panicked; it was that night all over again. His hot breath on my neck, his hands on my arms. I pulled away from him and watched as he began to crumble.

His hands were on his own body now, holding his chest, trying to stop the blood from oozing out. But it was no use. There were too many entry wounds. He was bleeding out. I'd punctured a vital organ.

He was making these unearthly sounds. Animalistic, almost. It was frightening yet satisfying all at once. He fell backwards, then sideways, and slid off the couch.

I don't know how long it took him to die, but I stood there and watched until I was sure he had stopped breathing. Once he was dead, I removed the black marker from my bag. And right there beside him on the floor, where his dead body lay and his blood seeped through the cracks of the tiles, I wrote my initials: SAD.

I don't know what it was exactly that caused me to do that. I hadn't planned that from the beginning. It was sudden, spur of the moment. It was almost as if I wanted to take credit for the work I had completed, like an artist leaving a signature on their painting. I didn't want to be caught, but I wanted something for myself. A reminder of what I had been through and what I accomplished. And in a way, it was one last fuck you to the man who had ruined my life. Beside his dead body would indefinitely be my name: Susie Dennicker.

It never started off as a hit-list, as you can clearly see. Never once did I think I would become what people refer to as a serial killer. Nor did I know that I would become the infamous Sad Killer. It all came effortlessly.

It was as though once I got a taste of vengeance, I needed more. It felt good. And again, please do not think me sick for killing these men — these human beings who everyone claimed innocent. Because they were not innocent. They were bad men. Terrible men. Despicable human beings.

It was the act of righting wrongs, avenging the people who needed it. Bringing justice and vengeance to those who had gotten away with it for so long.

It didn't take long to decide who would be next. I never intended for there to even be a next. But once I got that first taste, I couldn't stop. And so who did I choose? It would be none other than the drunk driver, of course. The seventeen-year-old boy who got away with murder. Who had too much to drink and recklessly made the decision to drive. Who, in turn, killed a family of four. Who brought havoc and misery to so many people. He had destroyed lives, ruined families. He needed to be taught a lesson. He needed to die.

Due to his age at the time of the accident, nobody knew who the boy was. But I was determined to figure it out. After a bit of digging and a trip down to the precinct, I finally had a name: Mike Darbyshire.

Mike was now twenty-seven, ten years since that fatal night. He was young and free-spirited, happy and content. Everybody loved Mike, just as everyone loved

Mark. Nobody knew the truth about either one of them, and that is what bothered me the most. That these men had gotten away with indisputable acts and no one had even batted an eye.

It was three weeks later when I finally made my move on May 7, 1965. I didn't choose that date accidentally, and quite frankly, given my timeline, I would have preferred to wait a tad bit longer before my next kill. But it was the anniversary of their deaths for Christ sake. The ten year anniversary. Mike's death needed to carry significance. He needed to understand that what he did was wrong and that there were consequences to his actions.

That night, I began my routine. I dressed up nice and did my hair. The weather was warmer now. I wore a strapless dress, even put on some heels. I was more experienced now. I would know what to do, how to behave, how to execute my plans thoroughly.

But this time went a bit differently. I met him at the restaurant, flirted my way to his table. He had a few drinks. We laughed, talked about our lives. He told me about his childhood. I made up a childhood I never had. He never noticed.

We went back to his place, my arm linked through his. We sat in his kitchen talking for a long time. He didn't make a move on me until nearly forty-five minutes had passed. I appreciated that. At least he wasn't a pig like Mark Irving.

He led me to his bedroom. I took his hands in mine. Then I pushed him backwards onto the bed and straddled him. But before I gave him the chance to kiss me, I began to speak.

"Do you know what day it is today?" I said to him light-heartedly. He seemed confused. "What?" he laughed from beneath me. "The date," I said. "What day is it today?" He thought for a moment. "Friday May seventh," he said. "Very good," I smiled. "And do you know what happened on this day, ten years ago?" He tried to sit up but I pushed him back down. He stared at me, his eyebrows furrowed. "I'll give you a hint," I whispered, getting closer to his ear. "Your accident." He pulled away from me suddenly. His face was contorted into a look I did not recognize. "What are you talking about?" "You killed them," I said. "Craig and Karen Weller and their two children, Joanie and Kyle." He stared at me, awestruck. And before he could say anything else, the pillow was over his face.

I pressed down as hard as I could. He was struggling underneath me. It proved more difficult than I had initially predicted. But I held my ground. I pushed down as hard as I could, thinking about the Weller's and how they died, knowing that I was doing the right thing.

His body was jerking feverishly, grasping at anything he could. If it wasn't for the alcohol in his system rendering him weak, he surely would have overpowered me.

I straddled him harder and pushed the pillow further into his face. At one point I almost believed that he would knock the pillow away and free himself – and then what would I do? Run away? Scream for help? He would know what I tried to do. I would be charged with attempted murder.

I couldn't let that happen, couldn't let him get away with it. So I kept pushing, kept holding on for as long as I could.

It wasn't long before his body ceased and his muscles relaxed. His arms dropped to the side, motionless. Yet still, I held the pillow longer, with all my might, just in case. I couldn't be too sure.

After another minute or so, I removed the pillow and had a look at his face. His eyes were closed and his mouth was slightly ajar, a tiny pool of saliva dripping from his mouth. I reached my two fingers towards his neck and felt for a pulse. There was nothing.

I placed the pillow gently on the bed next to him, unhooked my legs from around his body, and stood. On the wall, I scribbled one word.

I know what you're wondering: was the pillow my plan all along? It seems quite spontaneous, if you ask me. But yes, the pillow was in the plan all along. Because although stabbing Mark Irving had brought me great satisfaction, it was risky. There was so much blood. And it was tiring, I must admit. Stabbing a man seven times – it took a lot out of me. So while I was planning Mike's death, I was brainstorming other ideas. Other modes of killing that might prove easier.

Suffocation seemed straight-forward, and I wouldn't even need to bring the murder weapon. It would already be there, at his place.

I cleaned up as best as I could, took one last look at Mike Darbyshire, and headed out the window. It was becoming my new favourite way to leave a man's house.

The next was Patrick Brooks. Let's rewind three years prior to the death of Mike. After getting fired from my job at the diner, I became desperate, looking for any job I could find to make money. My mother had told me about a man named Patrick Brooks who needed an occasional sitter for his two children, Angela and Joey. Of course I inquired and was met by a wonderful man who was happy and relieved to have found a sitter. He explained to me how his wife had recently left him and he was all alone with the children. I understood and empathized with him. My parents separated when I was young, so I knew more than anyone how difficult it could be on a single parent. Little did I know that he was the very reason that his wife left in the first place; a bruised eye and a broken rib to boot.

He didn't need me often, only on the odd night that he went out, or when he had a busy work schedule during the day. I enjoyed spending time with Joey and Angela, they were good kids, kind and gentle. We would play hide and seek around the house, solve puzzles, play board games. I'd tell them stories about other worlds and they would get lost in them, imagining themselves in a faraway land.

It didn't take me long to realize the undisclosed abuse that was happening in the Brooks' household. Patrick was a very good actor. I had seen men like him before. How they were able to put on a phony smile and show their charm, all while beating their wife and children behind closed doors.

It was a difficult thing to come to terms with. Mind you, this was two and a half years before I began my act of vengeance on Mark Irving, so I was unsure of how to proceed with the situation. Of course, I could never prove anything. I couldn't go to the police and risk having the children's father taken away from them on a false claim – that would ruin their lives.

But I was so sure, so certain about what he was doing to them. Their behaviour, his mood swings. The odd bruise on the arm, or cut on the leg, dismissed as falls and accidents. It made me sick how easily the children learned to lie for him. But there was nothing I could do about it. Until the summer of 1965, that is. Once Mark and Mike were taken care of, I knew who had to be next.

I hadn't sat for them in a while as Patrick felt that Angela, at the age of ten, was old enough to look after herself and her brother. It had been about seven months since I had last been around their place and my body was buzzing with nerves the night I went over there. I waited until just after nine p.m. when I knew the children would be in bed. Then I knocked on the front door and waited for Patrick to answer.

He opened the door and was surprised to see me. I smiled. He invited me inside.

He asked how I was doing, executing a phenomenal performance of the caring man, the hardworking dad trying to support his children. I told him what was new with me: that I was looking for a new job for the summer and was wondering if he needed me at all. He told me he didn't, but would keep in touch in case the odd out of town job came up where he needed someone to watch the children.

I didn't chat with him for too long; the small talk was irritating my head and I wanted to get it over with. I had already chosen my modus operandi – a garrote. It came down to the decision being between a cable tie and a rope, but I ultimately decided on the latter. In my mind, that was easier.

We were sitting at the kitchen table. I stood up and walked behind him. Perhaps he thought I was going to get a drink of water, so he didn't pay much attention or turn around. I didn't want to risk my perfect opportunity by speaking and catching him off guard, although deep down I wanted to so badly. To be able to tell him that I knew what he was doing. To make him see the kind of horrible man he was and let him know that he was getting exactly what he deserved. But instead, I kept my mouth closed. Once I was behind him, I put the rope around his neck and pulled.

His hands were up in an instant, clawing at my hands and arms. I stood my ground, holding my body as far away as I could from his. He was kicking, jolting in the chair, gasping for air. More noises erupted from his throat. I listened to the sound of Patrick Brooks choking to death.

Finally, after a few moments, his body ceased and went limp. I waited longer before reaching forward and feeling for a pulse. There wasn't one. I then dragged his one-hundred-and-ninety pound body to his bedroom and plopped him in his bed. I didn't want the children walking into the kitchen the next morning and seeing that. At least when they found him, he would presumptuously still be asleep. Angela would call the police, and they would take it from there.

I looked at Patrick as he laid on the bed. His eyes were still open and I left them that way. I searched inside myself for any feeling of remorse or guilt for what I had done, but it was difficult to find any. He was a terrible man. A wife beater. A child abuser. Those poor kids couldn't go on like that, living in secret, hiding what was happening to them from the outside world.

Of course it would be hard for them – there was no doubt in my mind of that. And if anything, I felt for those children who would no longer have a father. But in due time, they would understand. They would come to appreciate the gift I had given them. For it was not the gift of life that mattered, rather, the gift of taking one away.

Three weeks after that on June 16, 1965 came who you refer to as victim four, but who I knew as Robert Baldwin.

Oh, Robert Baldwin. Perhaps one of my favourite kills of that summer. All of the men deserved what they got, but Robert was very deserving.

He was a charmer. Kind, friendly, a real gentleman. Everyone in Briarwood adored Robert Baldwin, including his wife, Flora. She was a sweet girl, only four years older than I was at the time. I had met her a few times around town, at social gatherings, the local pub. She was beautiful beyond belief with her white blonde hair and gemstone green eyes. He was older than her by fifteen years. It was a wonder by nearly everyone in Briarwood how she was chosen. How Flora became so fortunate to be married to Robert Baldwin. They were married six years when I ended his life.

It was the year prior when I first began noticing the signs. Flora and I weren't very close by any means, but I developed a knack for sensing the victim in people. Ever since that night with Mark Irving, it was as though I had a radar in my brain, and other victims radiated their griEthances. I was certain that no one else would be able to detect such a thing. Flora was always smiling – glowing, really. She was happy, hopeful, and radiant. She would talk about her marriage and how wonderful things with Robert were. But I didn't believe her. I knew she was lying. There was something in her eyes that gave her away. As though she were reading a script, or rehearsing lines.

It was mid-August of 1964 – the summer preceding his death – and a few of us were down by the lake having a few drinks. It was scorching that day, everyone was in their swimmers either in the lake or lounging on the rocks. I recall this day specifically because Flora Baldwin showed up in a long sleeve t-shirt. A few of the guys were teasing her, trying to get her to go in the lake, but she refused, said she was coming down with something. Everyone simply shrugged it off and allowed her to do her own thing, which consisted of sitting on the sidelines of conversations, watching silently and never speaking.

I realized, then, the severity of her situation. Because not only was he abusing her, but he was silencing her, taking away her voice. The poor darling couldn't speak, let alone go for a swim. He was killing her, slowly but surely, and nobody knew except me.

On June 16, 1965, I made my move. The weeks leading up to that night, I had studied and did my homework, as usual. I knew when Robert would be home and when Flora would be out. On this particular day, she happened to make a trip to the beach with some of her girlfriends. I knew that was my opportune time to strike. It would be one of the only times that she was out of the house, out of his sights. And he would be alone.

This was my earliest time yet, just after five-thirty p.m. The sun was still shining and the weather was warm. I didn't know how long I would have until Flora and her friends returned from the beach, so I made my move quickly.

Because of the situation, I had to change my method, once again. There was no relationship between Robert and me – no chance of easy proximity. The other victims simply let me into their homes because they either knew me, or wanted to. But Robert and I didn't know each other. And you may think that that would prove difficult, but clearly you do not know me.

I rang the doorbell and waited. Robert had a large home – larger than any of the other men's homes I'd been to that summer. There was a garden out front, I assumed where Flora did her planting, where she went to relax, her happy place. I pictured her kneeling in the garden, surrounded by flowers, a tear falling from her cheek, the bruises covering her arms. Anger bubbled up inside of me. I was ready.

Robert opened the door. He didn't know who I was. I told him that I was a friend of Flora's and that she had asked me to pick something up for her. He was a tad hesitant, but eventually let me inside. We began walking through the house, through the living room towards the hallway that would eventually lead to the stairs. I didn't have much time. I pulled the knife from my purse. He was walking in front of me, leading the way, his back to me. I walked closer towards him and in one quick motion, shoved the knife through his back where it would in turn puncture his heart.

He stopped moving. His body froze. He gasped for a breath and tried to turn around. I wouldn't allow him to. I kept the knife inside his body, holding it there for a long time. He dropped down to his knees, and still, I held the knife in place.

Finally, I removed it, slowly, wiping it with the napkin I had readily on hand. That was all. A single stab wound through the heart. Nothing too sadistic or violent. That would be unnecessary and reckless, and reckless led to being caught.

I then walked in front of him. He was crumbling on the floor, both hands clutching his chest. The blood was exuding through his fingers, dripping from his hands to the carpet below him. I stood there staring at him. He looked up and we made eye contact. He was gasping for air, trying to say something. One word: Why?

I knelt down so that we were at eye level. I did him the courtesy; I answered his dying question. I explained to him why I did what I did. I was doing it for Flora. I was doing it for all the women out there, for all the victims of abuse who were silenced and without a voice. I told him that he would no longer be able to hurt anybody. And that was all I needed.

Once his eyes closed and he collapsed to the floor, I checked his pulse. Then I grabbed the black marker from my bag and left my mark.

Surely you remember Jason Morgan? The man who burnt down his own house in 1957, killing his own wife? You probably know him more formally as victim number five.

It was July 1, 1965, the beginning of a new month, the peak of summer time in Briarwood. The sun was shining, the flowers were blooming, the lake was glistening. Everyone was enjoying themselves that day. Everyone except Jason Morgan.

After their house burnt down and their mother passed, Adam and Jason Jr. moved in with their aunt and uncle. They saw their father on occasion, but to be quite honest, I think the boys were scared of him – scared of their own father. Fearful of what he was capable of.

No one ever did find out what happened that day, what made Jason Morgan snap and set his house aflame. He was known to be a bit of a heavy drinker, and authorities believed that alcohol was involved. One too many and he grabbed the gasoline.

After the house burned down, Jason Morgan moved into one of the cottages down by the lake. It was where the elderly folks went to retire. Where people emigrated to when their spouse passed, or their children grew up and moved out. They were quaint little places, the cottages. A place where people went when they were alone.

Jason Jr. and Adam were twenty-five and twenty-three. They had moved on with their lives, found loving women to marry, and were beginning to settle down. To my knowledge, they hardly saw their father anymore, which would subsequently prove beneficial to me. No one would be with him. No one would notice – or care – when he was gone.

Around the time that I began my duties that summer, I knew in the back of my mind that Jason Morgan would be on that list. Just as I always knew that I would end with Paul Monoghan. But it wasn't necessarily that I planned each one out accordingly. One thing happened after another, and eventually, circumstances simply led me to each one. A chain reaction of events.

After Mark, Mike, Patrick, and Robert, I was feeling invincible, on top of the world. As though I could do anything and everything. I was powerful. I had finally regained all of the strength that had once been so selfishly taken from me. And let me tell you, it was a magnificent feeling.

The authorities were on the hot trail of the person who they were now calling The Sad Killer. It was catchy, I must admit. It was never my goal or intention to create a name for myself. I was simply doing my job, performing my tasks. The signature was of lesser importance. It was simply a final thought, a last act. But they ate it up, fiend over the signature, made a big commotion over it. The Sad Summer, it would later be called, referenced to multiple times in years to come. The man who got away with it.

As though a woman could not be capable of such a thing. This is what I was telling you about earlier. The women of Briarwood were invisible, unseen. No one paid attention to them. No one cared. As long as we remained in the kitchen with a ring on our finger and enough food in the fridge for dinner, no one was complaining.

It wasn't difficult killing Jason Morgan. I chose a day – a Sunday – the first of July. Everyone was out enjoying themselves, not paying any attention to the small cottage at the end of the row. I made my way over to his place, the method I would use swirling around my head. It would be perfect.

Now, given the circumstances of what he'd done to his family, the ideal way to end Jason Morgan's life would be to set his house on fire. It would be the perfect murder. A beautiful way to avenge the death of his wife and the damage he caused to his two sons. And it would be believable. He set his house ablaze eight years ago, and here he was again, history repeating itself.

But I couldn't ensure his death that way. And do you know how much work that would be? I'd need gallons of gasoline. I'd be putting myself at risk by being visible while I doused his house, both externally and internally. It simply would not work. I had a better idea instead.

I arrived at Jason Morgan's cottage-home and knocked on his door. I knew he would let me in, it was never a question. Every other man had let me into their homes thus far. That was the gift of being a woman. I was not threatening in any way. The perfect culprit. Unseen and invisible. Hiding in plain sight. The Black Widow of Briarwood.

He answered the door and took in my appearance. I asked if he remembered me from all those years ago. The girl that lived across the street from your house. The one you burnt down in 1957. Not those exact words, but he claimed to remember me. Once I mentioned my father, he was nodding, oh right, yes yes. The Dennicker girl.

The conversation came naturally. He offered me a tea and I declined. We sat on the couch, chatting about life and what he was doing living out here all alone in a cottage by the lake. As usual, I kept things brief, skipping ahead to the good part.

"Why did you do it?" I asked suddenly. "I'm sorry?" he was taken off guard. "Burn your own house to the ground. Kill Anna." He stared at me, wide eyed. "I," he opened his mouth. "That was a long time ago." "It was eight years, Jason," I said. "And because of you, she's never coming back. Anna will never have the opportunity to live the life she wanted. And your sons," I said. "Jason and Adam. You ruined their lives, destroyed everything they knew, diminished the small bit of happiness they had left. And for what? What did you accomplish?"

He remained silent, staring down at his hands. He was ashamed of himself. Disappointed. Remorseful. But none of that mattered. His emotions now didn't matter. The damage was already done. There was no changing that.

Before thinking about it any further, I removed the knife from my purse, and in one quick motion, shoved it into his chest. I slid the knife out and stabbed once more, aiming for his heart, just as I did with Robert Baldwin.

His eyes widened as he realized what was happening. He tried to lurch forward and grab me, so I pushed the knife further into his chest and twisted. He froze.

After another moment, I swiftly removed the knife and retreated from him, standing as quickly as I could. I watched as he clutched his chest, mumbling words that I couldn't understand. Something about why and how could you? Why are you doing this? Help me.

But I didn't help him. I stood there and watched, waiting for him to take his last breath and die. And I must admit, it took a while. God, that one took a while. But eventually his eyes fluttered closed and his breathing stopped. I slowly moved forward and checked for a pulse. There was nothing.

He died from blood loss. In my opinion, that was an easy way out – a polite way to end things. It could have been much worse. He could have suffered like his wife, gasping for air, dying from smoke inhalation and burning to death. He had it easy, and even then he didn't deserve easy.

Be patient, now, there are only two men left on this list. Do you want to hear about them or not?

The sixth was David Hill. He was thirty-eight-years-old when I ended his life on July 23, 1965.

I had my sights set on David for a while. Much like the other men I ridded society of, David Hill was a "good man." A hardworking husband, a proud father. But his wife and little girl didn't know the evil's he possessed. Nobody did. And that's what made him so dangerous.

David Hill was a classic con-man. I observed him from a far, pulling tricks and stealing money. He would make trips to the local thrift store, buy the cheapest jewelry he could find, then resell it to people for ten times the amount it was worth. And people fell for it. They bought it. And he made a huge profit from this business.

But that is not the reason I killed David Hill. Petty theft is one thing, not enough to kill a man for. No, what he did was far worse. And it was something that struck close to home for me.

He was eighteen-years-old when he raped Natasha Watts. She was two years younger, unsure of her place in the world. When a popular guy like David Hill showed interest in her, she was swooning. But much like Mark Irving and I, things did not end well for them.

I came across Natasha Watts years after the incident, when she was a cashier at the local bakery, age thirty-four. She was married and had two children. We bonded over our love of sourdough. Although she was ten years older than I was at the time, we got along splendidly. This was two years before I would avenge what David Hill did to her.

I would go to her place and see the kids, Millie and Jonah. Her husband was a good man, someone that she deserved. At the time that I became friends with Natasha, I was still trying to recover from my recent tragedy, and Natasha helped me with that. I opened up to her, told her about what happened to me that night with Mark Irving.

Her eyes were empathetic, her hands on mine. She wasn't just consoling me – she was connecting with me, resonating with everything I was telling her. It was after that that she revealed to me a similar thing had happened to her when she was just sixteen. A tragedy, really. It nearly ruined her life. She couldn't go to school. She became scared of everything and everyone around her. And when she finally did recover and immerse herself back into the world, she could not come in contact with men. She was fearful of them, fearful of what they were capable of.

She didn't date or have a boyfriend until she was twenty-three. By that time her PTSD had finally loosened its grips on her and allowed her to find love and happiness. Natasha met Antonio and the rest was history. They had Millie and Jonah. They moved into a beautiful house. And everything was right in her world again.

But I couldn't simply let go of what had happened to her. She told me his name – David Hill – and I kept it with me for two years, slowly turning it over in the back of my mind. By the time the summer of 1965 arrived, I knew my plans for David Hill. I knew that he needed to face a similar fate of Mark Irving.

I watched and waited. I memorized his schedule. I knew when his wife would be out with their six-year-old daughter, Poppy. And then I made my move, making my way to his front door.

I told him that I was friends with his wife. He smiled and let me inside. He told me she was at her sister's place for the day, but he would tell her that I dropped by. When he asked for my name, I had no reason to lie.

"Susie," I said. "Susie Dennicker."

He brought us two glasses of water and sat them down on the kitchen table, taking a seat on one of the chairs. Shortly after that was when I pulled out the rope. I brought it around his neck and pulled as hard as I could. And as I pulled, I spoke to him.

"This is for Natasha Watts," I said. "For what you did to her all those years ago. You didn't just rape her, David.

You took away her happiness. Prevented her from living her life. Scarred her in a way that no one should ever be scarred."

I pulled harder and he fought harder. His feet kicked backwards from the chair he was seated on and nearly tripped me. But I regained my balance and held my ground.

When it was over, I checked for a pulse to ensure that he was dead. Then I placed the rope neatly inside of my purse and took out the black marker.

Alas, we have finally come to the last one, the concluding chapter of my story, the final victim. Number seven, you call him. Paul Monoghan.

You might recall his name from the beginning of my story. Paul was married to my mother. After my parents separated, my mother was all by herself. She was working two jobs, trying to provide for us, as well as survive. She met Paul and all of her struggles seemed to disappear.

He was a nice guy. Friendly, approachable, willing to help. He charmed her and she fell for him. We all did, really. I was only twelve when my mother first introduced us to Paul. We all loved him. He brought us toys and candy whenever he came over. He would take my mother on dates, spoil her rotten. They were in love and I was so glad that my mother had finally found happiness again.

I was fourteen when the bruises first appeared. Fifteen when I finally took notice and realized what was going on, understood the severity of the situation. I had never witnessed abuse before, especially not first hand. I didn't understand. Paul was a great guy. He was always smiling and laughing. I couldn't understand how my mother could go from happy to closed-off in a matter of seconds. How her facial expression could change so drastically when he entered a room.

Eventually, I put the pieces together and realized what he was doing. But when I confronted my mother, she brushed it off, said that I didn't know what I was talking about. Everything's fine, she'd say to me. And I accepted her words. I listened to my mother and let it be. It wasn't until years later that I was able to look back at the situation and see how trapped she truly was. Women don't stay in abusive relationships because they enjoy it. They stay because they have no other options. They stay because they are in love, and they don't want to face the reality that the men they are devoted to are harming them.

We didn't have much money. Paul did. In a way, staying with Paul prolonged our survival. We were comfortable. We could go out for dinner once a month. We each had clothes to wear to school. And so I didn't complain any further. My mother told me it was fine and I believed her. Paul was, after all, a good man.

I was eighteen when she fractured her arm and broke a rib. She told the doctors that she had fallen down the stairs. Clumsy me, my mother had said. The cat ran between my feet and I slipped.

We didn't have a cat.

I began to take more notice. I watched her closely, observed her behaviour and his temperament. Some days he would be fine. Others, not so much. He was very controlling. He wanted my mother to be at his beck and call at all hours of the day. He wanted her attention on him and him only. If she even glanced at another man in the grocery store, all hell would break loose.

She tried so hard to be this perfect woman, this ideal image of whatever he had in his mind. But that's the problem with trying to conform to somebody else's standards of you – they're not real.

The abuse went on for years. She never left him. Things never changed. Not until August 14, 1965. The Sad Summer.

Now you see why I had such a vendetta against these abusers like Robert Baldwin and Patrick Brooks. Because I knew what they were capable of. I was familiar with how they worked and operated. I knew how they ruined lives. And I couldn't let it get to that. I couldn't let them do to Flora, Angela, and Joey what Paul did to my mother.

Perhaps everyone else that summer was just practice. Paul was the real target. He's who I had been aiming for all along. The other six helped me work towards my end game.

My siblings and I were planning a getaway weekend with our mother. Go up north to Ridgedale for three days to soak up the sun and lie on the beach. We'd pack up the tents, get the picnic baskets ready, and take off. This ensured two things. One, Paul would be alone and easily accessible. And two, my mother would be out of town with multiple alibi's. She would never be questioned, never accused.

I bailed at the last minute, said I was coming down with something. So my mother and siblings went off without me. I stood at the bottom of the driveway, waving as they disappeared down the road. I knew it was time.

I went over to my mother's house. It was nearly dinner time and I could see the kitchen light was on. I knocked twice, then let myself in. Paul appeared, holding a dish towel.

"Susie," he said, clearly surprised to see me. "What are you doing here? I thought you went away with the family?" "I had to cancel last minute," I told him. "I think I'm coming down with something. The flu, maybe." He rushed to my side, ever so caring as always. "Have a seat, Su. I'll put on the kettle and get some tea."

I did as he said and sat on the sofa. I looked around the room and studied it. The home I had grown up in. The home that Paul had invaded with his presence. He ruined everything. But he would finally get what was coming to him.

My mother had always been very spiritual. She was into meditation. She believed in the zodiac signs and moon cycles. She used crystals to heal her spirit. There were always tarot cards around the house. There were always crystals. More specifically, there was always a giant crystal that she kept in the living room, just next to the fireplace. It was about twelve inches in length, six or seven in height. A heavy rock. The crystal was white and purple with sequenced colours swirled into the center. It weighed eight pounds. I would use it to help me kill Paul Monoghan.

While Paul busied himself in the kitchen, I walked towards the crystal and picked it up. It was heavier than I remembered. I brought it back over to the couch with me, holding it in my lap. Paul entered shortly after that and placed two tea cups on the table, taking a seat beside me on the couch. He didn't even notice what I was holding. I glanced at him sideways, then without waiting another moment, lifted the rock and brought it down on his head.

My intention there was not to kill him. Not yet, anyways. He was unconscious. The crystal sat on the table, blood tainted on the side. I moved quickly, tying rope around his wrists and propping him up into a sitting position. I stared at him, analyzing his face. The bone structure, the wrinkles, how his eye fluttered at one point.

I waited over thirty minutes until he regained consciousness. He began to open his eyes slowly, blinking. His head was bleeding slightly, blood dripping over his eyebrow and down his cheek.

His eyes opened fully. He jolted upwards once he saw me, sitting in front of him, pointing the gun. After that, he didn't move once.

"Susie," he said exasperated. "What are you doing?" "We need to have a little chat, Paul." I sat up straighter and crossed one leg over the other. The gun felt foreign in my hands. It was his Magnum Revolver, after all. Dying at the hand of his own weapon. "Where's your mother?" he asked, looking around. "What's going on?" "Do you know what kind of man you are?" I asked. "Are you aware of all the irreversible damaged you've caused?" He only stared at me, eyes wide, mouth agape. "I want to know why you did it," I said. "Did your own daddy beat you? Do you enjoy hitting women? Do you feel powerful because of it?" "Susie —" "I'm not finished," I said. "I know what kind of man you are. I know what you're capable of. And my mother did not deserve this. She didn't deserve to be with a man like you. She needed to be with someone who loved her and cared for her. Someone who would look after her, not harm her. And my mother is not weak. She simply stayed because she didn't have any other options. You took that away from her, isolated her from friends and family, made her feel so alone that she had no one else to turn to. You did that to her. But regardless of what you did to her, what you made her become, she is one of the strongest people I know. And she raised me." He stared at me, processing my words, unsure of how to respond. "Don't worry about answering," I said, carefully constructing my next words. "No one's listening anymore." And then I pulled the trigger.

CHAPTER TWENTY-TWO

Ethan stood there paralyzed, his eyes on Susie, unsure of what to say next. She had told him everything, laid it all out in front of him. Yet he couldn't formulate a single word.

"After that," she spoke again. "I was finished. I didn't need to kill any more men because my task was complete. I had set out to rid Briarwood of those terrible men, and I succeeded. I'm sure there were plenty more out there, but I couldn't kill all of them. But it didn't matter – those seven were the most crucial ones. As long as I had them taken care of, my conscious would be relieved. I would sleep better at night knowing that I had brought a great justice to Briarwood. And as I told you before," she said. "I didn't enjoy the act of killing. I simply did what needed to be done. So after Paul, I never killed again. I didn't need to." Ethan swallowed, even though his mouth was dry. He parted his lips. "You have to know that was wrong, Susie. It wasn't up to you to kill those men, to take the law into your own hands. It wasn't your decision to make. You could have went to the police." "You don't understand," she said. "And you never will. You're a man. White, upper-class, living in the twenty-first century. You will never experience the injustices that people on this earth have to face. You will never know what it's like to be a woman. To feel so small and helpless. To witness the misogyny and the abuse firsthand and not know how to put an end to it. You saw what happened to men like Mike Darbyshire. He killed four people and got off scot-free. Jason Morgan – burned his house down and killed his wife, yet walked away without a slap on the wrist. So don't you dare tell me that I could have gone to the police. We both know that wasn't an option." Ethan inhaled slowly, trying to process it all. For once in his life, he was at a loss for words. He didn't know what to say. "I'm sorry that happened to you," he finally said. "You're right. I will never know what it was like, or what you went through. And I truly am sorry. But I just can't condone the murder of those seven men. It wasn't your right. As an officer of the law, I see injustice every single day. Believe me. You don't think I want to do something about it? To take justice into my own hands? Of course I do. I wish I could do anything to make things right. I wish I could solve every unsolved murder and bring justice to those who deserve it. But I can't. I can't do that. And I know I can't do anything about it now – it was fifty years ago – but what you did, Susie... it was murder. And it was wrong." She stared at him, her eyes tracing his face, neither one of them moving or saying a word. She looked down at her lap and smiled, shook her head slightly. "So what now, Ethan? What happens now?" Ethan inhaled deeply, thinking. His heart had been racing, nearly beating out of his chest. When he unclenched his fists, he realized they were drenched. "I'll need to alert the authorities," he told her. "There's no statute of limitations on murder. Unfortunately, you will be arrested and tried for your crimes." She shook her head again and laughed dryly. "You see, Ethan," her hand was moving beside her wheelchair, next to the window. "I can't let you do that." Before he had time to realize what she was doing, Susie was pointing a gun at him. Ethan's hand instinctively reached for his holster, which was empty. Fuck. He hadn't even thought about bringing anything with him. No gun, no badge. Just himself. "Susie," he held up both hands in surrender. "You don't want to do this." "Don't tell me what I want and don't want." "You said it yourself – you've only killed seven people. You don't want to make it eight." "I want to live how I want to live," she said. "And I want to die in my home, peacefully in my sleep. Not in a jail cell, going without food or clean water or basic human rights. I'm seventy-five years old. I still have many years left. But unfortunately, Ethan, you do not." "It won't work," Ethan said. "What, you're going to shoot me? Kill me? Then what? How will you get rid of the body? Look at you," he nodded towards her. "You can barely walk." At that, Susie stood from her wheelchair and walked towards him, perfectly capable. His heart pounded in his chest and he took an involuntary step backwards. She cocked the gun. "Please," Ethan said, desperate now. "What about Jordan – your eldest granddaughter. You're really going to kill me and take that away from her? We're going to get married," he said. "She wants a baby. We were planning a family." Susie sighed. "Begging won't do you any good, I'm afraid. What's done is done. You went sticking your nose around and now you know something you shouldn't, something that no one on this planet knows except for me. And I'm afraid that's a secret worth killing for." He was shaking, desperately willing to do anything. "Please," he said, tears forming in his eyes. "Please let me go home to Jordan. I won't turn you in, Susie. I won't tell a soul. You have my word." She was quiet for a moment, perhaps considering his plea. Ethan was willing her with every cell in his body to put down the gun. "I'm sorry," she finally said, looking him in the eyes. "But I just can't let you leave."

Then she pulled the trigger.

CPSIA information can be obtained
at www.ICGtesting.com
Printed in the USA
LVHW010452181022
730946LV00008B/450

9 781804 778333